Medusa Snare

AVONELLE KELSEY

Soggy Nomad Press

©2023 Soggy Nomad Press

ISBN: 978-1-957532-22-6

www.Soggy Nomad Press.com

Book cover by Nola Lee Kelsey

To thoughtful people who recognize Earth as a fragile home for life as we know it. For those who appreciate how rare the beauty of a flower, a rainbow dewdrop, clouds in a blue sky, a running stream, a poem and the hearts of loving, thoughtful people.

Loren Eiseley suggests we may be destined to seed the Universe or die—our CHOICE.

CONTENTS

PROLOGUE

Smog filled the air above the once lovely city of San Diego. Cars, planes and trucks spewed noise and noxious fumes, offending all the senses.

Increased population created increased demands, which wiped out each attempt to clean up the environment. Mankind wallowed in its own waste, seemingly unable to help itself.

But, other eyes were watching. Other beings were affected. It was time for intervention.

A detective, psychiatrists, a group of models and a crop of strange babies will be the connecting link to a better world or land without man. .An Unknown Author wrote:

> All things are bound together
> All things connect.
> What happens to Earth
> Happens to the children of Earth!
>
> Man has not woven the web of life
> He is but one thread.
> Whatever he does to the web
> He does to himself.

This little poem is framed and sets on Dr. Helene Troy's bedside table.

2030: The Mystery Woman

Detective Mike Lambert hesitated in the doorway of The Hungry Dolphin Bar, awed by the sight of a clear sky, a breath of fresh air and the beginning of a glowing sunset.

Ah, clean air and look at that sky. A rare occurrence! Colors flamed across San Diego tinting clouds with tangerine oranges, crimson and plumb purple hues against patches of blue. He breathed deeply, with pleasure, as he waited for a taxi, gradually, becoming aware of a light perfume on the ocean breeze.

Near Mike a tall, red-haired woman paused by the taxi sign in front of the Bar. She pushed back strands of auburn hair, tucking it under a green silk scarf. They watched the sunset together as they waited. Again he smelled the perfume and glanced at her strong, exotic, profile. Large eyes protruded slightly and the lips were unusually full. Kissable lips, he thought. She smiled faintly, aware of his admiration. Reluctantly, he turned back to look at the brilliant sky.

"It's as though Earth dresses herself for a New Year's Eve party," he said.

Dr. Helene Troy turned and looked directly at his scarred profile. It seemed to be lit, not only with color, but smoldering emotions. Troy, as she was most often called, felt her body stir at the sound of his voice. She looked at the sky and then glanced at him again in surprise. There was something familiar about him.

"You sound like a poet," her clear voice was self-confident, but blurred by a slight accent.

"My name is Mike Lambert. I'm a closet poet," he said in a teasing voice. "Forty-three years young, single, available and a reasonably happy man." His eyes twinkled in amusement as he looked into her upturned face.

She laughed lightly, "Are you always poetic and happy?"

Troy's quick laughter and rich, confident voice caught his attention. His body vibrated like a bell after the tone has faded. Mike glanced at her again. It seemed important to answer her question seriously.

"Except when I step outside and take a look at sickly brown smog, walk on oil-splotched beaches, listen to another greedy politician or ignorant millionaire preacher on TV," Mike paused, surprised at his own outburst with this stranger.

"My, my. I'm disenchanted. Now you sound like a man with anger in his heart." She watched him, thoughtfully. He turned toward an approaching taxi, frowning when it passed them by.

She wanted him to smile again. "I, too, feel anger when I know Earth could be like this every day," and waited for his response.

He scrutinized her with intense blue eyes. She was not slim. Curvaceous was the word that came to mind, almost as tall as his six feet. Those large round eyes of emerald green looked at him as though they scanned his very thoughts. They sparkled with passion and amusement as she returned his gaze. Her skin was creamy white, with a dewy look, as though she had just come out of the water. Extra thick, Titan hair escaped the scarf tied around her head. Mike's breath caught in his throat.

When air pollution was thick, women wore masks over the nose and mouth, as well as wrap-around glasses to protect their eyes. Except inside a building or after a rain, the naked face of a woman outside was unusual. Had he seen this woman somewhere before? Realizing he was staring, he tried to recall her last words and answer them.

"My inner vision of Earth is a turquoise globe with white, swirling clouds and no fences. Like those taken by space-satellite photos in the eighties."

A taxi pulled up to the curb. Troy nodded and stepped back. "You were here first."

"It's a great evening, I've decided to walk." He raised his hand in farewell. His brilliant smile blazed white against the scarred, tan face.

He must have spent time under a sun lamp when his scars were healing, Troy thought. She watched as he strolled down the street. An interesting man. He should smile more often. Troy sat back in the taxi after giving her Coronado Island, Ocean Street, address.

As they passed the man she turned, looked back, waved and mouthed, "Thanks."

Then, she remembered. Of course! He must be the brother of Madge, the detective. That's why the smile seemed so familiar. And the voice. The touch of a Maine accent still remained in his speech, as it did in his sister's. Troy knew it was silly, but she found it charming. If she remembered correctly, he was a private detective and worked with Ted, the husband of her friend, Jean, on secret government investigations. Their firm was called T & M Investigations. Well, well, she thought. Perhaps we'll meet again.

On Thursday evenings a group of friends often gathered at the Hungry Dolphin for happy hour and good conversation. Larry, a photographer who did piece work for T& M Detective Agency on listening devices, sometimes his wife, Lisa, Ted, his wife, Jean, and Mike was the core of the assembly. Mike enjoyed the unexpected twists given to a conversation by the women. The different points of view between men and women were fascinating. Larry flirted with the women added a joke now and again and sprinkled the spice of humor when Ted got too grave on a subject. He'd toss off a crazy remark, watch it sink in, throw back his blond curly head and give an infectious laugh. Ted would look at him, realize he'd gotten in deep water and add his slow, rich chuckle. The others watched the show. Their differences made them a wonderful group.

Mike was in a thoughtful mood as he watched the women. For the first time in years a woman haunted his thoughts. Jean, Ted's wife, worked at Scripts Aquarium. She always looked pristine. Her cheeks were rosy and dimpled and her body had a streamlined look. Lisa was tall and dark. She'd been Larry's model before they married. Three children later had softened the body but not her quick mind.

Mike had been musing about the mind vs. body ever since his encounter with the red haired woman. Was she familiar because he'd seen her before or was his body reacting to sexual need?

Jean said, "You're looking thoughtful tonight, Mike. What's on the platter?"

He grinned. "OK. Which do you think controls us more, the body or the mind?"

"Definitely the body," Larry said. "The inside already knows and goes its way. It performs, digests, goes through growth stages and ends up in the toilet." Lisa shook her head at him but her lips twitched in amusement.

Ted grinned and picked up the thread, "The mind listens to outside winds. It flexes and wallows in social opinion, shoulds and shame."

"Makes you want to scream," Lisa looked pale. "Government shackles, greedy bigots make laws. Even tried to tell a woman what she could do and not do with her body. Women doctors took care of that."

Jean reached out and took her hand. Her mouth twitched as she spoke dramatically, "Don't forget. The winds that shape the soul come from inside as well as outside."

Larry stood, "I rise on empty winds like a Phoenix greeting the morning sun. I'm hungry, wife. Let's go to dinner before Ted begins the sermon I see forming on his thoughtful brow."

The group rose and went to dinner. The laughter, good conversation and companionship ended in dancing until midnight. The women enjoyed having an extra man to dance with. Sometimes Mike asked an attractive single woman at the bar to dance. If they found a mutual attraction, he stayed after the others left. But, tonight, he felt thoughtful and sat watching the couples. In spite of his vow not to love again and his busy life as a detective, there was something missing. Why couldn't he adjust to bachelorhood and enjoy life?

"Guys. I'm tired. See you tomorrow, Ted, before you leave."

"I feel a poem coming on," Larry quipped.

Mike clapped him on the shoulder. "You got it." He kissed the women goodnight. Jean whispered, "You'll find her someday. In the meantime, Madge would love to see her brother."

Mike walked home, alert to his surroundings, yet thinking about his life. Ever since that sunset, he'd felt this emptiness. "Damn," he said and hit a fist into the palm of his hand. The three hoods that had been creeping along the shadows behind him, stopped at the violent tones in his voice and waited for another victim.

His apartment was masculine, except for the antique writing desk Madge insisted he keep after their Mother died. Mike sat at it and filled the emptiness with heart-filled words. What was mind? He'd thought he was getting a handle on this falling in love thing after Cinder's death ten years ago. Now, here his heart was fluttering like schoolboys over a woman he didn't even know, or want to know, for that matter.

In bed Mike tossed restlessly, slept and dreamed of a woman with red hair and large green eyes.

Finally, he rose and tried to write the restlessness away . . .

Why can't I control the mind? Is there a difference between the mind and brain or heart and body for that matter? Often when he wrote from a word's point of view, something took over and things seemed to clear themselves up; lifting a weight from his soul . . .

Mind Vs Body

Mind swirled up from the mists of helpless, larval nakedness seeking to survive, cradled in a crude brain encased in a clumsy body, fueled by a pounding heart. Elusive Mind wears brain like the heart wears the body. It pushes and probes, seeking some future inconceivable to the body-self.

Not being able to develop alone, Mind's own physical constructs, is built by an ignorant, socially-warped, child-like society, which has both impeded and intensified its existence.

Mind is a creature of dreams. Body seeks the plodding instinct of the animalistic and surrounds itself with vague ideas, religious beliefs, habits and customs. These crutches become a snare, trapping the mind. Mind feels misplaced like an orphaned child. Reality becomes distorted. It duels with the Body-Heart which seeks its own comfort, stares sightless at the new and different, trembles in fear at the unknown.

Mind also drifts in daydreams of ascetic: a great singer, a piece of art, a field of flowers. The slit dome of an observatory shows a midnight splendor for which it longs.

Body-Heart would hold time at bay. Mind-Brain would leave the slime trails of Earth gardens and live in an ephemeral moment, fly on vagrant mists, mount the winds of space.

Body chooses the uncomfortable now, fearful of change, denying that random, impulsive, sexual irresponsibility is the true reason for destruction of the environment; afraid to take control of Earth's destiny. The reality of Body is the moment. It gives birth to bigger, better, more people, a car for every body, like hermit crabs; floating blindly toward a Niagara on a river of restlessness and fear.

Mind-Body screaming within this sightless prison is drawn by longing, into purple shadows where thistles pierce. It longs to follow the siren's voice singing in the wind. Knowing the weight of a flower petal changed the earth, it seeks timeless memories, probing, giving birth to written words, spacewalks, love-linked minds, in spite of prehensile hands--an internet where only the brave dare project future realities. What is reality? Body says, "Here and now." Mind asks, "What makes you think there's only one?"

Dr. Helene Troy

Troy was famous in the woman's world. Not only as a published physicist, but she sat on several government boards, had been a representative at the UN, President of Now for several years, had published *Women Only* magazine and kept a small practice going from her office in San Diego. The new Women's Party had selected her for their presidential nominee. In a woman's world, she was 'The new woman of the century."

Her books were on the shelf of every Psychologist. Talk shows were Troy's food and drink. Even couch potatoes found her comments interesting. As she talked a screen behind her often showed examples of such things as child or spousal abuse, uneducated parents trying to raise a child, the drug of instant entertainment, and the death of imagination.

Troy and Jean had met as young women in college at the school of Oceanography in Portugal. Over the years they kept in touch with one another. When Jean and her husband, Ted, moved to San Diego where Troy practiced, they renewed their friendship.

"You must meet my friend, Madge," Jean said. "She knows so much about environmental problems and actually has some solutions, provided she can sell them to the United Nations. She says one or two countries alone can't do much. It's one Earth and all countries or we die together.'

"She's right," Troy said. "Where does she live and how soon can I meet her?"

Madge and her husband have this large organic garden on the northern coast of California near Eureka, but she comes to see Mike and me often. Her public nickname is 'Mite, as in 'The Mite Bites Again' headlines. They grew up in Maine and had gardens there but the growing season is too short outside of greenhouses—and they take power. Power causes other problems."

"Of course. "The Mite. She's on my contact schedule. Do you think she'd

swing some votes my way?"

"A given. Already converted her to you. That's one of the reasons for her visit to San Diego."

Jean introduced Madge, the leader of the strongest organic garden-environmentalist organization in the world, to Troy. The two women immediately began to discuss pollution problems and the influence a president could have who didn't give in to lobbyists and money power. "There's never enough money for campaigns. How are you going to handle the problem?"

"Well, I do have a rich uncle, several books which sell well, my talk show appearances, a good practice, and my father designed and built the water gardens in Portugal in which I have a vested interest. He died recently but Mother has promised me all the funds I need. "

"Campaigns are a bottomless pit you throw money into," Madge quoted. He brow wrinkled in thought, "Oh, yes, your father was an oceanographer professor, wasn't he? Jean spoke of meeting him in her college courses. He was supposed to have some secret power energy source. Efficient solar energy reflectors, as I recall."

Troy smiled in amusement. "Dad was always experimenting with power sources. The oil and car manufacturers were afraid he'd take over the market. They tried to blow up the gardens and destroy his inventions."

Her voice became sad, "He was injured and never well after that. Mother took over, closed the school to all but special study groups and students." She shrugged and turned to Madge. "But tell me about you and your husband.

"We're experimental farmers who try to make a small contribution to the food needed to supply the world. My husband grew up in a family of botanists and farmers in Nebraska. Their research over the years has been helpful. Loren Eiseley, an anthropologist, was Jacob's mentor. He reads his stuff like a Bible. Turned both Mike and me onto his work and ideas. "

"I've read Eiseley. He's a bit depressing in many ways. Yet, I can see how he might be inspirational to a writer and philosopher—maybe even a poet like Mike."

"I call them, 'Transition Wo/man'."

Troy gave a chuckle. "Ok. I'll bite. What's that?"

"A self-completed person like yourself who has cast off blinding hulls of the past, bursting forth full of new energy to implement great old ideas which were never allowed to be put into practice."

"Thanks! Is Mike such a person?"

"You've met Mike?"

"Only in passing."

"Let's say, in many things yes, in others, no."

Troy nodded. "OK. About the environment, how we can best help one another."

Something in Troy tingled when Madge spoke of her brother. She often mentioned Mike in their conversation. After their meeting on the sidewalk, Troy wondered if she had judged him too hastily. His presence had seemed to fill the cab, even though he remained on the curb. She smiled at the romantic bend of her emotions and turned her mind back to campaign issues. Would Madge introduce her? Surely they'd cross paths soon. Well, she had a campaign to run and an Earth to save, and here she was acting like a silly schoolgirl. There was little time in her life for an intense relationship. He wrote detective stories she remembered and asked her secretary to locate a copy and record it for video screening, if she ever got an extra hour to listen.

Madge gave her a copy of *Labels For Peace*. "Mike wrote the essay from my ideas. He might help you with speech writing. It was his idea to sell *Labels For Peace* in our environmental fundraising campaign. If you wear a label for a year and sell 100 copies of the pen and essay to other people, you received a golden pin, then bars for other environmental work. Instead of generals killing and getting bars, we get peace bars. Here's a copy of your own and a Peace Pin.

"Thank you. It's lovely." Madge did not tell her inside was a tiny monitoring device. If anything happened to her, they could 'home in' on her 'whereabouts' with one of T & M's tracers. Larry had designed the monitor. Madge, Lisa and Jean designed the pin, and at Mike's suggestion, used the Earth-space motif.

The blue-green Earth with a cloud swirl and golden sunset. A golden butterfly peered over the edge. Its antennas were tiny hooks for bars. Troy held it in her hand and remembered Mike's description as they stood looking at the sunset.

That night Troy laid it on the bedside table and read the essay which inspired the pin.

LABELS FOR PEACE

My lily pond is peaceful today. The air is a bit on the sultry side. A fish jumps, a bee buzzes, but the Butterflies seem to be resting. Their wings look like tiny yellow labels on slowly moving fans. A warm breeze rises from the other side of the pond. I, too, fan with my writing paper. A price label and name catch my eye on a scrap of newspaper floating nearby. I wonder about words and our ability to pin a thing down with a bit of print.

Labels come in all sizes and shapes to identify a package. Many people object to them but labels, like anything else, may be used for good or evil.

Harry Browne in *How I Found Freedom in an Unfree World* suggests that if we wear our labels, right away people know we have something in common or that the opposite is true. It saves a lot of time and guesswork.

I would like to call upon people everywhere to "wear a label' if they are for peace, a clean earth, and a goal wherein the population of the world is kept in balance with the food supply.

I accept the fact that this cannot be done overnight or in one year.

Therefore, I propose that the United Nations set up a Twenty, a Fifty and One Hundred Year Plan, rather like the Marshal Plan we set up for the recovery of Europe after World War II.

Goals which we need in order to save our Mother Earth and mankind could be set by the United Nations. Such as one language, one monetary system, an adequate food supply for the number of people Earth can feed without starvation, transportation and communication systems, clean air and recycling programs, etc.

Some things which appear difficult are simple. To control her population many years ago, Japan simply offered each person $20 to be sterilized. For $2,000 out of the war budget or health, education and welfare budget, people who could not afford children or would not make desirable parents would usually opt for the money and be sterilized--many problems would be solved.

Birth control could be encouraged through various means: Education, criminals, even euthanasia, so that excess population would die natural deaths and a limited number of new births would take place in each country. The 'so-called' haves' would share more and more over the years but the 'have nots' would not be an overwhelming mass.

Each country could do a study on where it is and how it would like to participate in a clean, peaceful, no starvation plan for Earth and its people. With the help of United Nation Counselors, each country would set five, ten, twenty, fifty, and one-hundred-year goals.

It should be emphasized that each country keeps its own unique customs. Without variety life would be very dull indeed.

Natural resources, machinery, large equipment, and manpower could be pooled, thus reducing the need for every person to own a truck, boat, or plane to be used once per month and set in storage most of the year.

Instead of labeling sharing as communism, or socialism, we need a goal of _Earthism._ The best part of all ideologies, including future inventions such as dimensional travel, space stations, or fusion could be incorporated in a flexible sharing program written in a <u>Constitution for Earth</u>.

Military units could gradually be phased out. In the meantime, their equipment, manpower, and knowledge could be used to rebuild cities, and highways, bring needed dams, bridges, and aid to backward areas which need help. Their bases schools and many of their personnel would make excellent teachers for these jobs.

There are many military people who want to see a better world for themselves and their families but do not know how to stop the natural spiral of militarism. A military complex lives on the lifeblood of the people who support it. National labor and materials go into unproductive adventures to keep jobs and kill.

Albert Szent-Gyorgyi, Nobel Laureate for Medicine, says, "This growth is dangerous because if the military-industrial complex exceeds a critical mass it becomes the master of the civil authority instead of being its servant; it dictates the nation's foreign policy and the distribution of its resources swallowing up great amounts of the national income; and it subverts all higher endeavor, causing, art, science, and humanitarian institutions to wither away. Our military-industrial complex passed this danger mark years ago. it cost the

United states $50,000 to kill each Vietcong...For the same money we could have sent each one on a luxury cruise ten times around the world...Armies are a threat to mankind, ...a blot on the face of human culture and intelligence...problems cannot be solved by bombs...we cannot fire them without destroying the world... who will defend us against the defense department...the United Nations is the solution..."

I have discussed many of the problems with people around me and we have come up with a variety of possible solutions.

The world needs leaders willing to look forward instead of backward. Leaders with faith in the future and willing to begin building a firm foundation for a peaceful, clean Earth . . . N O W! It also needs individuals like you and me to support and defend its new policies. The safety of mankind depends on each individual.

<u>We must find a way to stand together.</u>

I suggest a simple label as a symbol of our togetherness, the beautiful blue and white globe of Earth as seen from a spacecraft.

As I sit by a peaceful pond watching nature in all its beauty, I add a Butterfly to my sketch of Earth. The Butterfly, a symbol of freedom of the human spirit. The core within each of us. Love Mother Earth.

Wear a label . . . send a message. Such a little thing to do . . .

Troy brushed back a tear and vowed to wear the badge proudly and introduce it on her next TV show.

When Dr. Troy announced to the world she would run for president, she called Madge. "Will you go all the way with me on environmental issues?"

"You bet!"

"When we win, will you and your husband accept an appointment to the United Nations?"

"You sound so certain," Madge laughed. "I'll match you in confidence. Yes, we will, we'll do anything to help. Even in South America food crops are beginning to show environmental damage. That's our last food battleground."

Jean was on the conference line. She was pregnant so couldn't help with traveling and speaking but the three often consulted via satellite hookups.

Troy nodded sadly. "The problem may be too big to handle. Many people use religion as an excuse to reproduce excessively. China's euthanasia for the elderly upon request and sterilization of all boys at puberty has begun to show positive results. "

"That seems severe, but we're going to have to come to terms with nature. If you can convince the poorly educated to seek sterilization or at least control their birth rate . . . "Jean broke off in a tone of discouragement.

"The Responsibility to Earth Amendment and Television propaganda has had some response, but not enough."

"Mike might ask, 'Are the thoughtless ones worth saving?"

"Like it or not, we're all on this planet together. Keep the ideas rolling in."

"Oh, yes," Madge eyes sparkled but her mouth had its determined set, "Jean and I have decided you need a guard until you're established as worthy of a government protective force." Troy made a face over the phone screen.

Jean insisted, "No arguments. T & M are sending a couple of men over to your office. They'll check out all your patients, wander around the grounds and house."

"I refuse to have people wandering around my house and grounds. I've alarm detectors I use at night in the house and the grounds in the daytime. That has to do it. "

Madge shook her head, "I told Ted you'd say that so they'll be sending a motor home for headquarters. At least let them park on the empty lot next to you."

'I'll try it, but I insist on privacy in my home."

Jean or Madge often went with Dr. Troy when she left her home for speaking engagements. Both had been trained for their own protection. Like people in starving lands, the young reproduced hordes of children when they were very young. Society was not willing to take responsibility for their care. The results were small armies of unwanted, undisciplined young people who preyed on the unguarded, frail and helpless.

Police carried gas bombs, large stun guns, and patrolled in groups. The wealthy hired guards. White collar workers trained in self-protection and went about armed.

The in-between people, like blue-collar workers, were never safe.

Madge and Troy got together as often as possible. Only the privileged could fly these days. Many people had small planes and coast liners used sailboats which were an environmental vogue as well as necessity in many cases. Public transportation had finally taken over the car-ridden highways. In cities, mopeds and bicycles were everywhere.

Troy told Madge, "Oh, yes, I think I met your great detective brother outside a bar one evening."

Madge laughed. "Maybe not great, but he's a pretty good detective, should you need one. He's helped break up a lot of freak groups that attempt to set back every advanced program the government tries to invoke. What'd you think of him?"

"Well . . . I was impressed. It had just rained and we both admired the sunset while we waited for a taxi. Is he really a poet?"

"He told you that? It's usually the last thing he talks about . . .

"Mike's a lot of things, he's been with the CIA, under the guise of a reporter, a policeman, even a teacher once. He writes detective stories with a grain of truth and social commentary."

"Shades of John McDonald." Troy was amused.

"So you've read McDonald?"

"I met him as a child once."

Madge watched her face as it filled with anxiety, then relief and blanked off. "Nothing much. I . . . I was swimming and a fisherman hooked my wetsuit. John was on the boat nearby and heard my screams. He grabbed a knife, jumped overboard and cut me loose."

"The scar on your side?"

"I'd have bled to death if he hadn't been there. After that, he became one of us until he died. He was older when I met him."

"Imagine that. Wait until I tell Mike."

"No. Wait until he's ready." She looked at her wrist. "Almost time for my first patient." She hugged Madge and hurried away.

Madge talked of Mike often and spoke fondly of her brother, "On the surface he's macho, underneath he's a pussycat."

Troy smiled again at the thought of the tall man wagging a friendly tail. And again, she turned her mind back to the problems of Campaign Earth Issues.

When she returned home she waved at the guard stationed in a motor home on the street, unlocked the solid gate in the tall wall behind her house and stepped inside her garden. Except for a large pool, the yard was filled with vegetables and flowers. An ocean breeze kept some of the smog-blight from the plants. Usually Troy breathed a sigh of relief when she returned home, she hated the filth of the city, but tonight she felt restless. Perhaps it's the storm, she thought. She picked up an apple, ate it, sat on the porch swing and watched the last of a smoggy sunset fade into the sea.

Troy decided to go for a boat ride and swim. Her tiny craft looked like a normal boat from the air, with a small electric motor. In the darkness it slipped easily under the water tunnel from her house into the ocean. She headed for a special place known to very few people.

The Detective

Mike looked into the mirror as he shaved, skimming lightly over the scars. He wondered why he had dreamed about the red-haired woman and what she saw when she looked at him. In his mind he preferred to remember the attractive woman with sunset hair, rather than the sophisticated, presidential nominee on TV screens.

Would she have smiled at him so confidently, if she had known he was a detective? How could she know that he hated violence, but his trade often exposed him to brutal actions?

A knife slash on the cheek and a broken nose had left his average-looking profile on the tough side, he decided. His mop of wavy, brown hair softened the appearance to some extent. A mustache, which insisted on being red, covered part of the scar near his full lips.

"I do have kind blue eyes and a boyish smile," he said aloud and surprised himself with his own laughter. "Kids, women, and stray dogs like me." He felt so alive. "Must have been the toxic effect of clean air after the storm." He knew he was wearing a silly grin.

Madge had told him, "You're just a softie under that rough looking exterior." He smiled at the thought of his sister and turned from the mirror, whistling. Mike could hear Madge giving one of her lectures. He agreed with her theories but was not always certain her ideas were practical.

She seemed to enjoy practicing her lectures on her brother. "During the last fifty years thinking people have known the only way to clean up the environment is to decrease and balance the population of the earth with nature. Do you realize many young people in cities don't even know what clean air smells like? The damage to the environment is now so severe it may be past renewing."

"What makes you think this new 'woman's party' will be able to clean up the environment?"

"Because people other than politicians have decided to act. At the turn of the century," Madge said, "scientists, psychologists such as Dr. Troy, the Fearless they call her, the medical association, artists, authors, environmentalists and intelligent creative people decided to cooperate, speak out and act. They donated money and pay for prime time on TV to educate the public; the programs are broadcast all over the world in many languages. Dozens of organizations provide guest speakers, commercials and entertainment to educate the general public about improving the environment and becoming caretakers of both the earth and one another. The 'begin in you own backyard' motto sounds simple, and it is—Like Labels for Peace and One Earth."

Mike hugged her and said, "Don't forget to have some fun along the way. You only get one chance at living."

But she had inspired him. He sat down late at night and wrote an essay on Civilization which her Woman's website magazine published.

The Campaign Earth Group by the Woman's Party had formed a political group and began to collect followers. After they gained a great deal of support, a few other candidates dared risk speaking about the necessity of birth control, euthanasia and mass sterilization.

Religious people fought against population control until the sun could no longer shine through the smog, except for a few hours after a rain. Even then they promoted small revolutions in several countries. Many of their leaders went underground and were watched by local police and government agencies.

Finally, the private ownership of automobiles was banned. Only public transportation and small electric cars were allowed on the streets after 2015. Even the greedy realized Earth was beginning to die and they would go with her.

People became frantic and refused to vote until women came forth and run on the Campaign Earth Party. They felt if they continued with Woman's Party men might refuse to cooperate.

Could the women of the earth gain strength enough to solve issues that men had wrestled with for decades and failed miserably? Men doubted it. With the last resources of the earth, they were designing space cities instead of cleaning up their own planet. Mining the moon, Mars and comets kept the depleted Earth going, but polar caps were melting, the weather was capricious and natural disasters multiplied. So did people.

Mike shrugged his shoulders as though to get away from unpleasant thoughts. At first he'd tried to remember where he had seen the woman on the street. Television, he thought. Bet she was the woman Madge had been talking about and who was going to run for president. He had little time for TV and pseudo-living. The jobs his firm undertook were more exciting than screen pretend.

He went to the office one day recently to have a conference with Ted, his partner.

"We have a big job on our hands, Mike," Ted said. "Protecting Dr. Helene Troy, noted author, lecturer and Psychiatrist. She has taken on the population control issue and is heading up the Campaign Earth Party. The so-called 'abortion war' revolution by a few radicals, is over in theory, but many fanatics went underground and are still considered dangerous."

"You don't have to convince me," Mike agreed.

"Our firm has been hired as her bodyguard. She's a friend of Jean and your sister. Jean's old college classmate, in fact. Since Dr. Troy is local and her party hired us, the government has asked us to keep them posted on any subversive actions attempted against her, or anything else we discover. The CIA seems to have paranoia about some secret cult that's growing worldwide."

The firm often used outside private detectives to do the day-to-day' babysitting' with a client. Of course, they were well-trained.

Mike began watching and listening to her programs when he got an opportunity. Newspapers had given way to computer news. Even magazines could be read at computers or printed off in color, if one did not feel guilty about paper. "Papers are trees," Madge would remind him.

"I like reading, underlining and rereading. If it's worth reading again it's worth keeping for a reference," he argued. He'd kept his family's collection of books and kept a binder to keep order from the things he took off the web.

Their casual meeting at the taxi stayed fresh in his mind as he watched Troy on video.

"She is brave," he said aloud, as he listened to her answer question from callers and the television hostess.

A typical session went:

"Do you think people have too much sex, Dr. Troy?"

"Let's face it. Next to eating, sleeping, drinking and shelter, sex is our most important activity. Only highly sexual people have survived down through the centuries."

"Why the highly sexed people?"

"In primitive societies frequent sex was as common as eating. For a long time sex and babies were not connected. When the connections were made, other things began to be obvious. Women had the responsibility of raising children as well as providing for them. If there were too many children, the mother did not survive. Without her, neither did the children. Without children, the tribe would cease to exist."

"In other words, men and women were both enjoying sex but only women were taking the responsibility for children."

"True."

"What happened to change this?"

"Religion and education entered the picture and tried to give some of the responsibility of raising children to fathers and other adults. Priests hoped to discourage sexual activity by example and by insisting men be responsible for the results of sexual activity and marry. But, they did not take into consideration the basic, instinctive and overwhelming demands of the body to reproduce.

The priests began to encourage monogamy and discourage sex before marriage. Few people are willing to admit the race of man, by this time, had breeding mania simply because the act of sex is pleasurable."

"Are you saying that we're all over-sexed?"

"Yes." The audience let out a gasp, then began to laugh and applaud.

Dr. Troy smiled her rare, marvelous smile and looked straight into the camera and into Mike's eyes.

Mike told her later, "I think I fell in love with you then. I told myself it was the usual male lust for a lovely woman.

But, after that, anytime I was near a TV, I tuned to your show."

Word reached the T & M Detective Agency that religious fanatics were bragging, "We're going to finish off the devil woman, Helen of Troy." Ted put twenty-four-hour surveillance on her. He wanted to have someone live with her, but again, Dr. Troy refused.

Her secretary was given self-defense and weapons instruction. Ted also planted a suggestion in the secretary's subconscious via hypnotism. She would protect Dr. Troy at all costs. The doctor promised to take no new clients.

Since the gasoline shortage and the new laws about the size and speed of electric cars, there was no longer a parking problem. Dr. Troy often walked or rode a bike. She had an old converted Honda from the nineties in her garage which she seldom drove. The guard kept his electric car on hand and became her chauffeur.

Except for lecture tours once a year, or a cultural night out, she seemed content to stay home an unusual amount of time.

Troy lived in Coronado by the beach. One side of her house had an enclosure in which she kept a small speed boat. The firm couldn't cover all areas, but Ted said she had promised to call the motor home any time she planned to leave the house by boat.

So far, all the threats had been just that.

One night Mike was watching her 'live' talk show.

A caller asked, "If you become President, are you going to make a pill to curb our sexuality?"

"No and yes," she said. Mike waited to hear her talk her way out of this one. "The idealized pill is maturity. The only lasting pill available is education and self-discipline. Each of us must decide how much sex we really need. Which need is sex, for example, and which is just a need to be touched by another human hand?

"The bottom line on clearing up the environment, in order that it will become fit for humans as well as animal life forms to survive, is for each of us to face up to our sexuality."

"What good will that do and how do we do it?"

"We are a lazy society. Physical labor for the majority of people in the United States is unknown.

"Our grandparents lived through a couple of depressions so they worked, saved and valued objects too much. Our parents reacted against saving by becoming a throw-away society.

"The thrill was in the getting and moving on to more thrills.'Shop 'till I drop,' became a common slogan. For example, instead of a painting that would last a lifetime and be handed on to the next generation, prints were purchased to match the latest apartment wallpaper and dumped when they moved on. Furniture was cheap and disposable. The automobile is the worst example of overselling. It's expensive, mass-produced, pollutes and has a short life span.

"The lack of attachment to possessions is admirable, but when more and more is demanded by an increasing population, then abandoned, it uses up a tremendous amount of resources and clutters up the environment."

"Aren't you getting away from the question Doctor?"

"Again, yes and no." She smiled and tilted her head. Again those emerald eyes looked straight into Mike's from the television set. He caught his breath. He had to meet her.

"The more people we have buying and throwing away items which are made to wear out quickly to keep the economy functioning, the more polluted our environment becomes.

"Sometimes, each of us must look at ourselves and our environment with clear eyes. Know and accept ourselves. Take responsibility for our little corner. Decide between needs and wants and survival. Then, with self-confidence, move to change ourselves and preserve and maintain our square foot of Earth." She paused before continuing, "Sexual responsibility is the first step and perhaps the hardest."

"So I see myself as a sex fiend. How can that help me?"

"But are you really? Could it be that you don't know the difference between needs and wants? We are highly sexed, yes. Our bodies want and need loving, caring, and touching from the time we're born. Daily, not just until we're five years old and again when we marry.

"I'm inclined to believe if we often reached out and touched, hugged and stroked the people around us, we would be more responsible in choosing our sexual contacts, many of our physical needs would be met and we would learn the difference between love and sex."

"What about the biblical command, 'Be fruitful and multiply'?" The TV hostess quoted.

"There is a difference between understanding our sexuality, enjoying it with wisdom, and reproducing until we destroy Earth.

"A few people were fortunate enough to live in a time and place where they could choose how many children to have, as well as make certain they gave birth to a healthy child. If the world can look the population problem squarely in the eye, and take decisive action, the people of Earth may survive this crisis, even yet. I believe we can only do so by moving to the next step in evolution."

"Can you explain what you mean, Dr. Troy?"

"To those people who are willing to think, live simply, work hard at self-discipline, keep an open mind; and to those who are brave enough to discard superstitious crutches such as religion spawned in the dark ages with an emphasis on hate, not love and understanding, shopping, fear and greed; to these will be given true self-awareness. I believe unselfish self-awareness to be the next step in the evolution of mankind. 'Do unto others and you are your brother's keeper' will be automatic actions. Enforced legislation and threats of hell will be unnecessary."

"You're saying we would all be happier if we led simpler lives and were harder on ourselves? How will this clean up the environment?"

"Our world will clean up its act when people clean up theirs."

Mike snorted. How many people are going to use self-discipline in sex? He has no intention of punishing himself by giving up women. Normally, he didn't call radio or TV stations, but this woman with her green eyes and frigid body was too much.

Mike reached for the phone just as it began ringing.

"Mike. This is Ted. Better get down to the TV station. The guard for Dr. Troy just called from the hospital. He was surrounded and slugged by a gang of Bible thumpers. Said they had weapons and were threatening to blow up the station. I'm almost there and I'll try to slip her out. The police have been called. If my car is stopped, I'll wait for you to drive up by the parking lot for employees.

"Just slow down long enough to pick us up. Wear your monitor strap. Keep it tuned to mine in case we get kidnapped.

"Oh yes. Call the station first and tell them to get her to the parking lot by the freight elevator and to look for my car. She must not get into hers. They'll be watching it."

"Ok, Ted."

Mike dialed the station and watched the screen.

There was a surprised look on Dr. Troy's face when the hostess said, "We will pause for station identification and a commercial. Stay tuned folks." Her face was grim. Then, the screen went black.

"Damn you, you stupid jerks," Mike yelled at the television set. His heart pounded his throat and lips felt dry. He was numb with tension.

When they had been put on alert by the local authorities earlier in the month, both Ted and Mike had been issued an assault weapon. They laughed at the time and joked about the 'sex war.'

"Sounds good to me. Wait until I tell Jean," Ted said They couldn't decide what to do with the weapons.

Mike raced into the garage, paused in the car long enough to pull the gun out from the sling under the seat and lay it beside him. He longed for the speed of an old fashioned Thunderbird.

What in the hell happened, he wondered. Would they really be crazy enough to blow up a TV station, just to get at one woman? Was some rabble-rousing preacher behind it? Did she really stir up people's emotions and lives enough that they felt the need for violence? For all he knew she was dead and he hadn't even had a chance to meet her.

He put on the red light, which he was only supposed to use when doing piecework for the police department, and headed for the station.

The street near the station was sealed off a block away. There were smoke, fire engines, police and about a thousand people milling around outside the station. It was half an hour before he made his way on foot to the parking lot where he was supposed to meet Ted and Dr. Troy, if Ted had gotten to her in time.

The front elevator had been bombed, but the fire was out. A freight elevator was in use. The police at the door assured him all station personnel had been removed safely.

He hiked back to the car again and called Ted.

Finally, he answered. "Yes, Dr. Troy's all right."

Mike sighed with relief and listened while Ted updated him.

"The FBI as well as the local authorities have assured me she will have added protection, beginning tomorrow."

This sounded strange to Mike. He later learned she would be under the protection of the new, potential presidential-candidate custody law. T & M would continue to help with local surveillance.

"Jean wants Troy to spend the night. Will you stop by her house, and bring her suitcases to our house? She has an apartment, above her office. Also, her raincoat and hat from the closet."

Mike made a face at the phone. His silence gave Ted the message. Ted laughed. "They're already packed. She leaves on a speaking tour first thing in the morning."

"I'm not a butler. But, on second thought, we should check out her house. I'd like to see how the great lady lives."

"We'll pick up her car tomorrow. I think we'd better check the car for explosives before starting it. Or better yet, have the police bomb squad check it out. The station is back on the air. They say the police are making several arrests. I'll bet they can't make a case stick on anyone," Ted added.

"Just as soon as I deliver the sex goddess' nightshirt, I'm going to work on trying," Mike said. "How do I get in?"

"She says there's a key between two pans, under the potted ferns, by the back gate."

Troy's Worlds

D r. Troy's two-story house was elegant. A tall, white, stucco fence began at the sides of the house and ran to the back yard where a twelve foot high, translucent, wire fence, covered with flowering vines, enclosed a large lot. Waves pounded on the beach nearby as a speedboat raced up the bay.

When Mike opened the gate in back, he was in for a surprise. Lights flooded the yard. It looked like a miniature park and garden. On one fence grew a vine bearing a dozen pumpkins. Several stalks of corn stood beside a very productive garden climbing on risers and wires. A small windmill ran a waterwheel which dipped and stirred oxygen into a gigantic swimming pool containing a variety of fish.

On the back of the house the large wooden porch was furnished with a swing, table, chairs and a rack of farming tools. Everything was well-used, cluttered and the whole area smelled like his sister's farm. Baskets of fruit sat on tables and chairs, as though someone was going to can.

"Well, la de da," he said aloud. "Our lady has many personalities." Apparently one didn't have to live on a farm to be a farmer.

There were two doorways. One door led to her downstairs office, he presumed. The other door, which the key fit, opened into an old-fashioned kitchen with a staircase.

Mike peeked into the refrigerator, poured a glass of milk and helped himself to a couple of peaches. As he ate and drank, he soaked up the 'granny atmosphere' of the kitchen. It was equipped with a grinder, apple press, bread baking machine and a variety of antique tools. The ceiling had a rack of beans drying over a Ben Franklin, cast-iron stove which sat beside a modern gas one.

He opened a door leading to a basement. Telling himself he wasn't being nosy, just a good detective protecting a client, he went downstairs. There were shelves of canned food and bins of vegetables, just like in the history books. He felt as though he had stepped back a century.

This woman was planning on surviving the environmental revolution one way or another. She practiced what she talked about. Dozens of jars of canned goods sat on shelves. The smell brought back memories of Madge and her cellar of potatoes, onions, cabbages and salt pickles.

He continued to explore. One window looked into the pool at fish. Some strange equipment that looked like a submarine side with a rubber-plated door. He was about to explore it when he heard the phone ring, stop and ring again. It was Ted's signal.

"Hey. Are you all right?"

"Yeah. Mighty strange woman."

"I'll say. We like her. You should get acquainted, Mike. But then, you probably wouldn't appreciate her."

"Well. Do I hear a touch of criticism in your tone, partner?"

"You do tend to take your women lightly. This one deserves better."

"Thanks." Mike said feeling misunderstood.

"Get a move on. The ladies want to go to bed."

"The ladies want to go to bed," he repeated in a sarcastic tone and hung up.

The second-story apartment had skylights in the hallway. A large, luxurious bedroom-sitting room combination took up the top floor. He got a sense of someone who liked comfort and light. There was a fireplace with a few warm coals on the bottom. A box of small logs from recycled products stood by it.

Comfortable, leather divans, two reading chairs, and an old rattan rocker sat around the fireplace with a view of the ocean to the west. On the king size bed was a rattan lap-table with papers and an empty glass.

He picked up the pages. It was a speech about the educational process of preschoolers in relation to sex and virtues. Logic will settle of its own accord on the Ten Commandments in a civilized. Children need to be guided by logic, honesty and responsibility . . .

That lady never lets up, he thought. She must never get any sex to be so intense about it. She did have some good points. Overpopulation was the basic problem. But what was wrong with lots of sex?

He put down the papers and began to poke around in the closet. An overnight case and a suitcase were packed and waiting. She was going on a speaking tour, Ted had said.

Even though he didn't need anything other than her coat and hat, he snooped in a couple of drawers and an open jewel case.

A string of beautiful pearls with a cluster of stones caught his attention. He felt of their silken coolness. Other jewelry was made from polished shells and twisted shapes clustered with bits of colorful coral, gold and silver. These must have set her back a buck or two, he thought.

She was casually neat, but not excessively so. There were French doors which lead to a balcony overlooking the bay. Jasmine in bloom sent a sweet odor into the bedroom. He locked the doors and picked up the suitcases.

Before leaving, he stood in the kitchen and looked about regretfully, hating to leave. Then, picked up an apple, stuck it in his pocket, and listened by the door for a minute before going outside. Crickets and a frog sang. They became quiet when he closed the door.

There was a shuffling movement on the other side of the wall. Again he paused. Someone walked across the street. A car door closed, quietly. He leaned against the fence to listen and was surprised to receive an electric shock. He stepped back quickly. Leaving the suitcases inside the gate, Mike pulled his gun from the holster under his jacket.

The key was a strange one, long with an insulated circle at the top. Putting it in the lock, turning it as quietly as possible to unlock the gate, he stepped outside, quickly. A shadowy figure stood by a car parked across the street. The door opposite the driver opened. An overhead light came on for an instant.

Two men with strange large eyes, protruding lips and tight fitting caps looked in his direction. The motor started up. They drove away. He had a feeling they would meet again.

It was well after midnight. Mike circled the block a couple of times to see if anyone else was watching the house. Finally, he gave up and headed for Ted's across the Coronado Bridge to San Diego. The motor home with the guard was now parked in front of Ted's house.

Ted met Mike at the door. Dr. Troy had borrowed a toothbrush from Jean and both women were in bed. He told Ted about the two men.

"Were you followed?"

"I don't think so."

"Well, let's get some shut-eye. It's been a long day."

"I agree. When do I get to meet our client?"

"Dr. Troy leaves for a month on a lecture tour, tomorrow. She's invited Jean to go with her as a bodyguard, but with the time off for the baby, the sea lab doesn't want to give her more than a couple of days. We'll let the FBI handle the out of town stuff."

"Why are they in on it?"

"Something about TV Stations coming under Federal law. Also, she has the ear of a man up there, so they say. We may be guarding the next president."

Mike laughed. 'They' was a reference used contemptuously. "Goodnight, Ted."

As Mike stood outside the door letting his eyes adjust, he realized he felt let down. He had failed to meet the sex lady.

In his apartment, he felt restless. Should he go back and explore the basement of her house? Madge had told her Dr. Troy's father had invented a power source that had led to his injury and eventually death. Had he really developed such power and that accounted for the strange object in the basement? They'd had an underwater garden. Must be some design of her father's.

Mike kept a journal and often wrote late at night. Writing and poetry helped him solve problems. He named no names other than his immediate family, in case it was discovered and used by the unscrupulous.

"Why do I feel so intense about meeting this Dr. Troy?" he wrote. "She can't be that much different than the other women I've known. Could it be I still believe in fairy tales and am looking for the perfect princess? My mind tells me to be sensible, my body says, 'go for it'."

It was some time before he met the famous Dr. Troy, in unexpected circumstances. Ted and Mike were in their local office. Mike said, "I've been called for jury duty."

"In the old days you could have weaseled out of it."

"Yeah. Some things do change for the better. Let's hope we can get in and out in a hurry."

"Jean said even Dr. Troy isn't exempt. She's been called, too."

In spite of himself, Mike felt a quickening of his heart and looked up in surprise to meet Ted's questioning eyes. "Maybe I'll meet the great lady after all."

Ted grinned. "Behave yourself."

After the TV episode, T & M ask to be relieved of local surveillance and were no longer responsible for her welfare. Jean and Ted did not invite him over when Troy came to their house for dinner. She was still a popular speaker on talk shows and Madge insisted she was the most important personality since Kennedy. Mike was still skeptical, but kept track of her from a distance. Something about her fascinated him.

The courts had too many cases. Since the turn of the century, five laymen or peers handled the misdemeanors.

For the career criminal and murder trials a group of educated businessmen and women decided the case. They were given a week. The first day was spent before a television monitor listening to tapes on ethics, other cases and reviewing the law related to such cases. The next day the lawyers and clients presented the case to the jury committee on video and left the evidence in their hands. The jurors debated the merits of the case, interviewed the accused and accuser and any witnesses from a list of people interviewed by policemen, and then decided what the punishment should be if the person was convicted.

Instead of pay, the people reviewing the cases received a sizable tax break.

The courts were experimenting with several new systems of trials. The worst cases were presented to thirteen men and women who were experts in a variety of fields. These people retired to the jury room and decided the degree of guilt and amount of blame of both parties, or in this case, the murderess and the punishment she deserved and a two-thirds vote was needed to be found guilty. Then the jurors drew lots. The three with blank cards had to decide on the punishment. There was no judge.

Would Dr. Troy be in his group? His eyes roamed the people going into the courthouse.

He wrote, I remember when our eyes first met across the jury room; she was the most glamorous woman I had ever seen. During the trial, the tilt of her chin, her calm demeanor as well as her eyes and speech mesmerized me. I found myself watching her every captivating movement, hanging on to each word like a schoolboy. She looked at me strangely and turned away. Finally, I got my emotions under control enough to carry out my civic duty and talk to her.

With a bit of maneuvering, Dr. Troy and I were assigned to the same jury. Sometimes we were on opposite sides on the case, but more often than not, I found her arguments persuasive and intelligent.

"He was asking her to kill him when he tormented her," she said.

"How can you say that?" another juryman asked. "Don't you think you're prejudiced because the defendant is a woman?"

She smiled an enigmatic, Mona Lisa smile and explained patiently.

"He probably thought when he met her she was impulsive and fun—a party girl. She became pregnant and they married at his Mother's insistence. After they married, he expected her to act like his mother. She felt guilty when she failed to meet his expectations. Not feeling that she deserved to be loved because of a lack within herself, she accepted his verbal and then physical abuse as her due and just reward. She may have felt betrayed and lived in terror of being abandoned as she had been as a child."

"Then how did she finally get courage enough to blow that sucker away?" Irene, one of the women jurors, asked.

"The mother instinct. She was proud of her baby. For the first time, she gave and received love. In her eyes it was perfect. When he found fault with the baby and was wrong, she realized he had misjudged her and she was OK as well. It was he who deserved to be punished, she decided.

"As she said, "My baby is the only thing that ever really loved me and let me love it. I couldn't let him hurt the baby as he had hurt me. She didn't deserve it just because she was sick and cried, asking for help," she sobbed.

Then she wiped her tears and looked defiantly at the people in the room and the policeman at the door. "He'd wave the gun at me and make me do anything he wanted. Just because he was a cop is no reason he should put the gun to her little head and threaten to pull the trigger, if she didn't quit crying . . .

"She was just wet and hungry. I tried to explain it to him. He shoved me out the bedroom door and locked it, saying she could cry it out and for me not to go in there all night. He put the gun on the kitchen table and got a beer. Then ordered me to make him a sandwich while he watched TV.

"I began to make the sandwich. I looked at the knife and the back of his head. Could I kill him before he killed me, I wondered. I wanted to live long enough to get my baby to my sister where it would be safe. If we ran away, he would find me. I tried one time. He found me and chained me in the kitchen for a week."

By this time the only dry eye in the room was hers. She sat up proudly for the first time and announced, "I picked up the gun, walked up behind him and I shot him." Her eyes blazed as she looked around challengingly. "I'm glad I did it. My baby is safe now."

There was shocked silence for several seconds. Then, people began to applaud. Finally, the women gave her a standing ovation. Dr. Troy sat quietly watching the people react. I watched Dr. Troy.

I continued to watch her even after the jury released the woman to serve a sentence in a psychiatric clinic until pronounced well. When the jury members began to leave I screwed up my courage and went to her.

"Dr. Troy, I have a feeling that we were not in complete agreement about some aspects of the case. Could we go somewhere and talk?" She glanced at her watched, looked at Mike thoughtfully, then nodded. They discussed the pros and cons of the new jury system and moved on to more personal topics.

"In case you don't remember, I'm the errand boy who collected your toothbrush the night Ted rescued you from the TV station bombing."

"Really? Well, let me thank you now. Would you like a tip?"

"But of course. Why do you think I reminded you? I hope you feel obligated enough to scc me again?"

"How would you like to spend a quiet evening at my house, help me shell pcas and make a home-cooked meal? I much prefer my vegetables to restaurant food."

"If you'll let me help in the garden." She raised her eyebrows questioning.

"Remember, I even know where you keep your key."

"Oh, yes. Of course." He had the feeling she was annoyed.

"Hey. Don't worry. Your secret is safe with me. I won't use the key until you invite me to. Which I hope is soon. Scouts honor." He said holding up two fingers.

She looked into his eyes as though reading his soul. Mike's heart thudded and he felt nailed to the wall. Then she smiled that marvelous smile and he sighed in relief.

"When?"

"When, what?" He stammered.

"When do you want to come to dinner?"

"Oh. Tonight. Tomorrow. Every night." They laughed again.

"Tomorrow night at six? Oh, that's right. Being a detective you may have night duty."

"Six is fine. I'll wear my jeans and bring garden boots."

They did work in the garden picking the peas and digging new potatoes, and then sipped peppermint tea while the meal cooked. She threw a fishing line into the pool and soon had a trout. Mike sliced a lemon for her as she cleaned the fish and tucked it into the oven to bake. Naturally, they talked about Madge, the farm and her environmental work.

"We know her work well."

"We?"

"I mean, I read her essays and Jean introduced us before I asked her to help get my campaign off the ground. Her 'One Earth' pins have had a great deal of influence. In fact, I give one to all my patients as well as a copy of your Labels for Peace essay. It gives them something to think about besides themselves."

He felt proud of Madge.

After dinner they sipped apricot wine to soft music, sat on the porch swing and watched a full moon try to shine its way through the smog. It took all of Mike's self-control not to take her in his arms. There was a quiet, reserved strength and, yes, strangeness about her which he couldn't quite put his finger on. It wasn't just her unusual skin and hair coloring.

Somehow, he contented himself with watching and listening to her.

"This is a wonderful place," Mike said looking at the moonlit garden.

"Yes. I'm already dreading the trip to New York next month."

"Hey. I'm going on an investigation trip myself next month. I'm to be a witness in a case for a Federal Grand Jury. When and where will you be?"

In his journal he wrote: She had several speaking engagements in the city and surrounding states. I determined to make my trip co-inside with hers, even if it meant extending my stay. She said we'd compare schedules to see if a time could be worked out for us to meet. Before we parted, I invited her to a play and dinner. The rest of the month we continued to see one another every few days.

Usually, we ate at her house and sat in front of the fireplace or on the porch swing and talked.

One time I almost questioned her about the strange equipment in the basement but decide she might not like my snooping, so let it go.

Often I had the feeling we were being watched as we sat on the porch. She said it was probably the surveillance equipment she'd set up in lieu of a bodyguard. My detective instincts told me differently, but she seemed safe enough.

The abortionist's clinics had finally been accepted as a necessity of life for the most part and only an occasional attempt was made to slow birth control movements down. Better birth control and an aids vaccination had reduced the necessity of these clinics in the United States. Thanks to good Television Propaganda Programs and death-smog alerts, the governments of the rest of the world were beginning to accept the necessity of a near zero birth rate for the time being. However, getting the population to act responsibly was something else.

The week before they were to leave for New York, Mike invited Troy to a local play. He was determined to make a sexual advance for the first time. That night he wore a tux, took flowers and was on his best behavior. A gentleman in love.

It was one of those enchanting romantic evenings when everything seemed to go as planned. They went to dinner, the play was interesting. Afterward, they walked arm-in-arm to a nearby club for a drink before going home. The music was soft, sentimental stuff and they danced cheek to cheek. Their bodies hungered for one another and he felt her response as he kissed her lips lightly on the dance floor.

They were both experienced enough to savor the beauty of falling in love. Neither of them wanted to break the spell, Mike sensed.

When they returned to the table, he asked, "Where are you staying in New York?"

"I'm not certain. Since I avoid big cities as often a possible, I thought I'd leave it up to the travel agent and the government protection crew. Unless you have a better suggestion." She looked directly into my eyes with an enticing, amused expression.

His hands covered hers. "One room or two?" He asked holding his breath, lest I be rejected.

"One please," she whispered and leaned closer. Her silken hair fell across her smooth white brow as she swayed closer. Their lips brushed for a moment. It was like the touch of a butterfly that delights a person by landing for a moment on a finger. Time stood still. They moved in slow motion. She smiled.

"Mona Lisa," he murmured and touched her full lower lip with his finger. It was soft and firm. He held it there and thought of her lovely body. Would the rest of it be like the velvety touch of her mouth?

She kissed his finger. Then took his hand, turned it over and rubbed the scar on the back against her cheek. They continued to gaze into each other's eyes.

"Watch out," he whispered.

"What?"

"I read once that if we look into another person's eyes for ten minutes, we'll love them."

"Really," she whispered. "Perhaps you should just kiss me again." The table between them cut his chest, but he didn't mind.

When the waiter coughed and cleared his throat, they moved apart slowly. "I hate to break this up but everyone has left and its past closing time."

"Sorry," Mike said but wasn't sorry at all. His heart beat a rapid 'tat-too, tat-too. Surely she would let him spend the night.

They took a taxi to her house. When he attempted to pay the driver, she said, "Have him wait."

He felt let down and rejected as he walked stiffly beside her to the door.

She turned and asked, "Can you wait until next week? We'll be in New York, alone, and we won't have to feel rushed or get up early. Everything between us is so good. Romance is too soon gone. Let's cherish and anticipate our coming together." She put her hand on his arm and looked into his eyes, "Is that too cruel, too much to ask?"

He sighed in relief. "You bet. It will be the most exquisite torture I've ever had to endure." He kissed her long and tenderly. Her response was sweet and quiet at first. When he felt the stirring of her breasts and lips, he released her gently, turned and walked swiftly back to the cab before he became tempted to pull a 'me Tarzan you Jane' act.

Troy's secretary managed to get them seated together on the plane. Like honeymooners, they held hands, snuggled together, talked in low intimate voices. In the cab they kissed often, seeing practically nothing of the smog-weary city.

"We're here," the driver announced. "Thanks and Happy Honeymoon," he grinned knowingly as Mike paid him a handsome tip.

He looked at Troy and listened to her bewitching laugh behind the veiled environmental mask which she had drawn once again over her face before opening the cab door. The air made both cough before they ducked inside the hotel.

They registered and hurried to the elevator. Not touching each stood on opposite sides, gazing lustfully at one another. The ride seemed to take forever.

In their room the bellhop opened shades, gave explanations, asked if they wanted this or that until Mike shouted, "For God's sake, can't you do that later?" Troy giggled. The man looked startled, then smirked knowingly and left without thanking Mike for the generous tip.

He checked the lock and looked for Troy. The bathroom door was open and the shower running. Through the doorway came her dress. A shoe just missed Mike. As he undressed to join her, she began singing an old childhood song, adapting the words to the situation:

"Playmate, come in and play with me,
Take off your shirt and shoes,
Slide down my rain barrel,
(The clothes kept coming)
Shout down my cellar door,
And kiss me sweet and long,
Hold me forevermore..."

He laughed aloud with joy and anticipation, dropping the last of his clothing, he opened the shower door. The air was full of rainbow-colored bubbles. The hotel had one of the new bubble pipes for showers that were more popular than soap. He finally found her. She was slippery in his arms as they burst the beaded spheres between their bodies.

"Yuck," he tasted the soap on her lips and in his mouth.

She turned his face to the shower and said, "Wash it out."

He forgot about the taste of soap as he felt the beguiling softness of her breasts against his back. For a moment she rested her head against his shoulders. They stood in the steamy water enjoying the miracle of being together. Slowly her hands began to move down his body as though learning every inch of it. He let her explore. Her emotions talked through her hands. He felt her sympathy when she caressed the scars where he had been wounded in the war and stabbed by a resentful criminal when he attempted to save a friend's life. If she touches me sexually I will explode, he thought. He wanted that to happen for them together.

Taking her hand, he turned off the shower. Bubbles clung to her body and hair.

When he returned home he again wrote in his journal, not wanting to forget the moment of their coming together.

I will always carry a mental picture of her that day. Her white skin had peek-a-boo freckles in strange places. The lovely red hair, which was unusually thick in the center back, sparkled with tiny bubbles. Leaning slowly toward her I began to kiss her from the top of her wet silky hair, those bewitching eyes, the mysterious smiling lips, delicate neck, and sensuous breasts to the tips of her not-so-dainty web-toed feet. Then I threw her across my shoulder and carried her to the bed and began to work on her backside until she protested.

"Oh, Lord, I can't take it anymore,"

She rolled over and pulled me to her. Our lips met. I was inside her. There was no prolonging our climax. We erupted simultaneously and collapsed in a tumbled heap.

Perhaps it was because we had waited for this day for so long that made it memorable. Sex had always been enjoyable, but with Troy, it was special, a happening.

Mike lowered the journal and continued to think about Troy.

The time had gone by swiftly. He returned home before she finished her tour. Both had busy schedules. They continued to live separately. Each moment shared was precious. Months later, Troy still stirred his passion. She still retained an air of mystery.

It wasn't all sweet and rosy. Troy didn't always approve of the violence in his line of work, his sometimes macho attitude. In spite of his faults, he was glad she continued to find him attractive.

Solving World Problems

Today was another one of those rare afternoons. The air had been cleared by a hard rain. Mike whistled on the short walk to the weekly, happy-hour rendezvous with his old buddy, Larry Thorn. In their bull sessions they solved world problems as well as many of their own.

Larry and Mike met outside the door. Before going into the bar, they paused to watch a sunset in a fantasy sky. There was a strange mix of smog and cloud formations. Fluffy popcorn balls overhead, long-fingered streaks in the northeast and even a few thunderclouds in the south. Colors ranged from a savage red to salmon-pink against an ocean-turquoise sky.

"It's as though Mother Nature mocks pollution by using her enemy to make each evening swan song a memorable one," Mike said, remembering his meeting with Troy. Barry stood beside him quietly. "As though each day could be her last."

Mike turned, surprised. He had expected a humorous or sarcastic remark from Barry.

Mike studied Larry at him as they turned and went inside. Larry was different lately, he realized. He didn't wear his crooked grin or use his normal bantering, verbal personality. When had he begun to change, Mike wondered? I should have noticed sooner. Guess I did but I was too wrapped up in Troy to notice. Frowning at himself for not being more observant and taking a greater interest in a friend's difficulties, Mike threw my arm around Larry's shoulder. His body seemed tense. Instead of their usual place at the bar, Mike guided him to a booth.

"What's up Larry?"

He stared into space until Mike waved his fingers in front of his eyes.

"Oh, yes. I'll take a Coors."

The waitress raised her eyebrows at Mike. Normally, Larry would have paid her a compliment and perhaps told her an off-color joke. Asked her how she'd like to be in pictures or some such nonsense.

He ordered and returned to the inner world which, from his expression, was none too happy. Larry wasn't even pretending tonight. His thin face seemed haloed by the thick thatch of curly blonde hair. The pale blue eyes, which so often held a twinkle as he observed the world from a humorously and slightly satirical viewpoint, were dull.

"All right, Friend. Out with it. What's happening? Short of death, poor health and bankruptcy, I can't think anything can be as bad as you look."

"Have you seen the hologram in The Travel Agency window on Main Street, Mike?" Larry asked abruptly.

Mike watched him questioningly and shook his head, thinking he was trying to change the subject--tell him politely his problem was none of his damn business. He decided to play along until Larry was ready to talk.

"A hologram? You mean like the ghosts that waltz in Disney Land? Are you seeing ghosts?" Mike teased him.

He continued to look serious. "No. Yes. Maybe. I can't seem to get it off my mind."

"Why would a hologram bother you? You're an expert on pictures. By the way, what exactly is a hologram?"

Larry was a photographer and liked nothing better than to be able to explain an advanced step in the medium. Often, in detective work, the firm used his equipment or hired him to do piecework for the firm.

"Holography is a technique of producing a three-dimensional picture on photographic film using laser beams and without the aid of a camera." He went into a great deal of detail. Mike finally broke in.

"Hold it Larry. You're way over my head. What's so special about the ones at The Travel Agency?"

He laughed nervously. "Wait 'till you see the woman, Mike. You won't be able to get her out of your mind." A dreamy look softened his eyes for a moment. Then he became lost in space once more.

The curvaceous waitress approached. Mike waved her away, determined to get to the bottom of the problem or give up being a detective. But Larry was quiet and uncommunicative.

After finishing his drink, Mike decided to leave and try another angle.

"Gotta go, Barry. It's night and my work is just beginning. See you around or you can go night detecting with me." Mike clapped him on the shoulder. Even as he turned away, a glazed look came over his friend's face. His normally straight shoulders slumped.

Mike glanced back over his shoulder. Larry had not followed him. Instead he sat staring at nothingness.

Mike walked back, "What's eating you, Pal?"

"Huh? Oh, I'm fine?"

"Ted and Jean can't make it. Is Lisa coming?" No answer.

"Larry. Larry." Mike snapped his fingers in front of Larry's eyes before they focused.

"My wife. Oh. No. I guess not. I . . . I"

"So that's the problem?"

Larry waved him aside. "I'm fine. Fine . . . Just need to be left alone."

"Get a grip on yourself." Mike stood looking at him for a moment. "You know my key code if you need a bunk."

His glance made contact with the waitress. She walked by his side across the room. "Is he sick or something?"

"Why do you ask?"

"He used to be such a flirt and always had something funny to say. Now he wanders in and out at all hours of the night like a sleepwalker, orders a drink and often leaves without tasting it."

"I'll look into it. Keep an eye on him. Here's my card if anything happens. I'm going to see his wife and find out what the problem is."

"Good luck." They paused by the open door. "Looks like the rain's coming again."

"Yeah. We breathe for an hour."

Mike felt guilty about not staying, but, he was getting nowhere with Barry and a man has to earn a living, he thought.

Trouble at home, Mike suspected. Something tugged at the back of his mind. It would not come clear so he let it be for the moment. He had learned to respect this vague uneasiness over the years.

Being a detective is very much like being a psychologist, it seemed to Mike. What people say is only the tip of the iceberg. Larry's actions were screaming for help, and he wasn't certain as to the kind of help he needed to ask for. Mike would find out. Perhaps he'd talk to Troy and have her talk with Larry's wife.

By eleven o'clock he finished his assignment. Troy, would be expecting him, unless the job kept him out most of the night. They usually spent Saturday and Thursday nights together. She was an understanding woman. They never questioned one another's odd hours.

There were times when he arrived at her apartment at two a.m. and she was still downstairs in her office with a patient. It would be his turn to curl up with a book or be asleep by the time she returned to bed. When her soft curves fit themselves against his back, he usually woke. Sometimes they had long, quiet talks, if one of them was uptight about his work. Often, they were content to entwine, letting bare skin absorb the comfort of one body against another.

Out of curiosity, Mike swung by The Travel Agency on his way to Troy's house. San Diego is an average-sized city. Since the great water shortage at the turn of the century, no homes could be built or sold unless another house burned or was destroyed. No new permanent residents were admitted legally.

The once lush areas, yards and Balboa Park returned to desert vegetation. Many people moved north and into areas where there was more rain. The malls were filled with busy shoppers, but neither Mike nor Troy went there.

The downtown gas-light district still struggled to keep the feeling of a small town and a leisurely pace. It was a warm night, and even though late, many people were out strolling under the simulated, antique gas lights.

The holograms filled the large picture windows in front of The Travel Agency. Several people were standing quietly looking and listening to the weird music which accompanied them. At first Mike wondered what all the fuss was about. Then, a mysterious aura reached out from the woman. A flush of desire encompassed him. Mike heard himself sigh in longing.

There she was, the idealized woman, impervious, mystical, elusive, inviting each man to come to her. He watched her lively, black, shining curls bouncing against her bare skin. The blouse was off-shoulder, low-cut to a 'v' between rounded breasts which moved under the blue silken blouse. Long bare legs cast shadows through a gaily painted peasant skirt. Her eyes were alight with amused propositions.

She was surrounded by French houses with orange tile roofs which sat in emerald green meadows and deep blue, smog-free skies. Twisted trees fenced in pastures. Olive leaves danced in sunlight, throwing shadows across her sultry brow. Her scintillating walk made the curls hanging 'round her shoulders seem alive. The young Medusa would appear walking under the trees, smile invitingly over her shoulder, pause and speak in a husky sensuous voice, turn and enter a home. In the background the sound of the sea slammed and receded, slammed against the shore and receded . . . Wind whistled a lonely siren's wail . . .

This primitive background music produced the rhythm to which she moved and spoke. The illusory scene repeated itself, over and over. Each man who passed paused and Mike wondered if each was seducing her in his mind.

He stayed until he became tired of standing. There were others around him just as fascinated, but each had eyes, only for Medusa. That was the name which the music whispered, "Come! Medusa waits for you by the sea."

Somewhere in the back of his mind he knew he was being mesmerized, even as his analytical mind shut down.

Finally, he shook himself free of her spell and looked around. He felt certain many of the other shadow gazers had been here before.

Another window a few feet away was watched by a seemingly fascinated group of women. This hologram had a handsome man reaching out seductively. He murmured to them.

"Don't keep me waiting, Darling. Come to me soon. I'll wait for you by the sea."

Mike checked his watch. It was after midnight. Troy would have gone to bed hours ago, he told himself, trying to make excuses for not keeping their usual date. Feeling restless, he walked for awhile, wanting to be alone to think about the woman.

He never made it to Troy's house that night, or the night after.

Somehow, his investigations did not seem very important after he saw the holograms. Ted was out of town often and Mike managed the office. The workload was light. There were the usual divorce afternoon or night watches, a missing person, a lost or stolen item. Sometimes there were investigations for the police department or the government. The firm had security clearance. Using his office management as an excuse, he sent other employees on assignments or asked the secretary to handle things while he visited the holograms or just lay on the couch with the TV turned low.

Both Ted and Mike had worked in the military police during the drug wars of the late nineties. Now, they were often a link between the local bureaucracy and federal departments. For several years they had been keeping an eye on the 'abortion revolution,' as the police called it, and fed the government and state departments information only an observant, curious civilian picks up.

Environmentalists, and who isn't one these days, were calling for a One-Earth Resolution in the United Nations. But, as Madge often told Mike, "Just the fact that an individual is alive causes pollution. The greatest contribution any of us can make is to die quickly. The second greatest one is not to contribute to the population."

Even though Mike had a yearly sterilization shot, he'd been accused of impregnating several women in the past. Being a detective came in handy each time.

After seeing the holograms, Mike seemed to drift through his world in a light fog. He functioned at work but everything centered on his evening visit to the Medusa. He stopped seeing Troy. Often he and Larry viewed the holograms together.

Larry mentioned causally that Jean had a baby, but didn't act very excited about it. Just said, "It's a cute little duck."

Larry and Mike continued to meet weekly but their main interest was in the holograms.

"Funny thing," Larry said once. "When I first saw the holograms, I took Lisa to see them, they turned us both on and sex was really great. Then she became pregnant and seemed to lose interest in sex. For some reason, I don't care either. Unless I could meet the real Medusa."

"It's strange that a picture could have such a strong influence on us," Mike commented. He could feel his mind tug at the fog of his emotions.

"Sometimes I get this urge to smash those images, but when I get close to her, I can't do it."

"I know how you feel."

"Did you know I took a picture of her and enlarged it, but the picture did nothing for me? It was rather fuzzy. Ghostly. Then I taped the music. It is really weird when turned up high. For some reason I raced out of the house and ran all the way to the bay. After awhile I realized where I was and had to hike all the way back home."

They laughed and sat looking at one another for a long moment.

"You really have it bad, Larry."

"Well, the great Mike Lambert isn't so smooth in this case either, is he?"

Mike nodded his head in agreement.

Sometimes they drifted over to gaze at her until their eyes became fuzzy. Then, said a reluctant, goodnight.

His desire for women, including Troy, deteriorated. When they did have sex, he found himself fantasizing about Medusa. A detective seemed to turn women on. In this new century, 2020, women were often more aggressive than men. Sleeping around only succeeded in turning him off completely.

Mike talked to the manager of the travel agency and found The Medusa lived in Arles, France. He began making plans to go, but something always came up.

Ted came back for a week. He was still on an important mission for the firm. Even Mike didn't know the details, but it was taking a great deal of time. After a couple of days he asked Mike to step into his office.

"What's bothering you, Mike?"

"Did I do something wrong?"

"No. You act as though you're in a trance. Jean says you quit seeing Troy. Is that it?"

"I guess I've lost interest in women."

Ted had always been great at hypnotism. They'd learned it at Intelligence School in the military and he and Madge had played around with it in college. Mike used it for relaxing himself, but preferred the direct approach with suspects.

"Mike, you seem rather vague and this is a critical time. I'd like to hypnotize you and go back over past events since I've been gone. Do you mind?"

"Hell, no. But I can tell you without that."

"I've heard about the holograms. Just in case something happened that you missed, I'd like to hear from your subconscious."

"Be my guest." Mike laughed nervously and sat in a chair, closing his eyes. It felt good to relax.

"Count backward from one to ten, Mike . . . Relax . . . Have you felt differently, strange, recently?"

"Maybe. A little. After seeing the holograms in The Travel Agency windows, I feel distanced from people. Each evening after I finish work, I stop by to watch the holograms, then hurry home to dream of France and the lovely Medusa.

"Go on, Mike. Tell me about the holograms."

"Shortly after seeing the first hologram, I began to have erotic dreams about an elusive woman, a mermaid, bare-breasted with green sequin legs that swam toward me. She would appear with a usual walk but instead of going into the house, she went into the sea, then turned and beckoned, calling me to come into the water. I would try to follow, but there was something I felt I must do before I could meet her there. I couldn't remember just what." He paused. Even though under light hypnosis he wondered about the dreams.

"Go on."

"She might as well have been a real siren. I even found myself daydreaming about her. I guess this began to affect my work as well as my relationship with Troy.

"One day I went to the library and checked out an old book, The Odyssey. I spent two days reading it. The description of the scene where they tied Odysseus to the deck and filled the ears of the sailors with wax so they could not hear their calling of the siren, stuck with me as I pondered the holograms and the dream. Jung would have called my images archetypes, I suppose.

"Have you talked to Troy about this, Mike?"

"Troy nailed me on the spot after I failed to show up for our usual dates two weeks in a row. She called me at the office. I tried to keep regular hours."

"What happened?"

"She asked, 'Mike. Are you all right?"

"Oh, yeah, Troy. I've been meaning to call you," I stammered weakly.

Not one to beat around the bush, she demanded to see me. "I'll let you off the hook, Mike, but I want it face-to-face. Be at the cafeteria Del Mundo at twelve."

"She was waiting when I arrived. Neither of us were hungry. A frown formed between her lovely brows when she saw me. On her shining red hair was one of the net veils the women are wearing over their faces when outdoors. It is supposed to filter some of the dirty air. I suspect it's more for fun and fashion than practicality. But, even we men are wearing small nose filters and wrap-a-round goggles to keep out the grime."

Ted watched as Mike rambled. He had turned on the recorder and promised Troy he would let her hear it.

"Sometimes on the street as I look at the lovely long-legged women with yellow scarves and clean-scrubbed faces after a rain, I wonder how grubby cities can hatch these lovely butterflies. Troy is one of them." He paused and smiled.

"On her the delicate veil looked good. Real good. It gave her handsome face a softening effect. For a moment I forgot about Medusa and straightened my shoulders. Her frown eased up as she reached across the table, laying her hand on mine. The thrill of her touch and smell of light perfume reminded me of how long it had been since we last slept together. "

Mike paused and Ted prompted, "What happened when you met her?"

"She was angry. But tried not to show it.

"Let's be frank with one another," she said. "After all this time we owe our past that much." There was an awkward pause and she withdrew her hand. Again the frown appeared. My emotions gave a sob which shook my body.

"Talk to me, Mike. If it's another woman, I can accept that, but if it's something physically wrong, I want to know."

I shook my head trying to clear it. "There's nothing wrong. Just working too much or this damn air. Probably an allergy thing. I'll be OK soon. Just be patient."

"If I didn't know better, I'd think you were hypnotized. As though someone stole your libido."

"Troy is an astute Psychologist. That was just what it felt like inside. Except when within the realm of the Medusa hologram, my sexual desire was dead. As we talked there was a stirring in the back of my mind, as though there was something I needed to remember or she held a key to the fog in my mind, if could find it.

"Could we just be friends for awhile until I work through whatever is bothering me? There isn't another woman."

"You act as though you have the 'hologram virus.'"

"The what?"

"That just slipped out. Several of my patients are saying they feel vague. Only alive when they look at some silly holograms at The Travel Agency. It seems they think they need a vacation. The strange thing is, the women all want to go to the seashore."

"For a moment she slipped into her own thoughts. We have that effect on one another. As we talk together, problems often seem to solve themselves or solutions and clues become more evident. How I miss this woman, I heard my mind say. Then why was I being so distant? I wondered.

"Perhaps that's it. You need a good vacation."

"I gave her my charming boyish grin. It worked on other women, but she refused to respond. The frown only deepened.

"Promise me you'll think about it?"

"I nodded, leaning back in my chair, letting her clear gaze search my face, acting innocent. She looked disappointed and left for her afternoon appointments soon afterwards. The comforting presence of her voice and perfume remained and lifted my lassitude.

"A hologram virus. Leave it to Troy to put her finger on it. How could a picture give one a virus? I thought of you, Ted. You taught me to think in opposite terms.

"Give or more likely in my case, take. Yes, that was it. Something is gone from me, and Larry, too. Apparently, there are others. Guess my habitual detective inquisitiveness is starting to kick in. I'd like more time to investigate it, Ted."

"Take your time, Mike and report back to me as to your progress. I never thought I'd say this, but you're no good to the firm until you snap out of this lethargy."

Holograms

The secret to his lethargy and that of Larry had to be in the holograms. Mike picked up his hat and a bit self-consciously, slipped on his nose filter, adding wrap-around sunglasses before he stepped outside the office into the muggy air.

At The Travel Agency he turned his head and hurried past the holographic windows. He could feel the tug of the music but managed to push his body past and hurry inside. It took a minute for his eyes to adjust and his heart to quit pounding. Inside the agency the music was off and the shades were drawn to block out the window holograms. Giving the receptionist his detective's identification. Mike said, "I'd like to talk to the manager." She grinned knowingly, winked and when he just looked at her, showed him into the office.

"Detective Lambert to see you, Sir."

"Ah, yes. We've met, haven't we?" They shook hands. "Ah, yes. Once or twice at a Chamber of Commerce dinner."

Mike let him flounder around before coming to his rescue. "I'm Mike Lambert. A T & M Detective Agent.

"Are you investigating me?"

"Some people have been having a strange reaction to your ads in the windows. Or at least I'm here to find out what's so hypnotic about them. Can you tell me how they're made and by whom?"

"Sure. Be glad to show you what we have."

He showed Mike the projector for the holograms. It seemed rather ordinary. "Did you know that any piece of a hologram will make the whole picture?" He asked.

"How can it do that?"

"Beats me. I just turn on the switch."

"Would you mind if a friend of mine, Larry Thorn, an expert on cameras, took a look at this sometime?"

"Of course not." He looked at Mike closely. "Are you another spellbound Romeo?"

"No. Maybe, a little. But let me ask you a question. Have you been affected by the holograms in any way?"

"Of course not. Well, at first the staff and I were fascinated and we couldn't get much work done. Then, the technician from the Zinla Agency in Europe came. He spoke to us about the fascination of the holograms, and suggested that we keep the music out of the office and curtain off the windows. Now we hardly know they're there. The staff uses the back way to come and go. We also avoid the crowd outside.

"Besides, we're too busy selling tickets. I've never seen so many women with babies going on vacations. The women all want to go to the seashore and the men to Arles, France to see the 'Young Medusa.'" He smiled gleefully.

Mike could see him adding up his bank account. "So that's her real name. I thought Medusa was an ugly old woman who had snakes for hair?"

"Yes, but think of what she must have been like when she was young--before the snake curse."

Mike laughed for the first time in days, bought a ticket for France, thanked him and went out front to study the holograms in a more scientific light.

The music swept over Mike as he stepped outside. Once again the siren called and his being reached out in answer to the wail. It was as though the very earth was crying out to him. He stepped in front of the hologram and was immediately entranced by the woman again.

Mike reported to Ted the next morning. As usual, since the holograms, he seemed in need of sleep, his clothes were wrinkled and he looked as though he hadn't eaten for days.

"I have accomplished one positive action. I'm going to Arles, France and find out as much as I can about Medusa and the holograms."

Ted studied him for a long time. "Sit down Mike. I've been studying the last tape and I'd like to hypnotize you again to see if there have been any changes."

Mike frowned. "I said I was going to do something about it . . . I . . . oh, OK. Get it over with."

Again Mike sat silently before Ted and let himself be hypnotized.

"Ok. Mike. Open your eyes. Do you remember what you told me?"

"Yes. There was nothing unusual, was there?"

"I made a tape of what you said. Think I'll play it over. Do you mind if Troy hears it?"

"Well. No. When you two find out what's wrong with me, do you plan on a lobotomy or retirement?"

"Glad you can still joke. You're not too far gone. Let me know what you find out about the holograms?"

"The holograms? Oh, yes. My investigation. Sure, Ted. Meet Larry and me at the Hungry Dolphin Thursday, or will Jean let you out? You've been gone so much this past year. I've hardly seen your new daughter."

"I'll see you there, Mike." He patted his shoulder and watched Mike leave. Then he opened his desk and talked quietly into a strange looking device.

Relationships

Troy sat at her desk and listened to the tape.

Poor Mike. She wanted to reach out and call him, but she knew he must find his own road to maturity and action or they could never have a healthy relationship. If he was a good detective and was able to resist the siren's call, maybe . . .

She pretended not to notice his seedy appearance when she visited the holograms to check on her patient's reaction to them.

Her mind drifted to a woman who had visited her office in the afternoon. To lose a child was an especially traumatic event for a mother.

This one kept saying, "I can't believe she could drown. She swam before she walked. I'd swear she had tiny webs between her toes. We talked of having them removed but she swam so well, I decided not to mention them to anyone."

"What did your husband say?"

"Oh. He's traveling. As I said, he lives in his own world and I in mine. The baby was such a comfort. Bob even gave us the tickets for the cruise and joined us there. The vacation away from everything did us good. We were talking for the first time in months. Then . . . then Cindy just disappeared. If she fell overboard, no one heard a splash." She began to cry.

Troy tried to comfort her. Another victim of the hologram virus, she thought.

She played Mike's tape again. He was on to something, but could he push his emotional involvement aside long enough to find it?

Perhaps he needed a bit of help.

"Madge. This is Troy. Could you break off your lecture tour and go see Mike? He needs you, darling."

"What is it, Troy?"

"The same thing. Perhaps worse. I think he needs a shove from you to get past his inertia."

"OK, Troy. I'll leave after the speech tonight."

"How's it going?"

"I'm not certain. You know politicians. They tell you what you want to hear, and then vote where the money and power lie."

"When I'm president, I hope you won't say that about me."

"I won't. I think people would vote, if new ideas are put forth. It's the house in power and 'in groups' I worry about. You have them to fight as well as superstitious fanatics. I wish Mike were by your side."

"I think he will be. With a little help from you and Ted, I think he can be his old self soon. He's at least making an attempt to get his act together."

"He was such a handsome, funny brother. Maybe we all spoiled him because we enjoyed him so much. I never thought he'd get caught up in The Snare."

"Perhaps it takes a bit of male machismo to get other male's attention in our society, but he must work through this thing himself before he can be any good to us."

"Maybe. I believe if men had a choice, they'd be gentle and loving."

"You should have been the Psychiatrist, Madge."

They giggled and continued to talk.

"You'll come here after you see Mike?"

"Yes. Then I must get back to the farm, or I may have a divorce on my hands."

"Never." Troy felt a bit envious of the good relationship Madge had with her farmer-husband and Mike.

After the talk with Ted, Mike tried again to be objective.

But, as he wrote in his diary, Only Medusa offered that elusive, imperceptible something to which my male sexuality could respond. I forgot my resolution to find the answer and walked about like a...like a dog in heat, my mind only half on my work. My usual dress became slovenly; I didn't care about anything. At any rate, the windows were the talk of the town and nearly everyone managed to go by often. Going on European vacations were the main topic of conversations during the days. The night activity, none can say, but an unusually large number of babies were born in this spring and curtailed many actual trips.

Madge caught the midnight express after her speech and let herself into Mike's apartment with the key code when she got no response from her knock. She couldn't believe the man she saw slumped, unshaven; dozing before the TV set was her brother.

"Hello Mike."

He slowly turned his head. "Well, well. If it's not my famous, little sister, The Mite."

She could see him try to pull himself together. He stood up, swayed toward her. She caught him and gave him a hug.

What's happened to you?"

"Just busy, I guess," he muttered, vaguely.

"That's not good enough. Come here. Look in the mirror." She led him into the bedroom.

"Are you fishing for a compliment?" Mike looked at Madge, trying to avoid the figure of himself.

"Where's Ted? Isn't he still your partner?"

"Oh, he's on an assignment in California. Nothing here I can't handle."

"And Troy. Are you still seeing her?" she asked, knowing the answer.

He shook his head, looking at the sad figure in the mirror as though seeing himself for the first time.

"Is that what's wrong? Did you split up?"

"No, we still see one another off and on."

"All right Mike. Into a cold shower. Shave while you're there. Then we're going to get to the bottom of this."

When their Mom died Madge had taken her place, even though a couple of years younger than Mike. He'd played along with her all these years and listening to her became a habit. To please her and for his own amusement, he acted the child and she the mother. Madge was the breath of fresh air he needed.

After the cold shower she poured him a stiff drink and commanded him to drink it. "Come here." She patted the sofa, pulled a pillow into her lap and commanded, "Lie down and I'll give you Mom's velvet glove treatment. He lay down on the couch with his head in her lap. She stroked his forehead and talked softly; just like Mom when either of them was troubled or had a headache.

As teenagers and later at college, they'd dabbled in hypnotism. Mike often use it in his work. She stroked his forehead. He knew what she was doing and let himself slip into a relaxing trance. He would trust Madge or Ted with his life.

Perhaps she could help him help himself, he thought.

"Tell me, when did all of this begin?"

He told her about the holograms, remembering Larry's answer to the same question. As he talked the spell that had settled over Mike recently, began to withdraw.

"That's it, Madge. It's not the holograms. They hypnotize people, but . . . " He tried to sit up in his excitement. She pulled his head back down into her lap, continuing to stroke his forehead and talk to him. "The music. I hear the music even after I leave. It's like a siren's call. Odysseus knew it wasn't just the woman . . . "

"Relax, for now. You said they had been there for months. They won't go anywhere tonight. I think you should stay away from them for awhile. At least until Ted gets back. The two of you can work on it together like always. Promise me, Mike." She was so insistent, he promised. "After I leave, you'll stay away except to investigate. Don't listen to the music, Mike. Don't listen to the music . . . "

When Mike woke, it was morning. Madge was gone. A note on the table reminded him of his promise.

Even away from the holograms, the siren called.

Self-hypnosis, ear plugs and dark glasses, as well as distance, let Mike attain a more objective attitude toward the situation. Madge called every day at first to reinstate the suggestion she'd planted. He could do it if he didn't listen to the music. Now she called once a week and he told her what he was doing.

"Keep at it Mike," she encouraged.

It was Ted who originally advised him to become a detective. "You're like a bulldog. You never give up once you sink your teeth into an idea, so why not use your tenacity as a god-given talent and let it earn your living?"

At first, staying away from the windows make him feel like an alcoholic who no longer drank. As often as possible that month, he visited Madge on the farm. It felt as though he have been away from the green grass and blue sky for an eternity. Only the spray planes over the neighboring fields disturbed the tranquility he felt there.

Madge and he often watch the haze washing over the mountains from the cities and talked about solutions to world problems. 'Now, it's clean air and water, not jobs that immigrants seek." Their farm too had a windmill and pool of fish. The television programs had convinced many people to turn their yards into orchards and gardens where there was water. A cheaper fresh water from salt water device had been invented, for those living near the ocean, water was becoming available once again. Reused water from household appliances were allowed by the city for yards and gardens.

Drinking water was delivered to homes. Forests were being planted on vacant land and it was hoped in a few years a more frequent rain cycle would develop naturally. Schoolchildren and the unemployable were hired to water the trees by hand so none was wasted.

"There must be something more that can be done," Madge would begin, frowning in the direction of the brown horizon. All of them were wearing large brim hats, long sleeves and veils or sunscreens. Many people were building homes underground, but neither Mike nor Madge wanted to become a mole.

"Well, there are solutions but they include people's cooperation," Mike reminded her.

"Can't the government do something more?" she complained. "They keep spending money on space and seem to have given up on Earth. Maybe we need a declaration of war against pollution and overpopulation. Then we could sell Clean Earth Bonds. I'll have to talk to Troy about it. May God have mercy on us if she's not elected." Madge did tend to over-dramatize at times.

"Actually, the population of the United States wasn't too great and was going down, except for immigrants who came here and used our medical aid for a spawning ground at the turn of the century. In their short-sidedness, they believed they could take over the country and were being patriotic when they had children." Mike reminded her.

"We could still produce the food needed if pollution didn't kill the crops. It's the waste from the past and the demand for more and more products that people don't really need that's killing Earth. "

"That's true, but at the mention of birth control, a lot of religious toes are stepped on. We still hear their threats. It's hard to believe that anyone today could protest birth control."

"We're lucky Troy's still alive," Madge said and looked at Mike with a grin.

Nodding contentedly, he relaxed and soon fell asleep.

Mike's head seemed to be clearing. Like rising from a steam bath. Madge is right. The holograms do affect people in a strange way, he told himself as he shaved. She should have been the detective. She was a good worker for Troy and the environment.

His sister had always been a protester in peace marches, pro-this-or-that. She had a knack for gathering few people together for a good cause. Marriage only slowed her down a bit because she preferred to live in the country. Years ago she had been elected as a national representative to the president for environmental action. Her pins and the essay, Labels for Peace, won international acclaim. It also made a lot of money for the environmental group she represented. The beautiful jewelry pins of Earth from space with a sparkling butterfly were still selling.

They were the perfect camouflage for T & M spy devices. Ted and Larry wired them and, wallah; they had a lovely monitor or bug. Until recently, the women hadn't known about the bugs.

Mike picked up his journal scrapbook, opened it to essay ideas Madge had sent him, poured myself a cup of coffee and sat down to read. As he followed the words it was as though Madge's voice continued to soothe and strengthen the auto-suggestions she had planted in his mind.

Civilization. Was that the ultimate goal of mankind? For the first time in months, he felt the urge to write. He liked to look up words in a dictionary and let the word speak in his mind.

The dictionary blandly defined Civilization as an advanced stage of development in the arts, sciences and complex social, political and cultural structures.

But what was needed to make a civilization?

Civilization says, "I am the safe future for which all men search, yet out of fear and ignorance, they destroy that which they blindly pursue."

Civilization agrees that this may be the goal, "But individual men and women are the foundation on which I stand. These people live in the winding streets and twilight cities of everyday life. They work, plow, plan, dream and play. They dress me with clean streets, are courteous and thoughtful to one another and they are honest in their dealings."

Civilization continues thoughtfully, "The breath of a civilized man or woman smells of cosmic dust. She may be bare of foot, but knows herself to be the mother of mankind. Loving is her greatest attribute. He has compassion, raises violets and bridges, and has fetish oddities, boundless dreams and a smile as sweet as maple syrup for his family and friends.

Civilization is elastic and demanding. She believes criminals are a wart on her blushing face. A sign that those teaching virtues, the wonders and joy of life, have failed. Like a blade of grass pushing through a cement highway, crime is an erosion of the evolution of the human soul, a destroyer of civilization. It can be as small as littering, rudeness and vandalism, or as large as taking another's life.

"These diverse genes of wild forbears must not be allowed to reproduce," she warns, smiling sadly across chill vapors of time and space. Evening shadows creep across autumn's party splendor as her mystical face becomes one with purple shadows in a forest green tree.

Civilization says, "You will know me when I come. My middle name is Peace."

Troy spoke of Self Reliance. Mike wrote: Self Reliance woke from the realm of dreams to the pounding hoofs of reality. The unearned luxuries of his past were gone.

The world, a series of surprises, unpredictable, unreliable, stood in his path, dressed in an army of shapes and events.

Old men in suspenders chewed the tobacco of gossip and malice. Friends, with greed in their eyes, took advantage of his kindness. Unseen forces in the form of government claimed much and gave back pittance.

"Unfair," he accused. At their laughter, he slunk away as though he were guilty.

Wandering in brooding silence into the green forests of remembrance, Self Reliance sulked. His strange, gray iceberg brain listened to the night cries of faceless creatures. Cowering in the chill vapors of regret and remembrance of ashen splendor, his body trembled under an icy moon.

In nagging shadows of genetic memories stood his ancestors, with only a club standing before the wolf of hunger, cold icy winds, the sharing of food and body warmth. With this instinctive knowledge came the dawn of self-realization.

Sunlight sparkled cleanly on bubbling water, dewdrops rode rainbows, his clumsy hands tenderly stroked the lilies of the field, a kitten rubbed his leg, and a rib-thin dog snarled, barked, sniffed his hand and waited to be patted.

From the tree on which he leaned, an apple fell. Along the vine-covered path of life he wandered. A limping horse followed him with a hanging head, as though he, too, were condemned. Self Reliance now had a family to feed.

At first he saw only the seeds of a thistle to harvest. His eyes begin to pierce the shadows, the green, his nostrils the odors blown on a vagrant wind. Ears hear nature's music of whispering winds, babbling brooks, and animal walks. With pride and the fruits of the earth, he was able to survive. The discarded mansion became home. The horse provided transportation, the dog and cat brought food treasures. A lonely widow hired him.

Arms which had known silk shirts and soft woolens, now wore sunlit tan; muscles bulged from labor which left him exhausted but with a sense of accomplishment... Entertainment which had been sought in theaters and museums was all around in the beauty of nature, the frolic and courtship's of animals and birds.

Self Reliance had known many women but never love. In the arms of a simple widow, the purr of a stray cat, the greeting of a rib-thin dog, a limping horse and the pride in his own accomplishments, he found himself.

Mike sat thoughtfully looking inside the deep spaces of his mind. There must be a base of Honesty something whispered.

Honesty has been both exulted and shunned. Wise men know Honesty as the foundation of a nation. When she weakens, the sands of time soon blow across great capitols.

Honesty wears modest gowns, even when invited to visit the Prince.

"Let me give you furs and jewels," he whispers. "You're much too worthy for burlap. And your friend, Plain Jane, why bother with her stark words when the Kings of the World will flatter you with pearled myths about your beauty, promise you great deeds, wondrous things. You're too good for the average man."

Honesty warns both Prince and Kings, her hot breath flaming in silent rage, "Unless you share me with the average man, your kingdom will fall like a sandcastle before the incoming tide."

He was a wise Prince, "This day, with your help, we will build a nation. Will you, Honesty, be the architect?"

"It will be my honor to be your foundation. Upon this rock of Honesty, you will find peace and rest." She stretched forth her arms releasing the dove of honesty upon the kingdom.

They produced a nation such as the world had never seen!

*If you go to the Lincoln Memorial in an ancient city called Washington, you may still hear the name of Honesty wailing on the winds of time.

"I await a new Prince who values Honesty. Are you he?" she whispers to each individual who reads the memorial.

But what about the role of the individual in a society? He remembered a discussion they'd had one evening in the bar when Mike had been on a role. It went something like this. Mike wove the tenor of their thoughts together like a word-blanket.

Individuality is an undivided thing. He stands like a monument above the masses. His strength is as a mountain in the face of a storm. The earth would be chaos without him. Garments like steel clothe his loins, yet to touch him is to be warmed. In cities many feet trample the weak, the pigeon, by the indifferent who ride the tide of broken things. To be held in his arms is to feel protected. He holds not because he loves, but because you, too, are human. And humanity is what it's all about.

Individuality has waded through shards of scorn, seeming indifferent to society, yet knowing he, only this morning, rose from its seething ignorance.

Individuality is a builder of precision. His bridges and skyscrapers stand straight, strong, tall. In spite of the differences between himself and others, he commands respect. Like Van Gogh, too late, they learn to love him.

He stands alone, but not lonely.

He wouldn't have it any other way!

To Mike's astonishment, it was daybreak. He looked at the pages he'd written and felt as though he'd just started. Picking them up he glanced over them and realized they were the summation of many conversations he shared with family, friends and Troy. The only original thing about the whole mess was the way he put the words together. He shrugged and stood up. It was time to get back on the job.

As he placed the pages in his notebook a program slipped out. Troy—New York—their first time together. It had been so precious. How could he have let her slip away? As though trying to pull it back in place he fell back in the chair and tried to remember. He picked up the program and searched for the place it had slipped from to return it.

He found the place in the journal where he'd written about it.

His spirits lifted. He leaned back, closed his eyes and let the memories of their togetherness flow through him.

After awhile he made a new pot of coffee and drank another cup, knowing he was stalling his next moves, an investigation of the holograms, a call to Troy and a trip to Europe.

The scrapbook was full of Madge and many of his own escapades which had made the paper at one time or another. Also, some of Troy's writings and talks that she gave at the meetings as well as several of his own poems. Someday, he intended to organize it.

He paused to read one of his poems based on a statement that had caught his eye.

"Whenever you make a mistake, remember that you are God. God doesn't make mistakes. God only has experiences."-Rama.

THE PERFECTION OF IMPERFECTIONS
Mike Lambert

Change in crystal metals,
As in human beings,
Take place along the fault lines
Where boundary lines and forces meet,
Demanding change and compromise
In order to survive.

Diamond cutters and sculptors,
Work the places where imperfections
Rear their heads.
So the jewel of human beings
Would appear as imperfections
Where the insecure but malleable
Personality is flexible enough to change.

Mankind, you and I,
Have made the greatest advances,
Where the clashing of ideas
Are set up, uprooted,
Re-thought, refined,
And erected once again . . .

He turned a page in the scrapbook and looked at the program with Troy's speech, remembering. Tears flowed down his cheeks. He missed their togetherness. What is wrong with me? Why am I separate from her, he asked himself. Finally, he brushed away the tears, blurring his sight and read her words.

In his mind he sat in the front row proudly listing to her enchanting voice, applauding her mind as well as her splendid body as she talked about jails and social problems.

Jails, Dungeons, Anarchism

r. Helene Troy spoke, "It's a cold gray dawn as I stand before you. Shadows like those in jail cells cast long bars across this auditorium.

My mind is also shadowed.

Just as Dorothy Dix quit teaching and went to the rescue of people in asylums in the 1880s. I want to do something about county and state jails as well as the environment.

The first question most people ask when I show concern is, "Do you want all those people in the streets able to rape, kill, and steal at will? What else can we do with them besides pen them up?"

I ask, 'Is what we're doing now solving the problems'? Since no answer is forthcoming, I search for a few alternatives. A friend of mine was a parole officer for twenty years. I ask him, "How long do you feel a jail term needs to be if it is actually going to 'teach the criminal a lesson?"

"About six months," he responded. "It gives them time to ponder their crime and decide how they want to live their lives. They either come out changed or become a good citizen, or a hardened criminal."

We send people to jail in punishment for doing harm to someone or being destructive to something in society.

How often does the punishment fit the crime, I wonder? In a Child Growth and Development Course I learned that if we give a harsh punishment for a minor mishap and vice versa, we warp the child's way of responding to life situations. Even though the sentences may be for less than a year, often the conditions inside crowded prisons, for even a week, are traumatic and dangerous. They hurt not only the body, but self-esteem and spirit as well.

When I attempt to discuss crime and punishment with my colleagues they say, "Don't complain about jails unless we can let's hear some concrete solutions. What do you suggest could be done that might work to change the situation?"

"I've given it a great deal of thought and do have some suggestions.

First, we should spend more money on prevention than punishment. We could set up a Marshall Program against crime. One, five, ten, twenty, and fifty-year goals. At the end of fifty years, we would expect to have eliminated crimes."

The audience laughed, but she had their attention.

"Second, I would take five percent of the military budget, five percent of the health, education and welfare budgets and five percent of the prison budget to research ideas, genetics, DNA, etc.. Endow Psychologists, Geneticists, and Scientists to study the brain, mind, heredity, and the environment of criminals.

"For example, ancient societies had wise men and women. Usually they were long-lived, had experienced many things in their own lives as well as being observers of people, ideas, and their environment. They directed the affairs of the community and passed their wisdom down to others who were perhaps called Prophets, Wise Men, Priests, or Ministers, and today Psychologists. Psychology is not a babe, having been given birth by Freud and Jung. Let the wise people in our society present programs.

"Wisdom cannot always be passed down, however. Especially since words do not always mean the same things to everyone. Words presented without experience are often misinterpreted. Thus, we get Preachers instead of Wise Friends, Psychologists, and Ministers. Many Psychologists do not understand that they are the Ministers of society and Ministers do not realize they are the original Psychologists and these all took the place of friendship . . . a caring person or family to share problems with you.

"Or, that the basis of any teaching for a quality life must be honesty. Not in the form of commands, "Thou shalt not kill," for the ignorant, but based upon self-understanding and a knowing that with honesty comes a world free of crime. A paradise on Earth. Simple honesty can do this. But we must reason it out and desire it, not do it out of fear.

"Life is complicated because we make it so. Many lawyers, politicians, cheats, and liars build false plastic worlds and tell us that's all there is. With self-confidence which comes from knowing ourselves and seeing actions clearly, we will say, "No thanks to dishonesty."

At the end of each year, I would expect a complete report and pursue actions which the researchers proposed.

"Third, anyone who received a lifetime sentence or was a second timer would automatically be sterilized. We have too many people in the world now who are not fit to be parents. Don't give me the Hitler genocide thing. We all want and need the healthiest, most intelligent children we can have.

"I would pay anyone who volunteered for sterilization a thousand dollars. This is more than most two-bit criminals get for a crime. If they buy dope with it and kill themselves off, at least they will not be on the streets making other children to be future criminals. Japan controlled its population by offering money to anyone who would be sterilized.

"Fourth, just as we used Television to inform people about cigarettes, we could use it as propaganda against dishonesty, killing, and stealing. There are two things being left out of our educational system. They are, knowing and understanding ourselves and the importance of honesty in any society. Parents need training to be good parents. Being a parent should be a privilege, not an accident of sex.

"Thoughtless politicians say, "Johnny has to have more readin,' writin', and 'rithmetic." They never once look around and ask, "Why haven't our educational programs and religions given us honesty and peace? Is anything else needed besides these three which will add to the quality of life, better government, and a clean, peaceful world? If they learn the three biggies and have no art, culture, music, creativity, freedom to experiment, languages, etc., what will they write and read about?

"With Television, we can educate people to become angels or devils. To kill or to love. At the moment, we are a society of 'Parents trained by Untrained Parents.' Sometime, someplace, adults will need to be trained along with children to know themselves and their world. That which makes life a hell and not heaven is often man-made. Each of us has a piece of Earth to use wisely or throw away. Never in history have we had a propaganda tool like television. Nearly every shack, no matter how impoverished, has a TV antenna or a place in town where people gather to watch it. So, let's use it. If ten minutes several times a day were devoted to education and quality of life, we would be able to change the attitudes of nations in a few years.

"Fifth, Let's look at some of the old punishments that were supposed to be so inhuman. The Scarlet Letter gave an example of a woman made to wear an A on her outside clothing. Every person was aware the she had committed a crime. We might smile at it today, but the marking of the criminal was effective.

"I suggest that for certain offenses, the first-time criminal wears a yellow jumpsuit for six months to a year, with a monitoring tag. Thus, we all know who committed a crime and can keep an eye on him or her. The crime could be printed on the front and back. If they ever remove the suit outside the home, the neighbors report it and they receive a double sentence inside.

"For example: If a teenager steals a car, put him in the stocks or pillory. (A punishment where the criminal was put on public display with head and hand through holes of a board.) Thus, everyone takes a personal part in the punishment.

"Today's criminals are put away out of sight and their punishment is an abstract thing, like napalming. We don't see the eyes of our enemy so we can mete out inhuman punishment without a qualm. Also, it should be automatic that criminals pay back any money or damage expenses to the person against whom they committed the crime.

"Sixth, We have great trainers in the military as far as physical fitness is concerned. Many of these people are idle. I believe boot camp would be a tremendous sentence for a criminal. A daily ten-mile hike, learning how to be clean, keep busy doing projects to improve society, and eating only healthy food each day, raising his own food and flowers in a small garden patch, would turn out healthy people at the end of the sentence. It would be much better than being cooped up under crowded conditions. After six months of clean living and hard work, he or she could be allowed to take vocational courses for half a day.

"A criminal would not be released until he learned a skill and could become a contributing member of society.

"Seventh, Society itself could learn to accept the fact that once a criminal is not always a criminal and forgive but not forget. People must once again take part in the punishment system as well as rejuvenate criminals.

"Eighth, Serious crimes such as cruelty, rape, killing, and third-time offenders should have a jury of Scientists, Psychologists, and Medical Doctors to study the person. Theirs would not be to forgive but to decide if the person had a right to continue to live in society, the right to penalize society by it's having to pay for food, shelter, and guards for the rest of his or her life.

"The criminal could have the choice of being frozen until Science developed a way to rehabilitate them, or taking their own life. A Socratic Hemlock so to speak. (No one should have to live in a tiny cell and no one should have to share living quarters with another person where he or she is unsafe.) Neither should the taxpayer have to pay for people who pose a threat to themselves.

"Ninth, The Basic Goal for each person would be: A clean environment, a world free of war, food and shelter for all, a life free from fear of one's fellow man. Not one of a race to see who gets the most toys. Boats, trucks, luxury homes unlived in most of the year can be shared. A basic income for each and an opportunity to earn should be available for all, just excess amounts of income at the expense of cheap labor should not be allowed.

"The study of values for civilization, human relationships and simple honesty based on knowing ourselves, taking responsibility for our acts and doing unto others as we would want them to do to us, will lead to this kind of world.

"We have been innocent children learning to crawl and sit up. Now we have the knowledge and tools to stand up and walk together, to complete the circle, from Eden to Eden, if each of us clean up our act. I thank you for your kind attention!"

They gave her a standing ovation.

Who or What was Happening?

After hearing Troy they went back to the hotel room where Mike sat down and wrote a poem.

WINGLESS TIGERS
It's so fortunate that tigers have no wings.
Napoleon could have conquered England
With the help of old James Watt.
Heil Hitler had the power
An Atomic Bomb to Build!
He trusted not his scientists.
Again the world soared.
It's so fortunate that tigers have no wings!

Politician-tigers start their
'War to end all wars'.
Religions support the tigers
And harass the wings of science.
Waiting for a god to save,
Not believing in the strength and power
Of their own Humanity!

When we fly on wings of science,
Not superstitious finks,
Filled with hate and greed,
Put politicians-tigers in a pen,

Humanity, not tigers will have wings!

It is fortunate that science is based on:
Where is truth, not who is right!
It is fortunate that tigers don't have wings!

Mike let the book slide to the floor.

When he arrived home, his first instinct was to call Troy. No, he told himself and pushed back his hunger to touch her. This fascination with the holograms had to be worked out first. There must be someone behind them. Or was it just another way of selling, a commercial trick? If so, it needed to be stopped.

The phone rang. Mike ignored it. It kept ringing until he answered it.

"Larry here, Mike. Are you coming to the bar this evening?" Glancing at the clock he saw it was nearly 6 p.m.

"Be right there."

Mike decided to stay away from the holograms without earplugs and study Larry. He'd been exposed to them for over a year, whereas Mike had only been hanging around them a few months. If he could get past Larry's restlessness, it would tell him how deep the trance-like state went. Ted pulled into the parking lot on his mo-ped behind Mike. They walked toward the bar.

"You're looking much better, Mike."

"Thanks. Now we have to pull Larry out of his funk. Find out how his mind is functioning after long exposure, provided we can get his attention."

Troy's speech was still on Mike's mind. After they ordered, he glanced at Ted and switched the discussion to the group's favorite subjects--Laws, Rules, and Government. "How do you suppose a

Senate and House full of lawyers are going to like a woman psychiatrist for president, guys?

Larry gave a crooked grin. "I heard a good lawyer joke the other day." For a moment he brightened, then slumped again.

Mike quickly waved the barmaid away and said, "Tell. I need a good laugh."

"Let's see if I can remember it . . . Oh, yes. This man went into a curio shop and found a large brass rat. He took it to the clerk who said, "It's a splendid piece of work. I'll take it."

"You'll note our sign, we take nothing back. Shall I wrap it?"

"I'll take it as is. Thanks." The man carried the rat to his car, set it on the seat beside him and drove home in the direction of the Coronado Bridge."

Larry paused and stared into space. "Come, on," Mike urged, "Don't stop now. What happened?"

"Where was I?"

"Driving toward the Coronado Bridge with the brass rat on the seat."

"Oh, yeah! The man looked in his rearview mirror and saw rats pouring out of alleys and racing down the street behind his car. He glanced at the rat on the seat—it seemed to vibrate. God, he thought, what did I buy? I can't take these rats to the island. In the middle of the bridge he pulled over, rolled down the window and threw the rat into the bay. The rats behind him followed the brass rat into the bay. Well! How about that?

The man became thoughtful. On the other side of the bridge he made a U-turn, went back to the shop and began to look around.

The clerk saw him and said, "I told you sir, you can't bring anything back."

"Oh, I liked the rat fine. I want to buy something else."

"And what would that be, Sir?"

"I thought you might have a brass lawyer!"

It was great to see Larry chuckle at his own joke. Mike and Ted glanced at one another and Ted nodded.

"We do seem to have a few too many lawyers," Mike agreed.

"Who the hell began making laws, anyway?" Larry asked.

"Good question." Ted frowned. "I think a law was invoked when two people couldn't agree upon a fair settlement about an action or thing, such as a piece of land.

"I suppose when we won't compromise, a third party is called in to help settle the dispute. Usually, each person has no interest other than his own. Both parties may get a settlement, but they may be better off if they'd made a compromise without having to give the third person a piece of land in payment."

"It would behoove us to try to work out our problems." Mike decided, watching Larry intently. At least he was paying attention. Maybe the effect was wearing thin.

"Too bad each decision becomes set in concrete, called a precedence," Mike continued Ted's thought.

"What happens after precedence is set?" Larry asked.

"Usually it becomes a law which fits average but not the individual situation. Like wearing shoes on the wrong feet. True, we have shoes but the fit isn't very good,"

Mike laughed, "A couple of drinks and we're all authorities."

Ted liked to pursue a topic and was just getting warmed up. "It seems to me all laws and contracts should have a time limit. Say, after five years, we're all pretty well conscious of the law, it should become obsolete. Laws are not sacred. They should give us more freedom, not less." The group sat thinking and contemplating the subject.

Ted continued, "I don't remember if there was ever much mention in the classroom about the why and wherefores of Government. We memorized countries and leaders' names but why we needed them was not questioned. Animals seem to get along pretty well without laws other than their natural ones and a few instincts that help with survival."

"Like boundaries, laws only exist in minds and on paper. Maybe we need a good fire every few years." Larry was sounding a bit violent these days. Ted was watching him with a worried look and caught Mike's glance.

Ted and Mike had one of those relationships where each could often read the other's mind. It was good to have Ted back, Mike thought. He'd been out of town so much the last couple of years. They often saw one another only in passing and did most of their communicating by phone. Since Mike had caught the 'hologram virus' there hadn't been much of that.

Also, when Ted was home his children were in their teens and demanded a great deal of time; then he and Jean had surprised themselves and everyone else with a late baby, just last year.

"I've wondered if the Governing powers, such as the President, really have a job description. They often act as though they don't know what they're doing." Larry liked to worry a subject to death.

Ted hadn't been in on a session for quite some time so he waded in again. "Education is set up by the Government to create good citizens they told us in college. Before that, I'd always thought it was to learn as much as I could about many things. To be a good citizen means to obey the whims of the leaders in power, I presume." The others nodded.

"Jean would like to see education set up to teach people how to think, logic out virtues which are a must for a civilized society, to enjoy learning, and for all ages. Every seven years, adults could take a school sabbatical and be paid to renew their education, along with the body cells which are completely changed every seven years.

"If we understood ourselves and others, would we need so many, laws, fences, and signs, Troy asked me recently," Mike said.

Ted nodded, "She, Madge and Jean make a good team. They hit it off well. Sometimes I think if we left the women alone to govern us, they might clean up both the world's and men's acts. Women seem to be the only one's really speaking out clearly on issues."

"Maybe it's because they have us to protect them," Mike said feeling macho.

"Why not?" Ted asked. He loved and admired his wife, Jean, Troy, and even my sister, Madge. Both Larry and Mike nodded in agreement and sat in silence thinking.

Ted stood up. "How about an early session at the office, Mike, so you can fill me in? I'm back to stay. The next out-of-town case that comes in is yours."

"I think I know what it is, too?" Mike said. Ted looked at him with a question on his face.

"No emergency. We'll talk about it tomorrow."

"Let's go by The Travel Agency," Larry said standing up.

"No. Not tonight Larry. There's something wrong there and I'm going to find out what. I'd advise you to lay off, too. Doesn't Lisa resent your spending so much time there?"

Lisa doesn't seem to care much anymore what I do. Spends all her time with the baby," he said resentfully.

"Well, I don't think it's good for us. I'll talk to you about it later.

Mike wanted to do some more thinking. Clear his mind and summarize his knowledge as well as strengthen himself away from the holograms so he could investigate them objectively.

Mike went home and gave himself some strong hypnotic suggestions as he lay on the couch thinking about his life. His thoughts roamed to Troy. Even if they got back together, could the two of them have a good relationship? Was he lacking something men like Ted and Larry had to give to women? How could they be so trusting? Mike's relationships hadn't been all that reliable.

When Troy and Mike first met, she insisted he take a course in Intimacy and Friendship. At the end of the course, they were each to turn in a paper on what they had learned. The instructor liked Mike's essay so well he'd read it to the class.

Troy did not congratulate him or say anything when they went out for coffee later.

"What's wrong? Didn't you like my essay?

"Are you certain you want an answer? A truthful one?"

"Go ahead! Shoot! I can take it."

She told Mike, "Unless you really felt what you wrote in your guts and live it, the whole thing was 'a tub of bullshit'."

"You're laying it on a bit thick, aren't you? Are you sure you aren't just a wee bit jealous?"

"Maybe we should let it rest," she said with a faint smile. "It was a lovely sermon. Perhaps I shouldn't complain. You did go to the sessions with me and you did apparently get some ideas from them. Let's just let them gestate for the time being. OK?"

Deep down, Mike had to admit she was right. He had mouthed words and parroted them back. But, damn it. He did get a lot out of the class in spite of what she said. However, each time he reread the essay, he began to understand a bit more what she meant.

Except for writing poetry, or making love, Mike seldom expressed deep emotion.

Perhaps I was disenchanted about love too often, he thought. Losing Mom when I had just reached my teens and Pop soon thereafter, might have made me afraid to love deeply again. Madge seemed to give me the only continuous relationship I had ever experienced, until I met Troy.

The journal was open on the table. He had showered but didn't feel sleepy. After getting a beer from the refrigerator he picked the book up and thumbed it open to the essay. What had Troy meant? He read:

Intimacy and Friendship

INTIMACY is a word which we usually think of in terms of sexuality. Yet the dictionary gives several other definitions. Intimacy is developed by friendship through association, warmth and privacy.

The dictionary gives rather cool, impersonal interpretations of words but I find my thesaurus digs into meanings more precisely by giving nouns, adjectives and pronouns.

When I gave it the word intimacy to define, it started off with the sexual ones such as fooling around, adultery, entanglement, fling, etc., but it also gave attention, awareness, carefulness, cognizance, concern, consciousness, consideration, heed, knowing, knowledge, mark, notice, observation, perception, regard, sense. All of these seemed to be characteristic of not only a good relationship with the opposite sex but words which cement a friendship as well.

The definition of Friendship in the dictionary is showing goodwill, favor, cheerfulness and comforting. In the thesaurus, it gave friendship as being an affair, closeness, rapport, familiarity, and companionship.

Next to our lover or spouse and families, friends are the most important people in our lives. In fact, many of them outlive our marriages and even family relationships. Like an adoption of a child, a friend is chosen, not thrust upon us by accident of birth.

It amazes me how such an important person as a friend is often treated so lightly. In marriage, there are ceremonies to celebrate the engagement, the wedding day, anniversaries, etc. On a national level we celebrate, Labor Day, Memorial Day, Christmas, Groundhog Day, but where do we honor one another as friends?

The time we share with one another, the confidences, the knowledge of what makes us happy, sad, frightened, or angry is chosen. Sometimes even a spouse does not know as much about us as our friends.

We meet a person of the opposite sex and often marry within a very short time, but is he or she our friend? Does he understand our weaknesses and accept them? I believe the old fashion engagement was arranged in order that two people would have time to get to know one another well. They would have time to discover and value one another as friends.

How do we make friends which last a lifetime and are there for us? It takes a long time to make a good friend. Is there a way to shorten this process?

In two weekends of a Group Therapy Course, twelve strangers met. We chose someone we'd like to get to know, took his or her hand, this couple chose another couple, etc., until all linked hands.

Then they were asked to sit on the floor on pads, or if they were uncomfortable doing so, they could fold out a chair.

Two people chose to sit above the rest, a young teacher, and a middle-aged teacher. One businessman in his fifties sat stiffly apart against the wall.

By the end of the first two days, each of these people who seemed to have a polished smiling veneer, dissolved in tears. A softness appeared around the edges. Their outside appearance no longer held us out. They slid from their chairs to cushions on the floor. By the end of the sessions, it was as though there was no surface where any of us began and the other ended.

I've seen the same thing happen in church when people come to the altar and asked to be saved or, in other words, wish to change their way of life because they are so unhappy inside—they forgive and accept themselves. When we lose a loved one or get a divorce or some other tragedy, we are vulnerable once again to crack the shell of our beliefs and remold ourselves. A group known as EST uses group encounter principles. When utter strangers tell us how they see us, both our faults and strong points, it often makes us embarrassed and we deny or become resentful because of their comments; then when we realize they have no reason to find fault with us, we have to accept the possibility that what they are telling us may have some validity. Finally, we accept how we are and decide if we want to change. It is as though in a very short time we go through all the steps in The Time Frame of Grief.—Denial, anger, acceptance, etc.

In a traumatic situation, remolding can cause us to build up a harder shell than before, or it can help us regain sensitivity to our surroundings that we may have lost. With friends around us at this time, our world is a safe cozy place in which to run for shelter, somewhat like a child into the arms of a parent.

How do we make supportive friends? By being a friend. Being self-aware. What does that mean? We love the people we really look at, and the people who really look at us. People who listen to us and we them. Looking and listening are arts. If I look down at my plate and see that it's still full of food and my friend has finished his or hers, I realize that I've done too much talking.

If it's his problem, I'm giving too much advice. If it's my problem, I'm probably repeating myself and becoming a bore. Learning to both listen and talk is an important aspect of friendship. It is not taught in school. If people avoid us, it may be that we're either taking too much or too little.

It is important to give attention to the person I'm with. If one of us is constantly interrupting, looking around the room, or going off to the phone, the friendship may be pretty one-sided.

Getting to really know one another, not just the food or drink we prefer, or where each went on a vacation, but how each of us think and feel about ourselves as well as others, our joys and sorrows, builds a foundation for a continuing relationship.

It may be religion, philosophy, secret longings, politics, favorite music, authors, etc. Observation, perception, and recognition show regard for the other person. We develop another part of ourselves each time we share our lives with another person.

One friend said she learned a new sport with each new man she dated. I wonder what he learned from her.

A spouse is only part of one's life. It's lovely if the two of you agree on most things, but even identical twins feel smothered once in awhile and need a release.

Sometimes we may live a bit too vicariously in our friends' lives or our spouse's and fail to reach out to others who might help us develop other aspects of ourselves.

It has been suggested that when we go to a movie, read a book or have an orgasm, we forget the burden of our lives for a time. In friendships we share and develop other sides of our many-faceted selves. I find I have different personalities with different people. The 'Many Faces of Eve' may be true for more of us than we realize. I read somewhere psychologists have found that we can have up to 87 different personalities. Wow! Our friends and environment help influence the face we are showing now. Mine is glowing from being with this group. Thank you for your friendships!

Mike laid the scrapbook on the couch remembering the group session and the disagreement he and Troy had afterward. Tears flowed down his cheeks. Troy had been right when she called him on his attitude. It was bullshit. He had professed to care about those people, but except for Troy, had never tried to contact any of them afterwards. Had he ever really told Troy how much he cared about her? Why had he held back?

Each of them had past relationships that had ended for one reason or another. They'd decided they wanted a steady, monogamous one for a change. "In many ways we're alike," he told her. "You spy on people inside; I do the same on the outside." It had seemed to him to give them a great deal in common, but had Troy needed more?

Mike thought because they had found one another sexually fulfilling it was enough. They had drifted along, until he discovered the holograms. If he had really given of himself or asked for help, Troy would have been there to share his problem.

He reached for the phone to call her, and then pulled back his hand. When he worked out this haunting thing with the dreams and hologram, he felt he would be ready to have a real relationship. The way he was now, he would only be a burden at a time when she needed to be working on her campaign. He could only hope she would be waiting.

The Travel Agency

The next morning Mike scanned the headlines in the local paper and read with interest:
Travel Agency Windows Broken Again.

The entrancing windows of holograms which many of us find lovely are apparently the victim of vandals. The company is installing surveillance cameras and asking the police to patrol Main Street more often . . .

He reached for the phone and dialed the police station.

"Is Dr. Handley in her office? This is Mike Lambert. Have her call me when she comes in."

She returned his call within minutes. "Mike. How can I help you?"

"I wanted to know what you thought the breaking of the hologram windows was all about."

"A great deal Mike. I've been wondering if I should talk with Dr. Troy. There's something strange about them. Why are you interested? Has the woman got to you, too?"

"You might say so, and I don't like it."

"Why don't you come down to my office and compare notes?"

"Thanks. I'll do that."

Dr. Handley was easy to talk with. Over the years they'd shared many cases. Mike admired her. She was a new breed of policewoman, pushing innovative action in the treatment of possible criminals. Some of the new court practices were beginning to have an effect on the crime rate.

Psychologists were becoming an important part of the police and criminal system. They weren't just called in now and then to testify as they had in the past. One of them usually sat in on each jury case.

"You don't look well, Mike."

"I seemed to have caught the "hologram virus" like so many others, but I'm determined to get a handle on it." He grinned. "If I don't I'm afraid Ted's going to fire me."

Dr. Handley smiled and inclined her head as she studied him. "Tell me about it."

"Something about the holograms puzzles me. After talking with people and a dream one night, I finally realized the strange music was actually the sounds of the sea. Apparently, my subconscious had picked up on it more quickly than my conscious mind. I caught myself longing to see the ocean. I wondered aloud, 'Was it the music or the woman that so many of us find fascinating?"

"Subliminal ads were outlawed in the seventies, "Dr. Handley said thoughtfully. "Maybe we should look into that aspect."

"If a conscious mind is behind it, why? It does sell tickets, but the manager of The Travel Agency here says the majority of ticket sales are to women with babies, or men who want to go to Arles, France to see Medusa. With my logical mind, I've tried to find a way past my biological responses, to no avail."

Dr. Handley said, "I'm hearing more and more about the holograms. Some of our policemen and women are showing lethargic symptoms. They say something about holograms now and again but I hadn't given it too much thought until the window breaking episode. Been meaning to take a look."

"Wear earplugs. I'm going to Europe as soon as Ted can spare me and talk to the source of the productions."

"Keep me posted, Mike."

Mike kept his distance from the music but continued to watch the people. He thought about Larry and his strange reaction to them. Not only had Mike's sex life gone to pot, but he began to find a pattern among the married couples he knew. Asking questions brought out similar answers that went something like when he'd first talked to Larry. He tried to recall Larry's responses. They went something like:

"Hello, Larry. How's Lisa? I haven't seen her around lately?"

"Oh, fine, I guess. To tell you the truth, we're thinking of getting a divorce."

"I thought you two had a good marriage. What happened?"

"Well, the woman, you know. After I saw the holograms last year, Lisa became pregnant. Then, I started having strange dreams and our sex life deteriorated. I don't seem to want anyone but that woman. I know I sound like a schoolboy, but I'd like to go over there and actually meet her."

"Larry, is Lisa restless too? Does she dream about the man?"

"Well, I don't know. She hasn't seemed interested in sex since before the baby came. We don't talk much."

"You've had other children. Why should that make a difference this time?"

"Well, it does. It's a strange child. Don't get me wrong, it's loveable and cute in a duck-like sort of way. Very smart." He paused, and then continued, "Lisa wants half of our savings--to take a Mediterranean Cruise," he said, looking off into space and rambling in a dreamy sort of way.

"Hell, I told her I want to take one, too, but I can't get the time off. She says it might do us good to get away from one another for awhile. I refused to give her the money. Know what? She borrowed it from her folks. Can you believe that? Lisa has always been the conservative one."

Dr. Handley called again the next day. "I stopped by the holograms. Good thing you told me to wear earplugs. Felt as though I was being sucked into an ocean wave and remembered your warning. Dr. Troy's trying to get time in her busy schedule to see me."

Mike summarized his talks with Larry. "That's not much to go on, Dr. Handley, but it's happened to me and I'm an investigator. I feel as though I've been on a long voyage in the fog. The only way I can go near the holograms is with earplugs. Larry made tapes of the music and listens to them at home. He's really been involved. But, he's promised me he'll stay away and give you the tapes for analysis that is if you can trust your sound technician. Maybe he can break it down with machines and wear earplugs. See if there's some sort of subliminal message in the music."

"I think you're right, Mike. It sounds like a form of hypnosis is being attempted and as though it has something to do with the ocean. What would anyone have to gain other than selling travel tickets? Do you think it goes deeper than that?"

"That's one of the strange things about it. Why should it matter where anyone goes, if only ticket sales are the goal?"

"There's another mystery I'm trying to solve which takes precedence over this one, I'm afraid."

"What's that?"

"Babies drowning. Do you realize more babies have drowned this past year than in all of the last twenty years? It makes me wonder if we're having a lemming's suicide with terrible twists. The mothers say the babies have an excessive love of water. Nearly everyone who takes their child on a cruise loses it in the water. It's driving the ship captains crazy."

"Water again," Mike mumbled.

"What?"

"It is somehow connected to water. Have there been any other strange reports about water that you know of the past year?"

"Well, let's see. We've lost an atomic sub and so have a couple of other countries. Then, there was the one newspaper item about an alien watercraft being captured by the CIA, but it was hushed up."

They talked for awhile. Mike told her, "I'd better get my butt to Europe, me thinks. Tackle the problem from that end. I need a vacation anyway. I'll let you know when I leave. "

It was time to put an end to the mystery. The agent assured him Medusa still worked at the head office in Arles. Mike decided to go and meet her first. I'm not going just to see Medusa, he told himself.

Mike talked to Larry again before leaving. They were in the bar on their usual Thursday night meeting. Mike finished his drink and shoved the glass toward the bartender, who refilled it.

"Larry. Listen to me. Someone's been throwing rocks through The Travel Agency windows where the holograms are displayed; at least nine times in the last couple of weeks right here in our city. The owner keeps replacing them because the holograms sell so many tickets. I've been to the police department. They're trying to make the owner turn off the holograms for a month. We want to see if it's the holograms that are having strange effects on people. From what I've found out so far, the music is what's doing it. If you must go see them, wear earplugs. Promise?"

"You really think it could be them and not Lisa and me?" He asked, a gleam of hope lit his eyes.

"Yes, I believe it's possible. I don't go near them without earplugs and the holograms are just interesting pictures. I'm going to ask Troy to talk with some of her patients."

"How is Troy? Come to think of it, we haven't seen much of either of you lately."

"Your relationship's not the only one that's been affected, my friend. I'm worried, Larry. The Travel Agent manager told me the advertising's going to change next month. There's one for children's vacations coming up. I'm afraid of what it may do to children. Keep yours away from it. Go home and talk to Lisa and both of you stay away from those windows and especially the music."

"Jesus. What can a person do about something like that? Isn't there a law against subliminal advertising? We may not be the only ones who've been affected. What can I do to help?"

"Just talk to Lisa, pass the word along to others and keep away from the holograms. Don't forget to leave the music tapes at the police station with Dr. Handley. I wish you could have gotten inside the projector devices."

Larry nodded, "Don't think there was much there except the computer disc to program the music and action, as far as the holograms are concerned."

A few days later Ted and Jean came in for Happy Hour. She worked at an Aquarium and always looked fresh and clean. Her short hair shown around her pixie face like a halo. Ted teased her about being a fish doctor and said she could practically talk to them.

"Did you see the papers?" Ted asked laying it on the table. "That killer we sent to jail just announced that he has 'got religion. Can you imagine making headlines out of crap like that?'"

"What the hell kind of religion?" Larry asked.

"Sounds like the seven-year itch to me," Ted said and began to scratch a sunburned shoulder. "Think I have it."

They laughed sipped drinks and sat in thoughtful silence.

"I wish I knew if there was any Meaning in Life," Larry was despondent. They weren't watching the holograms, but Mike gathered he and Lisa still had a ways to go before he was his old 'happy-go-lucky' self again.

Mike saw Ted wink at Larry as Mike drug out the little Thesaurus he kept for writing poetry: "Affiliation... Relationship...Re-union...are a few definitions in the dictionary for the meaning of religion. Surprisingly, commitment, love and passion are some others. Life means, among other things, spirit and essence. Meaning is significant and understanding. We put these together and find Meaning in Life."

"Are you looking for Paradise, Larry?" Jean asked.

The waitress served another round and they watched her sway across the room.

"Maybe a good lay would do it," Ted said. "Look that up, Rev. Lambert."

Mike didn't mind a laugh at his expense if it would brighten up Larry.

"Is paradise different for each individual, just as each of us chooses different things from our environment?" Jean wondered idly.

"Dr. Frankl in Search for Meaning suggested that to find meaning we need interesting work, loving relationships, and reasonably good health. Meaning is a by-product of these," Ted said.

"Ted reads nearly everything and retains a great deal of it, I read a few things and think most of it isn't worth remembering. What do you say, Larry?" Jean teased.

"Who reads?"

Ted was on a roll, "Scientists suggest that we're a part of it all, like a ripple in a pond. The question, what is the meaning of life is a nonsense question in relation to life. Accept and enjoy it, they seem to be saying. Biologically, life may be heaven or hell depending on an imbalance of hormones."

"Now who's giving the sermon?" Mike teased.

Ted grinned and continued expanding on Larry's comment. They liked to get Ted wound up on philosophy. He was better than any preacher Mike had ever heard.

"Troy says the best part of religion is just good psychology," Mike quoted.

"Speak for yourself, John," Larry said trying to be witty. Mike made a face and looked at Ted. He was fired up and Mike wanted to hear what he had to say.

"Many of us wouldn't recognize paradise if we stumbled into it. As Shaw said, 'Everywhere I go, I go, too, and spoil everything'. We drag our past into each moment, not trusting the beauty of now, or we project the future into today and it looses its shining possibilities."

Larry seemed to have babies on the brain. "Except ye become as little children, ye cannot enter the kingdom of heaven," he quoted. Mike suspected it was because their latest baby was such a strange looking child. When Mike asked him about her, he always insisted she was fine and super-intelligent. "Just slow walking."

Ted nodded and picked up his train of thought. "We teach children to pay attention to what has worked in the past. By the time they become adults, most of their time is spent responding to the past to protect the present. When we reach the future, like retirement, we've forgotten how to enjoy each day," he paused.

"So what is paradise?" Larry asked. "I didn't enjoy being a kid that much."

"Is 'now' the key?" Mike asked, feeling a poem coming on.

Jean chimed in again, "Maybe it's keeping life simple. We need to clean house both mentally and physically often. Don't carry around lost causes, past hurts, and fears. Liking ourselves. Knowing that we are learning a little more each day about living life. If we learn to crawl, and then walk maybe we can run into the future with open arms."

"I guess life is the greatest adventure we have, alright," Larry said. "That would mean this is paradise. I'm not sure I'll live through it." He slumped down and stared at his drink.

The bartender approached, "Sorry boys and girls. Bar's closed. See you next week. Hope you got the problems of the world solved." Sometimes he sat down and listened to Ted and added his two cents. Tonight, he just wanted them to leave.

They found Larry a cab, Ted and Jean went home, and Mike walked back to the apartment, thinking.

He couldn't understand why his deepest emotions and thoughts only bubbled up in poetry and never flowed out of his mouth as ideas did from Ted's.

Mike stayed up another couple of hours writing 'exploratory' poetry. With poetry he seemed to explore his thoughts and emotions to a depth he couldn't express in spoken words. Maybe he could understand Troy better through a poem. Her main interest seemed to be in the environment and running for president. She was probably glad to have him out of her life. Gave more time for herself and her goals. No, not her goals but those of Earth. She, Madge and Jean were determined to clean up the world. Sounded like a bunch of housewives with scrub pails.

Maybe that was what was needed, he thought, as he looked through the swirling smog outside the window. The government should issue scrub pails for everyone. "No rest until you've cleaned up 6 sq.ft. each day . . . " He smiled and picked up his pen . . .

EARTH MIRACLE

Such a strange round structure
Floating about like a lonely bubble
Of blue-white atmosphere.
Self regenerating,
Making oxygen to breathe,
Stirring up storms at the surface of rain forests
Planting nitrogen in its own soil.

A Troy upon Troy
As it builds on fossilized layers
Meshing life together like one single creature
Clinging to itself
Turning, turning in the sun.

A lonely lovely jewel
Of many cells,
Giving birth to that one thing which can destroy self.

Will it allow its human sucklings
To turn it back to dead brown dust?
Can it survive its own wild prodigy?

A vague uneasiness tugged at the back of Mike's mind. There was something obvious he was overlooking. This time, he would pay attention. Mike remembered dreaming of Odysseus and the siren who fed sailors to the swine. How, he had himself tied to the mast so he could hear, but not leap over the side in answer to her call.

It was obvious that music was a part of the disturbing influence. Perhaps Dr. Handley's technician could isolate parts and come up with something. These days he carried a pocket full of earplugs and passed them out to people he encountered at the holograms.

Ted thought Mike was exaggerating, but he accepted the earplugs and promised to wear them when he checked out the holograms. Also, if Mike felt that strongly about them, he should go to Europe right away and checked out the source of the holograms.

"I forgot to ask Jean, how's Troy's campaign is coming?"

"They work well together. Troy's spending most of her time making television tapes in her garden."

Mike nodded. He seldom missed one of her proclamations which asked people to live more simply, recycle, save, use and buy as little as possible, raise a garden, if only a few plants in a pot, be aware of each decision we make and what we're doing in each small act such as: leaving water run, buying things we don't need, reusing everything. "Whether or not you're rich enough to afford a thing is not the issue. The issue is: Will this shorten the life span of Earth, my children and I? Change your attitudes and change the world."

It was a strange campaign plea. Mike was certain she would never get elected. However, what she said made sense.

"There seems to be an attitude change needed more than anything," Madge had said. "I went with her to the United Nations last month. Her words seemed so simple they had to agree. However, they probably won't do more than rebroadcast a few of her tapes."

"Madge has a minor in psychology and is into attitudes and new age stuff."

Ted looked at him intently, "Troy asks about you. You seem much better now. Why don't you call her Mike? "

"I am, soon. But first I have to figure this thing out and get rid of my strange dreams. There's something going on and I don't like it. When I get to the bottom of it, I'll work things out with myself and hopefully with Troy."

Mike went to say goodbye to Madge before leaving.

She looked at him strangely, laid her hand on my arm and said, "Mike, I want to tell . . . " A tractor pulled into the yard. "Oh, there comes Josh for dinner. I'd better get busy."

Mike looked after her wondering what she had started to tell him, and then shrugged. She'd tell him later or perhaps it wasn't too important. He stayed outside to listen to the night birds sing and to think.

Ted was busy with his own cascload. He wondered about their new baby. Both Ted and Jean were in their forties. They didn't seem as enthused about it as new parents usually did. Ted just said Jean took her to the aquarium every day because the baby loved the water. So had the babies who drowned, Mike remembered. He must pay them a visit as soon as he returned . . . and Larry, too.

Larry's Crisis

The last evening before leaving Larry met him for happy hour; Mike saw a change in his face. Maybe it had just been a mid-life crisis. He teased the waitress and his eyes flashed with good-natured humor.

"Have to be going. Promised Lisa I'd come home early for a talk, after the baby is in bed."

He gave Mike a punch on the shoulder and stood up. For the first time in months, Mike thought, a bit of the old Larry had returned. "Hate to leave you alone, on your last evening. Or, do you have a date with our holo-ghost?"

"Don't mind me. I think I'll have a date with a real woman for a change."

Talking to Larry clarified his own thinking and gave him courage. He suddenly had a desperate urge to see Troy. The pay phone was busy. He had another drink and waited impatiently.

"Hello, Troy. This is Mike. I realize it's late, but I need to talk with you. Can I come over?"

"Well. I'm rather tired Mike. Couldn't this wait until tomorrow?" Even though they hadn't seen one another recently, she had never put him off before.

"No, Troy. It's important. Not only to us, but perhaps to a lot of people."

"Okay, Mike. Come on over." She pushed a new gate buzzer when he arrived.

Evidently she had been in bed. Her silky red hair swung free around the heart-shaped face he had kissed so often. A soft gown and robe clung to her body in all the right places. He tried to take her in his arms. She yielded politely and then turned away.

"Sit down, Mike. How can I help you?" She asked in her office voice.

He smiled to cover the pain and sat opposite her in a chair tossing his hat symbolically on the couch beside her.

She laughed in the way he remembered so well. Troy leaned back against the low-covered sofa and they studied one another. Other people might have been uncomfortable but they had always enjoyed their silences together.

"You can help me in many ways, Doctor," he murmured. Then, sat up straighter and took on the voice of his profession.

"Troy. You and I have both been acting strangely the past year and growing farther and farther apart. I think I have a clue as to why. Before I jump to any conclusions, let me ask you some questions. You're one of the few people who can give a straight answer."

She nodded, but said nothing. Mike shoved back an impulse to put his head in her lap and smother himself with the perfume of her body rather than talking. Breathing deeply, he managed to set the image aside and continue.

"Please don't put me off and say its private information. This could be very important." She remained silent, waiting.

"Have any of your patients talked about erotic dreams, becoming distanced or divorced from their spouses shortly after the birth of a child, perhaps dropping everything and going on a trip to the sea? Anything along that line?"

"How did you know, Mike? 'Course they're our symptoms also. I haven't had a child, but I sure as hell would like to take a sea voyage. Some of my patients have told me the only time they feel calm is when they see the holograms or go to the ocean. I've looked at the windows myself and I've been reading up on holograms. On the surface there doesn't seem to be anything especially different at The Travel Agency. But I, too, have suspected a relationship. What have you found, Mike?"

"Nothing definite I can put my finger on, but a lot of things I don't like. People I care about are hurting one another. The hologram windows on Main Street are broken too often to be insignificant. Tomorrow, I have an appointment with the Chief Psychologist at the Police Department, Dr. Handley. Remember her?" She nodded, thoughtfully.

"We're going to work on this thing together. I'm going to Europe, to investigate Zinla's Illusions in Arles, France where the tapes are produced."

"So, you're going to Europe to meet the sultry Medusa, Mike. Even the 'man for all women,' can't resist," she said frostily. It was not like Troy to be jealous.

"Troy, yes, I do intend to meet Medusa, but no, I am not going just to meet her. Part of the reason I'm taking this trip is for us. I liked our relationship and I don't like feeling distant from you. We really have something and I don't want to lose it. Do you?"

She raised her bright, emerald green, intelligent eyes to Mikes. A breeze from the open window blew a strand of hair across her face. Her familiar perfume clung to his nostrils. He was struck with such an intense longing for her that his body felt turned to stone.

Their eyes locked. There was no need to answer. As one, they stood up and walked toward one another. For the first time in months, they kissed passionately, and then he picked her up and carried her to the bed.

Her lips were full and inviting. There was no time to remove all their clothing. He pulled up her gown and helped her unzip his pants. They caught on his shoes and he kicked them off impatiently, rolled over on his back and she rode him like a galloping stallion until she screamed with passion, then he was on top again and he, too, climaxed.

They lay back exhausted, looked at one another and laughed. A tear rolled down her cheek. He lazily reached over and wiped it away. Women often cry when they are happy as well as sad, he'd learned many years ago. Tears fell from his eyes as well. He felt whole again. She licked away his tears and leaning on her elbow, looked into his eyes.

"You've changed, Mike. I think you're finally maturing emotionally."

The old Mike would have pulled back or made a remark and laughed. Instead, he held her gaze for a long moment, and then kissed her gently. "With the help of a good woman, I may yet become a man. Any volunteers?"

"I'll take it under advisement, darling," she said softly. "Until you return from Europe."

He knew she was giving him space to work out the Medusa thing. For some reason the tears continued to flow. Inside he felt a crusted slab of emotions break off and wash away.

Memories of his parent's death and Madge's sad little face floated before his vision. Then, they blurred into prison camp, torture, a knife wound and the gunshot which left him paralyzed for months. Although Mike didn't say anything, it was as though she read my mind.

This was one woman who accepted all of his emotions. She sat up, slipped the gown over her head and used it to wipe his damp face. Then she kissed him tenderly. Sitting up, she finished undressing his exhausted body. As she slipped off his remaining shoe and sock, she began to massage and kiss his toes, feet and legs. By the time she reached his lips, he was ready again. This time their lovemaking was slow and tender as they re-explored one another's bodies and came home again.

For the first time in months, Mike overslept. No dream sirens reached out to him, leaving him unfulfilled.

Troy was up. She was all clean and gleaming femininity in hose, heels and suit. It was as though she had never been touched by his hands. He reached out for her, but she smiled seductively and blew him a kiss.

"I'm going to talk to some of my colleagues and do some investigating of my own. Call me," she said softly, blew another kiss, gave him a Mona Lisa smile and left.

Showering and shaving quickly, he let himself out and hurried uptown for his appointment, feeling light and free. The world was once again a wonderful place and he felt ready to meet any challenge.

Dr. Handley met him at the door of her office. "Thanks for coming, Mike. You look more rested than the last time we met," she said smiling. "Did you and Troy make up?"

"You bet." He smiled like the cat that ate the canary. The city is large in size but the same people seem to run into one another when their interests and jobs are connected. She knew both Troy and Mike, not intimately, but in a friendly, business sort of way.

After pooling their knowledge, they planned a counterattack on the effect of the holograms.

Until they could legally be turned off, Mike would go to Europe and investigate the source of the advertisement.

"There is also a government investigation in progress," she informed him. He raised his eyebrows. Surely Ted would be aware of any such work. She smiled, not giving away any secrets.

"It seems many coastal cities all over the country have the same set of circumstances. I'm going to call a meeting of several Psychiatrists and Psychologists. Try to get them to compare notes on their client's symptoms. Would Troy have time to help?"

"I've already talked with her. She's working on it now. In fact, indirectly she's been working on the problem longer than any of us. She even has a name, The Hologram Virus."

Dr. Handley smiled and nodded. "A good choice of words and a brilliant woman."

Then she asked reflectively, "Did you know that the number of babies who have drowned recently both in our city and others is even higher than we had estimated?"

"There's more here than meets the eye," Mike muttered in a sinister tone. Both laughed nervously, even though it was no laughing matter.

"You bet there is. There may not be a connection, but we have to find out. Something is going on worldwide. This may be more of an emergency than anyone realizes. It's beginning to have the taste of both local and international intrigue."

"But babies, drowning? That seems a bit far-fetched unless some pro-birth fanatic is loose. But then, this whole thing is strange," Mike mused.

Dr. Handley nodded. "Glad you're leaving for Europe today. You already have your ticket. I've talked the department into giving you an expense account for investigating the European source. That's the best I can do at the moment. As usual, lack of funds for anything out of the ordinary are slow in coming." She studied him for a minute, and then said warningly, "This may be more dangerous than meets the eye, Mike, so be careful. Keep us posted. Here's a package of official licenses, gun permit, etc., and a number where I can be reached day or night."

He grinned. "Yes, Mother," leaning down to give her a farewell peck on the cheek as he took the papers.

He headed uptown to the office, a four-room suite. Their secretary occupied the outside room. Mike's office connected to a third room which was furnished with a comfortable couch as well as a shower bath. He spent more time here than in his apartment during a busy case.

Ted had returned to New York for a few days working on an inter-state connection on illegal waste dumping. Mike hated to leave before he returned, but both Dr. Handley and he felt time was important.

"Sarah I'm leaving for Paris, then on to Arles. Try to locate Ted and Troy, in that order. But first, order me some breakfast. I'm starved."

"Yes, Mr. Lambert. Yes, Mr. Lambert," she kept repeating until he stopped giving orders and laughed.

"All right, Sarah. Good morning. How are you today? Is that better?"

She was thirty five, blue-eyed, and plump, with a twinkle in her eyes. When he took himself too seriously, she could bring him back down to earth in a friendly sort of way.

Mike made a tape for Ted on the talk with Handley and the investigation in general. He'd been sloppy and careless recently. A bad sign for any detective. Storing it in the safety deposit box in case of an emergency, he ate quickly. It was his first good meal in several days.

At his apartment he packed a recorder in his carry-on bag along with the gun permit from the police department and the temporary badge Dr. Handley had thoughtfully supplied.

His phone rang. "Dr. Handley here. Just wanted you to know I contacted the local authorities in Arles. They're expecting you and have begun an investigation of Zinla Studios themselves. You'll be updated when you report to them. Be careful, Mike. This could be bigger than either of us imagined…or it could be a wild goose chase."

"Got ya! I'll keep in touch."

When he called Troy's office her secretary said she was with a patient. "I'll leave a message on her tape."

"Troy my love, Mike here. Leaving for Europe this afternoon. Sorry we didn't get time to talk. No—I'm not sorry. It was a wonderful night. God how I needed your touch . . . Call Dr. Handley at the police station with any information you gather. She'll fill you in on our plans. I'll be in Arles, France at the Van Gogh-Terminus Hotel. Will call you from there within the next twenty-four hours.

"If I get this mystery solved in a couple of days, how about taking a long weekend or a few days off and joining me? We haven't had a holiday together for a long time. Don't you think we're long overdue? Will call you from Arles. I . . . I love you, Darling!"

Van Gogh

The first time Mike had gone to Arles, France he was a younger man, inexperienced in love and the arts, except for an affinity for Van Gogh paintings. He had kept a poetic journal about the experience. Besides a military investigation, he'd done the usual things, fell in love with a French girl, learned the language, and acquired another scar not only physically but emotionally.

The second trip was on their honeymoon. After a year of passionate E-mail letters and phone calls, he'd returned to Paris. They'd married and she'd gone along happily with his desire to go to Arles in pursuit of Van Gogh memories. He loved the sight of twisted trees and golden fields.

On their honeymoon they'd fallen out of love. She became homesick and returned to Paris, alone. He received another E-mail:

Dear Mike. Even though I love you, I know you can never live in Paris and I prefer to remain in my own country. I wish to have our marriage annulled . . . .

He'd written her a sizable check and stayed on in Arles to write introspectively about love, life and illusions. For the first time he was able to write with abandon.

The 'stream of consciousnesses writing broke loose again after the death of Cinder, his second attempt at love and a relationship. Ah, the lovely, mysterious Cinder. She'd gotten mixed up with a gang of hoods in her youth. To get free of them, she had to spy on firms like that of Mike and Ted. Was his love for her more deeply ingrained because they'd killed her when she tried to protect him, he wondered, or was it partly guilt?

Mike had put the little book of poetry in his briefcase thinking it would be interesting to compare this trip with the others. Unexpectedly, the pain came flooding back. He wanted to burn the book, but forced himself to read and remember it. Gradually, his heart settled down. He could once again gaze objectively at the scene below him and read the words in his diary without tears blurring the words.

In pencil his new young bride had proudly written her name under Mikes. Mrs. Mike Lambert. Later, he'd crossed it out. After reading, Letters to Theo, Mike's own disappointment and anger had helped him write passionately about the artist's life.

So much time had passed he'd almost forgotten. The past was a bittersweet memory. Or was it? Except for short affairs, he'd never let anyone get close to his heart again. That is, until Troy. Compared to Van Gogh's disappointments, his were mild. In that long ago past with his bride waiting bored nearby, he'd written:

VINCENT VAN GOGH

Such a crazy mixed-up day. One moment the sun shines, then a gust of wind flings thunder clouds overhead, lightning flickers, rain pounds, thunder roars, threateningly. I'm tired of being inside so I'll put on a raincoat and walk.

All the swirling and swaying reminds me of a Van Gogh painting as I stand looking down upon the town of Arles, France where Van Gogh lived and killed himself. I sit on the hillside under a tree and write my thoughts:

Ah, Vincent, Man of golden fields and starry skies,
Seeing beauty where other eyes saw only toil and tears.

I stand here where once you stood, remembering . . .

The town of Arles, now that you've gone,
Proudly acclaims your name.
Too late, they 'love you', so they say.

Ah, if just once or twice in times gone by,
They'd rubbed your weary back, or praised your name,
As you did theirs
In your brilliant paintings,
Giving their life meaning,

Would your eyes have grown dim,
Or golden paintings been touched with blacks,
And deep blue colors of the night?

You gave your love in spite of all
They did or didn't do.

Tell me Vincent, would the world have ever seen,
The beauty in gnarled hands and worn out shoes,
Ever dared to look at suffering
Through eyes of love and colors richly gold.
If you hadn't added humanness to poverty,
Letting each share others pain?

Yes, Vincent, your love of earth and man, still comes shining
through,
But for the way we treated you,
I am so ashamed!

Mike remembered his Art Instructor reading a headline in
grade school and showing them pictures of Van Gogh Sunflowers.

He'd copied one and his mother hung it on the refrigerator. Later, she'd framed it and hung it by her mirror. He'd been so proud. Madge had placed it with her collection.

The headlines in the newspapers read: "Van Gogh goes for $39.9 million dollars. London--In a spectacular bidding due to some of the world's richest art patrons . . . pushed the price of Dutch painters Vincent Van Gogh's Masterpiece, 'Sunflowers', to an auction record . . . "

Was it too much for a painting? He wondered later. What were they really buying? An investment? Will his works be after all, hidden away in some mansion or storage vault and for how long?

Mike had thought museums were full of dusty junk when younger, but Van Gogh's paintings helped him see the world in a different light. In college, his mother sent him a copy of Letters to Theo. His writings again inspired Mike.

Don Mclean once wrote a lovely song in tribute to Vincent Van Gogh's work. Mike hummed his tune and, suddenly, felt compelled to write his own song:

Vincent,
You must have felt such torment
In your burning, wrath filled heart,
 At man's inability to love
With lofty, intimate, sympathy and strength.

At children in darkened bee hive mines,
Women, faded young, worn out, Boys like men
All pale from fever of poverty and dust.

At fattened greedy parasites,
Without a soul, who throw crumbs

At lonely dying feet.

At those who cannot understand,
That each of us has love enough for all mankind.
At all who turned your love aside,
In fear and carelessness each day.

But you would not be stayed.

On canvas,
 You poured out beauty of Starry Nights,
Golden Sunflower Days,
The Plight of Peasants,
Glorified in work.

You gave to Man a wealth of Mind,
Beauty borne of Love.
40 Millions not enough!

Like Christ, you suffered,
Took you life.
 When human misery became too much.

So let us strive to understand . . .
The Loneliness and VOID
Of one who loved, without a Touch!

   Mike read his own words with interest. He remembered the blue skies and burning the sun. So different now . . .
   During my reverie the rain has stopped. The sun is coming out and a butterfly lights nearby. I'm determined that I will share a touch with someone each day who seems lonely."

Mike tried to smile at the memory of the sentimental young man he once was, and yet, he also felt a nostalgic longing for innocence lost . . .

Arles was still a charming town. Underground transportation took him to the heart of the city. Van Gogh's golden skies were brown and dreary. Trees were blighted. Even the residents who had been so friendly before seemed to have lost their sparkle. The Roman coliseum, bridges and artifacts added to the gloom. Before reporting to the police station, he checked in at the little off-beat hotel called the Terminus Van Gogh. Larry and Lisa had also discovered it on their honeymoon in France. Their glowing stories of its charm had made Mike determined to spend a vacation there once again. In spite of the gloom, nostalgic charm gripped his heart. He missed Troy. She would understand.

With pride he'd shown his young bride the market, an old cemetery and the Roman ruins. They spent a week here, wandering the street, going to the market and getting to know one another. It took only a week for the physical attraction to give way to boredom. Homesickness was her face-saving excuse. He could have kept her there but once over the disappointment, there came a flood of relief. After she left he wrote frenzied poetry. His ego was injured more than his heart. In spite of this knowledge he wallowed in self-pity and spent a great deal of the time at their sidewalk cafe pretending he was waiting for her to come back from shopping.

He'd shared his passion for the place with Cinder. Not knowing she was running away from the past, he'd left her alone. The past caught up with her. They'd found her body in the river near the roman wall.

After Cinder's death, he'd walked away from her funeral in a trance of grief. He would see her in a distance, race down the street to find a petite blond tourist who looked at him strangely because he had just grabbed her arm and turned her face toward him.

In those days, he would have stayed, perhaps even made it his home and become a writer. He often wondered how long he would have played the grieving lover game, if Larry and Ted had not come for him, packed his bag, took him back to the states and put him to work.

The memories kept flooding back as he walked up the stairs to his room in the little hotel, relieved to find them painless. They were like a lovely story he'd heard once and would remember pleasantly when he heard a certain song, smelled lilacs, saw a short blond woman, or heard a tinkling laugh.

For months Ted and Jean, Madge and Jacob, Larry and Lisa, took him into their homes and lives. Gradually, the black and white flatness in his heart gained color once more, but he was determined never to fall in love again. His poetry was the only true outlet for his emotions.

A promised job to finish, visiting Madge at the farm, or a meeting with Larry, gave Mike a reason to get up in the morning.

Then, he'd met Dr. Helene Troy. Once more, in spite of his distrust of deep feelings for women, his daily life had regained extra dimension and color. That is, until the holograms. How he could have let Troy slip away for even a few months, he wondered.

Mike realized he had opened the door to his room and had been standing for some time, reviewing the past. Then, he deliberately closed it and planned his day.

He put his briefcase on the desk and suit bag in the closet. Thank goodness formal suits and ties were no more. One-piece jumpsuits or shirt jackets with soft Velcro closures and lightweight shorts made life comfortable for businessmen. Not much had changed inside the hotel. He opened his briefcase, talked to his comp-recorder and felt an overwhelming desire to sleep. Slipping off his clothing he slid under the sheets and felt wide awake.

Each room was set up to resemble the artist's room in his paintings. Copies of Van Gogh's artwork adorned the walls. Mike's eyes rested on a picture of this room. The rough Spartan look had taken on softness in today's interpretation.

During the Second World War, Van Gogh's small house had been across the street from the hotel. Bombers aimed for the railroad station three blocks away and hit his house. The land on which it sat was a small dusty park the last time he'd been here. Now, some enterprising Chamber of Commerce had an architect design and rebuild it. Even knowing this, Mike's first priority would be to visit the monument. Beyond that was a Roman Coliseum and an old shopping center. Even a Greek Theater had been built by those industrious Romans.

On the other side of a stone wall was a large river guarded by Roman Lions and Cinder's spirit. The whole setting was artistic.

For centuries a weekly fair had been held on the streets. It is said that anything could be purchased there. In the old days, even a slave.

Mike gave up. He was too excited to sleep. The nap he'd caught on the plane would have to do. Showering down the hall in a communal bath, he slipped into comfortable clothing and headed for the little café on the lower flower. European coffee was still a treat.

Music and people wandering in all directions told Mike the street fair was in progress. He walked along the street and saw a cow, chickens, fruit, flowers, art, sculpture, clothing and tools for sale. The Saturday Market was in full swing. Lovely girls were everywhere, but none could compare with the Medusa of the holograms. Perhaps one like her had caused Van Gogh to cut off his ear, he thought to himself.

Mike soon found out. A group of people stood in front of one of the chain of stores known as The Travel Agency, much like the ones in the states. This was a new hologram of a trip to Stockholm via a boat, to visit the fair. Tulips waved in the breeze by the dock. The picture was different but the haunting music was the same. Hypnotically, Mike began to watch along with the crowd, until he realized what he was doing. He slipped in his earplugs, took a deep breath, squared his shoulders and walked through the door, into the presence of the Medusa.

A line had formed in front of her ticket window. He took a number and sat down to wait and observe. Glancing around he saw several men sitting idly, or pretending to read travel brochures. They kept looking toward the dark-haired woman at the counter. Her thick black hair was stringy; she wore glasses and no makeup. It was as though she was trying to make herself plain. In spite of this, the movements of the sensuous Medusa still called. She was a lovely young woman, but just that. So where did the attractiveness of the hologram come from? He pictured her bouncy hair and swaying hips, but could not quite put his finger on what was missing. Could the music add all the mystery and hypnotic beckoning? Hadn't he written once that music was a language of its own? Would heaven-creatures speak in music language?

Finally, it was Mike's turn. He passed his card to her and told her he was not here on travel business but would like to talk to her privately.

"Could I take you to lunch?"

"Look, Mr. Lambert," she said returning his card. "I do not wish to go to lunch with you or even talk with you. I am here to sell tickets. Leave me alone.

"Next please," she said looking past him at the man in line behind Mike.

"This is business," he said. "Either you talk with me or I'll be forced to call in the police. Take a look at this." He handed her the note from local authorities given him by Dr. Handley.

"Who are you and what do you want? Is this just another approach?"

"No, it's serious. We can talk here or wherever you suggest."

"I'll meet you next door in thirty minutes. Now please leave. I have work to do."

Our lovely Medusa was even less seductive closeup, he thought. Her lips were drawn thin, there were lines between her brows, and she looked as though she needed a good night's sleep. The bouncy black curls hung lifeless. Did she ever smile? But, the voice still came through, suggestively low and sexy. It needed the siren music to cast a spell.

Mike went to the outdoor restaurant. The sun shown brightly on the swirling trees in Van Gogh paintings. For a brief time, dappled sunlight fell across interesting looking people strolling along the sidewalk.

Smiling grimly, he reminded himself he was sitting at a sidewalk cafe in Europe, a dream come true for many people. But the dream in real life was beginning to take on nightmare undertones. Arles was smoggy and crowded. His eyes watered and his head was beginning to ache. In spite of the fact that the other customers ignored the smog, Mike put on his filter mask and wrap-around glasses until his food arrived.

The lovely clear colors of the hologram must have been taken at another time or just after a rain. He tried to concentrate on his reason for being here. In the back of his mind he kept asking himself, what was missing from the picture when he saw Medusa, besides her appearance and the music?

It was important that he remember.

Medusa was on time for lunch. Two p.m. the late continental lunch period. Mike was starved.

"What do you want?" she snarled.

"Food," he snapped back. They both laughed. Medusa of the hologram flickered on for just a moment.

Mike felt the lure again. Fighting back desire, he asked, "Is Medusa your real name?"

"Yes, but my friends call me Med. What are you doing over here, Mr. Lambert? Does it have something to do with the strange effect of the holograms?"

"Yes. What do you know about them? Who made them?" She remained silent, looking off into space.

"Do you realize the trouble they're causing? Marriages are breaking up; erotic dreams ruin people's sex life. They seem to have a hypnotic effect on people. A beautiful woman like you must have problems enough with men without advertising."

Her lips curled sarcastically. "Just the trouble they've caused me alone is too much. I wish I'd never made the advertisement."

She ordered a sandwich when the waitress appeared, then continued. "Women mobbed John so often he quit his job and is growing a beard to disguise himself. Last night someone broke into my apartment for the tenth time. Fortunately, I've been hiding out at a friend's house. I need the job, but I may be forced to quit, too. Trying to make myself unattractive doesn't seem to help. I'm having my hair cut and dyed. Also, I'm getting a pair of ugly glasses. If that doesn't work, I'll have to go away." She paused, shrugged and smiled bitterly.

"My boss says he's trying to get The Travel Agency to quit the holograms for the time being, but no luck as yet. I don't think he tries very hard. Business has been so great that he can't fire me in spite of the trouble men cause in the office."

"You speak English like an American, look Italian and live in France?"

"My Mother was Italian and Father French. The Catholic school I went to was run by American Nuns. My English is flavored with their style. Also, I was an exchange student in Los Angeles for a couple of years."

Mike watched her and let her talk around the subject until she felt safe.

"My family knew some of the Hollywood Set. I stayed over for another year and did some modeling. It helped to get part-time modeling jobs here when I returned." She paused and looked down, remembering.

"When I was in your country, I took a tour across the United States and was very impressed by its size and diverse scenery. Where are you from?"

Listening to people often told him more about them than asking questions, so Mike answered briefly.

Suddenly, she glanced at her watch. "I'm sorry Mr. Lambert. Guess I can't help much, but I feel better. You know about the Zinla's Illusion Ad Company, I'm certain. That is where we did the modeling for the holograms. The photographer had a lot of strange apparatus. But then, I know very little about holograms. At the end of the filming, I felt as though something had been zapped out of me. My sex drive is nil. It's such a shame too, with all the attention I've been getting."

"Were any of the other models affected?"

"John's felt the same way, and yes, all of the models are affected." She looked embarrassed but pushed on. "Do you think it's possible for someone or something to steal a person's sex drive?"

He was tempted to invite her to find out. "I don't know Med, but I'm sure as hell going to find out. That's why I'm here." She let his use of her name go by with just a faint smile.

"Good luck. I hope you do. I need some peace, and to keep my job. It would be nice to live a normal life again." She smiled wistfully. Medusa stood up. "Sorry I snapped at you this morning. If you learn anything, you can call this number. I may not work for a few days. I've asked for a leave of absence." She hesitated. "To tell the truth, we models have decided to do some investigating ourselves."

"Why don't you leave that to the experts? This may be more than you can handle."

"How do you think I've gotten through the last couple of years? I can take care of myself."

"Famous last words," he said to her retreating figure.

Now he was worried. She had eaten very little. Mike reached over and took her plate of food. It was too good to waste. As a detective, he never knew when his next meal would be available. Pulling his hat down to shade his face from the smog-bound sun, he digested both the food and information.

The puzzle was getting more pieces. Some of the corners were beginning to emerge. Money was the obvious motive. So far, no one had been murdered, but he wondered how many castrated couples felt half dead. Has anyone been convicted for emotional killings?

How could drown babies be connected? He could make no sense of this bit of information.

Suddenly Mike remembered something both Ted and Larry had mentioned. Their babies were different. But how did they mean? He had noticed a slight difference but really hadn't been in contact with the babies much after their births. Had they deliberately been keeping them out of sight? Were all of the babies who drowned different in the same way? He must see one after it had grown older. That would be impossible unless an unusual intelligence or alien presence interfered. How often had he laughed at flying saucer stories? What about the alien craft story the government had hushed up?

When he got hold of Ted, he'd have him do some prying. It was time the Feds returned some of their favors. He hadn't really pursued the baby connection, but Handley had thought one possible.

Perhaps he'd find all the information he needed at the Zinla's Illusion Advertising Company. Surely a company as large as theirs would not want to jeopardize it's standing in the world market with illegal, subliminal advertising. Yet that's what it boiled down to.

Unless . . . The Ad Company must know what it was doing? Or did it? Had the owners foreseen the problems?

I don't need to kid myself, Mike thought, greed and ambition are the driving force for most people. They can blind their eyes to the most obvious things. One look at the sky proved that.

The local authorities, Commissar de Police, Milek, had talked with the Zinla Advertising Company. The owner insisted they only hired a holo-photographer to do a normal hologram. Disney Land and others have been using them for years.

"The photographer made a series of ads for us and left on another assignment. We tried to locate him after the ads had been so successful in order to have him do more, but he just disappeared." Quote Mrs. Zinla.

Finding him is a job for me, Mike decided, but wondered if his French would be sufficiently convincing for the criminal types he might have to deal with in France. A few U.S. dollars still spoke nearly any language. Glancing at his watch, he decided there was time to get to the Zinla Illusions Company before it closed.

Zinla's Illusions

An attractive secretary, Anna Quince, informed Mike the president of the company was busy.

"I'll wait," he said, giving her the benefit of his most charming, boyish grin before picking up a magazine and flipping idly through it. She glanced at him often. When he smiled, she returned it with a flirtatious air. Once in awhile he said something to her. She would pause and chat a minute, until the busy phone rang again.

He studied the woman as she worked. There was an exotic look about her. Her eyes bulged slightly, large kissable lips, and a long, slim, Nefertiti neck crowned by abundant hair braided heavily in the back. She reminded him of someone. He wondered if she added a hairpiece. Lovely, but a bit strange. Whatever it was about her that bothered him, he couldn't quite put his finger on it. Was she too friendly?

Finally, she got up and went into the office. Pretending to get a drink, Mike wandered as close to the door as possible. Two women were talking.

"He's a detective, for God's sake, Zin. Maybe he can find your baby."

"It's too late for that now." The woman's breath caught on a sob.

"I didn't mean to upset you. You know that. But we have to face up to it. Either turn off the holograms, or the police will do it for us, unless we cooperate. They may anyway."

"All right. You win. Send him in." They lapsed into fast French and he lost the 'jist' of the conversation.

By the time she came out, Mike was sitting on the couch again reading a magazine. He was surprised that even part of their conversation had been in English.

The secretary returned with an inviting smile. "You may go in now, Mr. Lambert."

"Thanks. Be here when I get back." He winked. She nodded.

He paused and watched the way her bottom swayed as she walked back to her desk. Women are beautiful creatures. As far as he was concerned, no sculpture on earth could compete with the lines and curves of a hot-blooded woman, be she wide or slender.

Troy agreed. They had often sat on a park bench after a rain, just watching people. Each body told a story about its life.

He turned, almost bumping into a tall dark woman in the doorway. She arched her brows knowingly as she caught his glance toward the retreating secretary.

Giving a salesperson smile, she extended her hand and said, "I'm Zinla. Won't you come in, please?"

They shook hands. She rubbed her hands on the skirt which covered slim hips, brushed back a lock of black hair falling across one tear-swollen eye and retreated behind her twelve foot long desk. The room was decorated in pinks, lavenders, blues and white. Touches of gold set off mod white furniture. The chairs across from her were high-backed and comfortable when he sat down.

"Now, Mr. Lambert. If you're here about the holograms, I'm afraid I can't add anything more than I told the Commissar de police. All this nonsense about hypnotic effects upon people is silly. Maybe lonely, heartsick people fall for one of the models and show up trying to date her, but that's normal."

Mike listened. She caught herself talking too much and paused.

"Perhaps. Sometimes after questioning, a few new things come to mind that didn't at the time. Have you thought of anything besides what you told the police?"

"No, I've been very busy."

"Would you take a minute, set back close your eyes and visualize the photographer?" By the annoyed expression, he could tell she didn't want to. However, her job was to be cooperative to a point, so she did.

Mike, Ted and Madge practiced the Erickson technique of hypnotism in college. Her English had a heavy accent. He'd been happy to find that most educated people in Europe spoke some English. Using her own way of wording was not quite as easy. But he fell in with her vocabulary and tone of voice.

Under the olive skin, the pallor of her face was pale. Gradually the lines between her brows and the corner of her mouth relaxed.

"Try to relax and visualize the photographer. Where did you first hear about him or meet him?"

"He appeared one evening just after Anna, my secretary, had gone out. He was tall, thin, with slightly protruding eyes, wore a trimmed beard, a hat, and dark glasses, even inside and at night. When I asked him about them, he said the glare of the lighting in photography made them sensitive. There was something almost alien about him. He seemed harmless, and in his way was quite handsome and charming. His card gave off a fascinating holographic effect. It was aqua and the waves seemed almost real, as I read his name." She paused. Mike waited.

"When I told him to come back for an appointment the next day, he said, 'No. We can arrange an agreement tonight and I will do the background work outside in the next few days and the indoor models at night. You have models, I presume'.

"He showed me some holographic film strips and played the background tapes. I was fascinated. Anne came back from dinner for a report she forgot and approved them, too. His references were good. From Disneyland and several reputable ad companies. I could not check them out that night, but after he showed me his work and I listened to the tapes, I really didn't bother to check farther. That is, until after he finished and I tried to locate him again. No one had ever heard of him. But, his work was fantastic. I know a good thing when I see it." She opened her eyes, tossed her head and looked at him challengingly.

Mike nodded understandingly. "That's fine. Just continue to visualize him with your eyes closed. It's easier to remember that way." She was about thirty-five or perhaps forty, tall, slim, sophisticated. A handful for any man, he thought as he watched her. "Was he an attractive man?"

"No. Yes. I guess so." She paused and frowned. A tear drifted down one cheek. "It might be a relief to talk about it to a stranger," Mike suggested, gently.

"My marriage had not been going well and I had nothing to go home for. I asked him if he would like to use the fold-down bed in the ad room after a late night filming. I often use the bed when I stay in town late. While he was here, he used our modeling room to set up his equipment and backdrops for the photography sessions." She paused for a moment.

"I supposed his strangeness was that of an eccentric American artist. Afterwards, I wasn't quite certain if his accent was American or not. His nose was platyrrhine.

"Anne said, "Quack, quack," after he left one day. We laughed. For such a thin person, he did waddle a bit as he walked. His voice was low and his words clipped.

"He seldom smiled, even when he received the fat check. Funny, I hardly noticed until now how alien he really was. "The holograms and music had a strange hypnotic effect upon me. They are charming and unforgettable."

"Did he associate with anyone else while he stayed here?"

She hesitated a moment and I held my breath as she stirred restlessly. Often in a light state of hypnosis, a person will refuse to cooperate when something personal is exposed. I had the feeling Zinla needed a Father Confessor and I was it.

"We stayed here together one night. We locked his equipment in the modeling room. He set up what he called a lock ray across the door and only he could reach through to unlock it. Anyone else would get a burn."

"Did you have a child by him, Zinla?"

"Yes, no." She sat up and opened her eyes. "My personal life is none of your business. How dare you come in here and question me about it?" she shouted.

"I dare a lot for the people of the world and for people I care about? For whom do you care Zinla?" Mike shouted back at her.

"Not very damn many people. Especially men. They all betray you in the end. And now even my baby is lost." Her voice broke. She put her head on her desk and sobbed onto the ink blotter. He had the feeling she had been in this position often.

When she finally quieted down, wiped her face and looked at him defiantly, she said. "Please leave, now."

"Mrs. Zinla, do you realize that your holograms are wrecking lives? That marriages are breaking up and people's sex lives are becoming erratic?"

"That's all supposition. I'm here to make money and a hologram is no more destructive than a film strip. When you take Disney's off the market, I'll consider doing the same with mine."

"What do you think will happen to children? Couldn't you at least hold that one back?"

"No. With the holidays coming up, people want to do things with their children to prove to themselves they love them. I get 1% of each ticket and hotel reservation sold."

Mike could see this line of questioning was getting her back to a defensive state. Before he allowed this to happen he talked soothingly to her for a moment. She must not be allowed to affect the children. Again she relaxed and leaned her head back against the chair, looking at him with half-closed eyes.

"Ms. Zinla. Have you personally been affected by the holograms?"

"Well, yes. I don't look at them anymore. Well, I still look at the one of John Sandos. My divorce was final last year. I'm so busy with work that instead of going out, I just watch John and masturbate. I tried to hire him to work for me and even get him to live with me. We spent one night together, but he just doesn't have it sexually. The holograms lie." She broke off.

"Don't you think, Ms. Zinla that all this emotional upset might have something to do with the holograms?"

"No," she said, but he could tell that some of her self-assurance was gone.

"Now, I suggest that we view the children's hologram and if you have a peculiar reaction, you consider taking it off the market. Since you're making so much money on the others, surely you can spare the children? Do you have other children, Mrs. Zinla?"

"Two." For a moment I heard a sob in her voice again. Then she stood abruptly. "We'll have to go to the viewing room."

We went into the other room. She quickly stripped the cover off a strange projector. "I've never seen one quite like that," Mike said. It resembled an undersea camera. Where was Larry when he needed him? He tried to memorize as much about it as he could see.

In a moment, a lovely scene of Tivoli, a famous recreational center in Copenhagen, Denmark stood before them. Children rode on slides, played in tulips, as ballet dancers swept gracefully across the screen. Loving parents hovered over them smiling. It made Mike long to be a parent showing his children the beauty life can hold. He felt a strange longing to see his parents, to meet them at Tivoli. Quickly, he stuck the earplugs in his ears.

"Stop the hologram! Do you have a camera that can take a photo of this scene and blow it up? Also, I'd like a recording of the soundtrack. It has a sound in the background common to all. Like the ocean."

"Mr. Lambert, don't you think you've spent enough of my time? I'll give you a copy as you suggest and then I want you to leave. Please wait in the lobby."

He had been too eager and let his hold upon her slip. While she made copies, he studied the locks and location of doors and windows in the room.

The secretary gave him an engaging smile. It was obvious she found him attractive.

Mike sat on the edge of her desk and invited her to dinner. They set a time and place. He had hoped to spend the evening with Medusa, but perhaps this might be more lucrative. If he could get the keys, it would be simpler than breaking and entering. Her mind might be easier to tap than Zinla's.

"On second thought, why don't I pick you up here after work, since I know where the office is located?"

"Sure Mike. See you at eight o'clock. I thought the boss would ace me out."

She had a charming accent as well as smile. She must be in her thirties; her skin has a moist dewy look. Almost like that of a young baby. Troy had that same kind of skin. As though they never allowed the smog or sun to touch their faces. Her eyes reminded him of Troy's as well. Rounded out just a bit more than the average person. I'm just lonesome for Troy and see her everywhere, he told himself. A common symptom of lovers.

A touch of makeup enhanced Anna's high cheekbones and coloring. Mike liked his women a bit more plump, but she had enough flesh in all the right places.

"I hope you like what you see," she smiled as he studied her.

"You bet, Sweetheart." Mike leaned over and kissed her lightly, feeling like a child caught with its hand in the cookie jar when the door opened just in time for Zinla to catch his act.

"Mrs. Quince, I'll see you in my office. Mr. Lambert is leaving. Good-by Mr. Lambert. I do not intend to be of any further service to you and neither will my secretary."

He looked at Anna, who winked. The date was still on. Mike made a hasty retreat.

Back at the hotel, he listened to the soundtrack. It was the roar of the ocean. Birds called, waves pounded against rocks and under it all was a strange siren call which made his psyche long to follow. Who or what could have sung or played such a song? He came to himself as the music finished, instead of replaying as it did with the holograms and Mike found himself wanting to pack to go on a cruise. He felt he must find the ocean and the singer.

The music, separate from the picture, made him certain it was the dangerous part, not the obvious hologram.

He turned off the soundtracks, ran a tub of hot water in spite of a sign saying, "Water rationed. ¼ tub per person." Sipping a cold glass of French wine he leaned back in the tub, closed his eyes and went over the clues.

First, the strong sexual desire and then a lessening, almost castrating effect. What could be the use of this?

To have children? Then a disturbed relationship? To free the parents and make them want to flee to the ocean? There must be a reason why water was involved. A great number of the cities of the world did not recommend drinking their own water these days. The babies had to be connected in some way, but how? Why? Who? He worried the questions.

He considered many answers, but did any make sense? Suppose there was a conspiracy, a large one. Some group wanted to influence or blackmail the whole world. And why children? Babies needed such a lot of care. Mothers would fight to the death to defend their babies.

The last tape was for children? How to get there? By boat. There would be thousands over the summer.

The other ships had been in the Med. Why the change? To throw off suspicion? The children drowning. How many had drowned and how many were missing? The local police and governments were compiling figures from cities all over the world. Mike felt beat. He should have put Anna off for another day. Hot water and aspirin revived his body temporarily.

Usually, the crimes he investigated involved adults and were straight acts of murder, missing persons or articles, thievery, and such. Once he had worked on a kidnapping case, but that was the work of a few and one child.

"Come to Tivoli," was the message, but what was truly calling? What effect would the strange music have on children? Would they be as lemmings rushing to their deaths? If not death? What?

Most of the babies were not over one or two years old. Barely walking, if he remembered children in that age group. He must talk to Troy. The children would be too young to hypnotize.

During the Moslem war, Mike had inadvertently stumbled into a spy situation. The CIA acquired him. They taught him to use hypnosis instead of torture to exact secrets from victims. That's where he'd met Ted and later Larry.

After the war, jobs were hard to find. He ended up joining Ted Wentz, in a detective agency. With the exception of their assignments for Federal and local police, a great deal of the work was boring. However, it paid well. Gave Mike time and money for a nice apartment, and to play around with women. That is, until he met Troy. Now he had money in the bank and was a full partner in the agency.

Just as her psychology and his detective work fit well together, so did their life styles. He missed her in more ways than one. Suddenly, he had a strong desire to be with her. He laughed as he noticed his erection. She should be through in the office by now. He had left his cell phone on the chair with his clothing. Without thinking he dialed the operator. While waiting he did a bit of self-hypnosis to lower his budding edifice.

"Hello, Tory, it's me, Mike."

"Mike. Where are you? I've been worried about you. There's something I need to talk with you about." She didn't wait for him to answer and plunged on. This was not like her at all. He frowned and sat up straighter as he listened.

"Something is happening here. I have several new clients and a couple of my old ones telling me about lost babies. No bodies were found in any case. They all say their babies drowned or had an accident while on a cruise in and around Europe. A few have disappeared off our own coast, according to Dr. Handley. It's too much of a coincidence. I checked with other psychologists at a convention yesterday. The same things have happened to many of their clients.

"All the women have been exposed to the holograms we discussed. Most seem to be easily suggestible. The infants have all been about six months of age or a bit older. Crawling stage. I suggested to Dr. Handley that the police department call in Geneticists. Even though the babies are different from their immediate families, they have a great number of characteristics in common."

"Such as?"

"Such as their preference for swimming instead of walking. A stiff mane of hair in the middle of their head and running down to the neck bone. All have a protruding mouth and a face more rounded at the sides. I remember seeing Lisa and Larry's child. It fit that description. Also, Ted's and Jeans. When they were younger the differences did not show up as much as it does as they get older, apparently.

"What are we going to do Mike? I talked to The Travel Agency and even went to the police.

Dr. Handley told me of your investigation and she believes they dovetail in someway. It's so sad." He could hear the sadness in her voice.

Troy was a strong woman. This hologram nonsense had thrown both of them for a loop. He could see how it must upset the average family.

"Brace up, Darling. It's going to be all right. I'm in Arles, France. That's where the holograms were made, but it is not the original source." He heard her take a deep breath...

"Listen to me, Troy. There are times when public citizens must take things into their own hands. This is one of them. The soundtracks must be turned off. Surely someone who is a presidential nominee has enough influence to get a few pictures turned off."

"I'll certainly try, Darling."

Mike felt his not being there to cast a ballot for her was letting her down. The holograms had taken over his life and now the investigation continued to separate them. He realized he didn't even know what her chances were for election. Madge had assured him she had a better than average chance of winning, even though her stands were considered radical by many.

"Troy, can you forgive me for not being there during the most important time of your life?"

"It's OK Mike. We'll talk about it when you come home. There's so much I have to tell you about myself, about us. I hope you'll understand."

What was she talking about, he wondered. This was no time to play guessing games. Probably just a woman's need to feel loved.

"I promise I'll make it up to you and get back as soon possible. Will you have time to get hold of Ted and fill him in? This is what I've found so far." He told her of his visit with Medusa and Zinla as well as the local authorities and his ideas about a possibility of an international plot or alien interference.

"The babies may be the key. Keep on it. Ted should be on his way back from New York. If not, have Jean contact him and tell him it's an emergency. Try to find out exactly where the babies were lost, ages, sex, or anything from other Psychologists."

"Tomorrow's election day, but I'll do my best. If I'm elected, I'll be pretty busy."

"Oh, Lord. And I'm over here. I'll try to make it up to you when I get back. You know my heart and love are with you, don't you?"

"Oh, yes. That helps a great deal. Madge, Lisa and Jean will be here after they vote. Where are you off to next?"

"I'm going to drive down the coast of Italy where most of the cruise ships come and go. I'll be here later tonight after dinner. Leave any messages with the hotel."

"Will do."

"Oh, yes, tell Ted and Larry to find a way to mess up the soundtracks on those holograms if they can't get them turned off. Especially the new ones for children. Dr. Handley is trying to find a way to shut them down legally.

"In the meantime, call Larry and Lisa and have them show you their baby and Jeans. Have them come to your office for a meeting. Use hypnosis to find out what you can about the babies' conception and how different they really are. There has to be a common thread between the children. Try to feed them suggestions that will block their wanting to go near the holograms. Pass out earplugs. Anything. It's not just enough for them to be aware of its power. Call an emergency meeting of your colleagues."

"Oh, Mike. Do be careful."

"That goes double, Sweetheart. We still have no idea who or how many people we're dealing with, but I suspect someone is holding a great number of children for a possible ransom or blackmail."

"No one would hurt babies, surely?"

"If I haven't gotten to the bottom of this in a week, or if something happens to me, call in the journals. The reporters will make a good story out of this and maybe expose someone's hand."

"OK, Mike. I'll get busy. I feel better now that we have a course of action. And Mike, I'm not very objective when it comes to you. I've really missed you these past few months."

"Thanks. I could use a vote of confidence. I really appreciate you taking time from your busy schedule to help. If the white house is what you want, I wish you luck." There was a pause and he said into the silence, "I've been a fool, Troy. When I get back, I'll show you just how much I miss you, too. I love you, for what it's worth. Be very careful, I'm not sure just who or what we're dealing with. This sounds a bit crazy, but I wonder if it's entirely human?"

Fighting Back

Anna was outside the office when Mike pulled up in the taxi. He hurried her out of sight before Zinla discovered their meeting. At the restaurant he plied her with attention, drinks and food, before he began to ask questions. "What do you know about the photographer?"

"His card had Quaternion Films on it.

"Do you remember his name other than A. Quinn and his waddle?"

"Well, he wasn't turned on by me. Usually, Zinla has her pick of the men and I get her leftovers, which isn't too bad."

She saw Mike's questioning look. Was she lying or didn't she know about Zinla and the photographer?

"Don't be too hard on her. She's had a lot of trouble in the past year or two." Her voice lowered and he knew the gossip was coming.

"Her husband asked for a divorce. Then a lover left her pregnant. For some reason she decided to have the child. It had a strange look. Reminded me a bit of Quinn," she said as though the thought had just occurred to her.

"Then a couple of months ago, she went on a cruise and the child fell overboard. They searched the ship and the area. It was never found. She's been bitter ever since. It's beginning to show in her personality and work." She looked at Mike thoughtfully, "You aren't the first ones to inquire about those holograms."

"What do you mean?"

"Just after you left, John Sandos and Medusa barged into the office. At gunpoint, they demanded the film and the soundtrack energizer that Zinla keeps locked up with the film. To keep the tapes current, a new one has to be sent to each customer monthly. That's part of the sales package. Only the contracting agents know about it, but somehow the models found out and took them all with them."

"Oh, my God." Mike slipped the keys he had pocketed back into her purse and took her hand. "This is very important. Do you have any idea where they might have gone?"

"Well, it's hard to say, but I looked out the window and the model that is in the ski holograms was driving the car." She looked nervous and quickly finished her fourth glass of wine, her face flushed, eyes bright.

"Just exactly what were the other holograms about?"

Anna patted Mike's arm, "You don't want to talk 'shop' all night, Honey? Let's go to my place and get cozy."

Mike took her hand and squeezed just tight enough to get her attention away from sex and back to the subject.

"This is important. It may be a matter of life and death, do you understand? People have disappeared and perhaps died because of those ads. You may be the next on the list. Do you understand?" He squeezed harder.

Fear caught in her eyes. Her secretarial training came forth. She gave him information as rapidly as he was able to ask questions. Her memory was remarkable. Or so it seemed. Mike had a feeling something wasn't quite right, even though she seemed extremely cooperative and a little tipsy.

"The addresses for the models are in the office. Zinla's gone home. We can get them if you really think they're important."

"Let's go." Mike paid the bill and helped Anna to her feet. She tucked her arm through his and squeezed it to his chest. As they got into the taxi she leaned close to him and he thought, she smells as fresh as the sea. Funny, it was the same kind of perfume Troy wore.

He felt a stab of guilt as Anna pulled his head down and kissed him. The taxi pulled to the curb and Mike breathed a sigh of relief.

Inside the office she seemed to sober quickly as she gave Mike the harbor where Quantra Cruises shipped out, the address of John Santos, Medusa and the other models.

"Do you have a list of all the agencies that have purchased the holograms?

While Anna looked them up, Mike made phone calls. None of the models answered their phones.

When Anna finished, Mike sat her down and began to talk softly and slowly as he looked into her eyes. At first she refused to go under but with more effort, she finally relaxed.

"Anna, listen to me, this is important. How many of the models have had babies?"

"None that I know of."

"How many women whom you know have had a baby within the last year, who might have seen strange looking and gone on a cruise?"

"Several. But so have I. Is there a connection between the holograms and the babies? Is my baby safe? Tell me?" She was becoming agitated in spite of his hypnotic suggestions.

"It's all right, Anna. Your baby is fine. Tell me. Who is the father of your child?"

"Why, my husband, of course. Or was, he? We're divorced now, so it's OK."

"Come on Anna. You were never unfaithful? "Not once?"

Mike saw her hesitate so put her deeper into the trance and then urged her to tell him about her lover.

"It may save your child's life, Anna," he said gently.

"Well. I guess I can tell you. One night after the filming, 'the Duck,' that's the name we called Mr. Quinn behind his back, asked me out for a drink. I thought it might be good for business. Even though I'm the secretary, the business is one-third mine. Anyway, he asked me, and I went. After a couple of drinks he seemed charming and invited me back to his room to look at holograms. An old line. I was lonely and I knew Zinla wanted him. It would be putting one over on Zin if I got him, I thought.

"That's about all I remember about that night except getting out of a cab at about midnight. My husband made a big scene and I insisted that nothing happened. We fought often after that. I . . . I've never been sure whose child it was. But it's mine and I love her," she said softly.

Something didn't ring true, but he couldn't put his finger on it. "You said, 'It's.' Is there anything different about your child?"

She bristled in anger for a moment, then sighed and said, "I guess there is. At first it was hardly noticeable, but now it looks more like a sweet duck every day. It loves to swim--never wants to get out of the bathtub."

"Where is she now, Anna? I'd like to see her. Do you have a picture of her?"

"I don't think so." Her purse was on the table and a picture of a baby sat on the desk by it.

"Is this the child? Is it a boy or girl?"

"A girl. They're all girls." Her hand slipped across her lips. He looked at her intently.

"All girls. All the babies are girls? How do you know this?"

"I don't know." He took her face in his hand and looked deeply into her eyes.

"Quinn," she whispered. She sagged back into her chair. Fear in her eyes. Mike questioned her at length, but either the blocks were too deep for him to penetrate or she didn't know anymore to tell him, he decided.

"Anna, where is your baby now?"

"Oh, we've been giving discounts to anyone with a child under a year who signed up at The Travel Agencies. My sister has been helping me with the baby and her children. I decided to give them a vacation, so she's taking the Quanta's Cruise Ship to Crete for two weeks. Oh my God!" Anxiety seemed to bring her out of the light trance.

Mike could see hysterics forming. Taking her by the arms as she came to her feet, he held her firmly and shook her a bit.

Then, he kissed her. A good kiss, he had learned from experience, makes a woman more pliable than a slap. Besides, he liked women. Where their children were concerned, no man was a match for them. They caught subtle nuances of events and followed them to the core of the matter more quickly than men. Perhaps they're more emotional because of the speed with which they do so. Men arrive at the same place, but usually through a more obvious objective method. Thus, they have a longer absorption period for the emotions to dissipate, giving the appearance of indifference. Mike had often contemplated this idea. Once again he saw it in action and decided to use it to his advantage.

"We may not have much time, if what I believe is happening is true. It's a long story. I'm calling a Psychiatrist friend of mine in the states and my partner as well as a Police Psychologist. You listen and I'll fill you in later on the parts you don't understand. After the phone calls, we'll go after your daughter and the models.

"Operator. I want a conference link between these numbers. It's official police business and very important, so move as quickly as you can."

Glancing at his watch he noted it was near midnight. Hopefully, Troy and Ted would be in their offices, as well as Dr. Handley.

Anna, while we're waiting for the connections, find the number of the Quantra office, see if the ship has a phone number listed. Also, dial Commissar de police, Minlek. Turn your intercom sound on so he can hear what I'm saying to the people in the states, do that first, please." He handed her the number.

Troy came on, then Ted and finally, Dr. Handley.

"Troy, we may not have much time, so let me ask you a question. How many of your patients talk about their latest child being different, perhaps slightly deformed and loving water and have discussed the possibility of a different father than their present husband?" He felt her hesitate.

"Don't give me that confidential crap. This could save the lives of their children and many others."

"All right Mike. I've been trying to call you about just that. After talking with you, several of us went into a phone conference and compared notes on the patients that we have been seeing the past year. Nearly all the women confessed to a phantom lover and that their child was looking more like him every day.

"They had all visited the hologram often and are very subjective. Not all have confessed to a child, but we're going to probe further. Many have lost a girl child, in or near the water, within the first year of its life. They all seem to think their child cannot possibly be dead.

"We thought it was because the bodies had never been seen, therefore, they were not able to accept the deaths.

"I'm trying to contact the local pediatricians who may have examined some of these children. So far, the one I spoke to confirmed the fact that the children are a bit different at birth and that they swim readily, talk early, but their legs weren't developing walking abilities as quickly as they should. Their mouths have a curious fishlike shape, but they seem exceptionally healthy and intelligent."

"Thanks for the quick follow-up Troy; you'll make some detective a good wife one day." He smiled as he heard her laugh.

"Ted, Troy filled you and Dr. Handley in so far. Were you able to get a handle on the soundtracks?"

"Oh, yes. Larry and I are working on it. We hope to have the problem solved tonight. Dr. Handley. Will we get trouble from the police department?"

"I don't know, Ted, but I won't bring it up unless there's a complaint along that line. The department may be relieved. More children are drowning. There's a rash of swimming classes. We've been getting reports from other states and cities that seem to confirm what you're saying, Mike. What are you going to do next?"

"Anna, the secretary for Ms. Zinla has a child and sister booked on the Quanta Cruise Ship. We're going to try to head them off or make connections with it as soon as possible. If Anna will risk it, we may have to use her child as bait."

As Anna started to protest, Mike said, "It may be the only way to save it in the long run."

"Do any of you have any ideas? If not, keep working from that end; try to keep it out of the press for the time being. This may be an international crisis."

The office door opened and in stormed Zinla.

"What the hell is going on here? Get out of my office. Anna, what's going on?"

"Shut up Zin. Just shut up. Wait until he's off the phone and I'll explain. The Commissar de police wants to say something to all of you, Mike."

Zinla's face was twisted with anger. Anna motioned her to a chair. The sound of the Commissar's voice seemed to quiet her down a bit.

"Go ahead."

"We have the whole collection of models at the station. I received the report from Zinla and brought them into my office. I've let them hear what you have to say. They have nothing to add except that they're trying to tell me that the man may be part fish or alien. They're very upset. We're going to keep them here overnight, if Mrs. Zinla presses charges. Would you like to question them?"

"Yes. While Mrs. Quince gets our reservations on the Cruise ship, I'll come to the station. Hold on a minute."

"Ted. The machine for making recordings of the music here has been taken by the models. The present tapes will eventually run down, but in the meantime, keep on the scrambling device, just in case someone else has one. I'd like a schematic sent to Arles via a fast international delivery service." Anna called from the other phone. "Just a moment."

"Mike. The Commissar de police says John Santos is pretty sure he can build something here that will do the trick. He's pretty good with electronics. In fact, he wants to go along on the ship with you."

Mike repeated the message on the three-way hookup.

"Did you hear that Ted? Gather as much info there as you can, in case we have to prove to the government that this involves international interests. And check out a news story about an alien craft with them. Dr. Handley can update you on it.

"All of you report to Troy at her home in the evening. Is that OK, Troy? I'll try to contact you between eleven and twelve each night and we can exchange information."

"Plays hell with a gal's nightlife," she said trying for a bit of humor. Then seriously, "You bet. I won't rest anyway until I hear you're ok and we get this mutant, phantom lover, baby kidnapper, or whatever.

"There's one thing, Mike. I believe the babies are still alive. You'll notice a pattern. Except for the interruption of sexual enjoyment, nothing really criminal has happened. A seducer of women, apparently to produce seed that makes nearly all become pregnant at any time, healthy happy, slightly different children, but intelligent and loveable. So far no bodies found. I believe the babies are alive and growing in some safe place. There may be thousands of them, or at least hundreds. Where and how could they be concealed? If you could just follow one of them . . . " She broke off thoughtfully.

"Good thinking, but it's still kidnapping . . . We need a child, though, in case we miss Anna. Any ideas?"

"I have one," Ted said. "Ours. Jean . . er, we have a baby that has a strange look about it. Jean's story is the same as the others. I believed her, but as you describe the child, it could be ours. Jean and I will fly over. You book us a cruise, either together or separately. I'll get a monitoring device for our daughter and the other child. If you have to go ahead of us, leave messages at the Zinla office or your hotel. I'll call Jean and we'll be on the first plane out. Larry can handle it."

"Yes. Let Larry do it. Give him something to think about. That's a good idea. To come on over. We're trying it from several angles. Anna alone with her child and you as a couple. You can head back to the states, if nothing pans out.

"Dr. Handley, can you keep an eye on Troy in case she gets on the track of something that may be dangerous? Alert her presidential protectors to be extra watchful. Keep a low profile, Tory. He laughed. "Are you president yet?"

"Tomorrow . . . It's looking good. But my mind is elsewhere. If I win, I won't have much time for a few days."

"I won't keep you. Unless anyone has something to add, let's get busy. Bye, Dr. Handley, Ted, Troy, take care. Talk to you tomorrow night. Let me know when you'll arrive, Ted."

Mike hung up and was immediately pounced on by Zinla. "I'm going with you and find my baby. You can't stop me. Please?"

"Well, well, Zinla. Please? I didn't know you knew the word."

"Mike!" Anna said warningly.

"Ok, Ok. But Zinla, your chances of finding your baby are almost as good if you remain here, as if you came along.

"You had more contact with the photographer than anyone. I'd like to put you into a deeper hypnotic state and go over things that may be buried in your subconscious mind. I suspect that all of you have been under a hypnotic influence off and on. The soundtrack itself may be set to induce certain actions. Different ones may trigger different responses. You might have been used more than you know." She looked unhappy at his suggestion.

"Whoever is behind this is a master. He may even have an instrument that is tuned to the wavelength of each person's brain patterns. I've read about their development, but haven't used one. Also, someone knows a great deal about genetics." The women watched him thoughtfully.

"We're dealing with a group of people, I suspect. Intelligent, mind specialists, hypnotists, psychologists, electronic and radio technologists. More than one person. Also nursemaids. We need to find a place where a nursery could be set up for hundreds of children. A place where the sale of commodities of milk and baby products may have increased recently." Mike was thinking aloud. He finally had Zinla's attention.

"Zinla, if you really want to find your baby, will you do as I ask? You may be our strongest link." She nodded her face pale.

"Do you understand the commodities market?"

"Yes, I do. You've convinced me. I'll work from here and be the clearing house for this area as Troy is in the States. While Anna packs and tries to locate her sister, I'll book the tickets. The business must go on Anna. You're past due for a vacation anyway." She gave her a hug and, for the first time, Mike noted a bit of warmth under the cold veneer. The businesswoman was shifting into gear. Mike had no doubt she was efficient and would be helpful.

Anna seemed to have overcome her earlier state of intoxication. She was nervous. Mike could understand her anxiety about the children and her sister, but it seemed to be more than that. He watched her closely for a moment. She caught his glance and pasted a smile over her frown.

"The Commissar de police is still on the line."

"Tell him I'm on my way to the station. You ladies do your thing. I'll be in touch."

Kidnapping

Several women and three men were crammed into the Commissar's office. Mike was introduced to the models. Since they had been tuned into the office conference, they needed very little additional information and said they didn't have anything to add. They all seemed exhausted emotionally and physically . . . Mike was close to exhaustion himself and knew he'd have to grab a nap soon.

Reluctantly, they promised to keep a low profile and let the officials handle the case. Meanwhile, they were advised, if they came up with anything, they were to call the Commissar and Zinla.

"If she isn't in, put a message on her phone recorder and I'll pick it up later." When Mile suggested they let him put them under a light trance, they protested. Too much so. He pretended to let it go and gradually relaxed the ones with the strongest opposition. The others soon fell into place. "Just relax and rest. You've had a long struggle and it's nearly over.

When the models were under, the Commissar opened a door and invited his superior and four men from the United Nations Peace Keepers who had been observing through a window in the wall, to come in.

Mike had been conscious of the two-way glass and had turned to face it, hoping he might get his observes to show themselves . . .

"A CIA man is on his way to the police station," an officer told the Commissar de police. The four men looked at one another as though annoyed.

Other than initial resistance, the models seemed to know very little on the first layer of the conscious mind. Mike tested to see if anyone was faking. Once a subject has been hypnotized, it is hard for them to resist going under again.

"Each of you visualize the photographer in your mind. Did any of you contact him outside of work at Zinla's?"

"If so, raise your hands." No response. "Did any of you feel that you might have been hypnotized as you are now?" All of them raised their hands. Mike took them deeper and began to probe.

"John, what happened?"

"The first time was in the office. He told me to think of my most attractive self. A time when I felt I could seduce nearly any woman. As I did the commercial poses for him, something seemed to go out of me. He used me in a couple of others films besides the sea in a harbor, but I can't remember where. He paused. Mike said, you'll remember. Just relax and breathe deeply."

John was silent for a while and then leaned forward, "I remember, I was fascinated by holographic photography. I kept trying to find out more about the extra box and some of the different equipment he used. The last time, I told him about my sexual drain, he assured me after a few months my sexuality would return.

"Then, he asked me to go with him to a lab and donate sperm for a special genetic project on which his company was working. Normally, I would have objected, but he convinced me it was of international importance. I believe he hypnotized me to get my consent."

"My God!" Mike heard one of the men mutter behind me. He silenced him with a glance. "Did you see where the lab was located?"

"No, but I'm certain it was on a large ship near the waterfront."

"John. I want you to go deeper into your visual mind. You see the ship, describe it."

"It is long, about 160 feet long. It is old. A mermaid is above my head as we walk along the pier. He told me the ship and memory of the night would be too far away to remember except as a hazy dream. Everything seems to be in a fog."

"Who is on the ship?"

"I don't know. A crew and I hear babies crying and being sung a lullaby." They looked at one another meaningfully.

"Go on, what else do you see and hear?"

"On the deck are cases of baby food and milk. The lab is where we are now."

"John, did you donate sperm?"

"Yes."

"Did you, Jose?" Mike asked the Spanish model.

"Yes."

"Can you add anything to what John has told us, Jose?"

"No, just shadowy fish. All look like Mr. Quinn only more fish-like. They are working in the lab and seemed excited about something. They keep saying, it works, it works."

"What are they talking about?"

"One race. The children of all will make it safe."

"Make what safe?"

"I'm not sure."

"Where are the fish?"

"Not fish. Fish men. Like Quinn. They're afraid of people. Afraid we'll kill them?"

"Where are they?"

"Hiding. Deep down in the ocean ... for a long time."

"Why are they taking sperm and babies? Are the babies hostages?"

"Don't know. He took me to the pier and put me in a cab." He stirred restlessly coming back to the moment.

"Medusa, did Mr. Quinn take you to his ship?"

"No, I didn't see a ship. Just the studio at Zinla's."

"Did you see him any other time besides at the studio?"

"No."

"Did any of you ladies see Mr. Quinn outside the studio?" There was silence. "Do any of you have anything to add about Mr. Quinn, the holograms, or the modeling job?"

There was no response.

"When I count from ten backwards down to one, you'll come back to this room. You will feel very rested and refreshed. If at any time you remember anything, you will call the Commissar de police here or Mrs. Zinla, if you can't locate me. You will leave the detective work to the experts. Your sex life will return to normal." Mike wasn't certain about the latter, but it was worth a try.

"John. Please remain available to help with the technical equipment, should we need it." He counted down. One by one they opened their eyes and looked around the room.

"As far as I'm concerned Commissar Minlek, you can send them home, they've had a rough time emotionally." They left gratefully.

Mike noted with satisfaction John's interested glance at the ladies' rounded behinds and that he fell in step with Med. They smiled intimately at one another as they paused in the doorway.

After the models left, the group of men sat around and looked at one another. Each seemed deep in thought. Finally someone said, "What are we to make of all this?"

After a moment Mike waded in.

"It seems to me that if we leave things alone, there may be a plan by someone to get us to accept them. Is it alien or from the earth? Perhaps we need someone from a genetics lab to supply us with answers."

Since Mike seemed to have the floor, he continued, "It would seem to me that the babies are not dead and may be in good hands. If the babies are half-human and half fish-alien, we wouldn't dare destroy them. It seems to me they have gone to a great deal of trouble to make certain we'll react peacefully to them. But, will it be blackmail for power and money, or a peaceful overture we can expect? I'm thinking aloud gentlemen. Anyone wish to add something?"

One of the United Nation's Representatives cleared his throat and said, "You seem to have given this a great deal of thought, Mr. Lambert."

He nodded and waited. Would they share their discoveries or would each department beat around the bush and work alone? That would make it harder for everyone and take longer. Were they bent on being cautious, or would they rush in like fools with too much power and not enough wisdom, as the United States often did, using the CIA as a club?

"If they averaged 50 to 100 babies in the past year or so, from several seacoast cities, there may be thousands," one tossed a crumb in front of Mike.

He nodded. His reaction was being studied by the two men and the Commissar de Police. They were holding something back.

The leader finally spoke, "The reason we are here is that we have a message from these creatures. We got wind of your investigation when following the trail to Zinla's Advertising Agency. The authorities at the police station sent us to this department in time to catch your hypnosis act. Very good work, Mr. Lambert."

"Could I see a copy of the message?"

Mike was worn out and in a hurry to be off. Time to be diplomatic later. They glanced at one another and nodded. Reluctant the leader pulled a copy from his pocket.

It read:

"Ladies and Gentlemen: It is of the utmost importance that representatives of the United Nations meet with us. All of the babies that were reported missing are safe. They will remain so, if the military is not called in. Have them come to the Zinla Labs in Arles, France on August 10. The place is under observation at all times. Do not call police action of any kind or many will die.

"They must come alone. A messenger will tell them where to carry on from there. We have ways of knowing if any harmful actions are to be carried out against us. Do not act in haste." A. Quinn

"I'd like a copy of this. I suppose you've checked out the stationary and any return postage marks?"

The UN President said, "It was delivered to my home. They seem to know intimate details about my life and activities. The stationary was just plain typing paper,"

"I'd give a pretty penny to be in on that conference," Mike said hopefully.

"That might not be acceptable. It may be wiser that each of us carry on as planned and keep one another posted. They may not have you under observation as yet, but they're getting information from someplace. We checked Mrs. Zinla out, and other than ambition, found no evidence that she might collaborate knowingly with anyone. However, we couldn't find much of a background on her secretary before three years ago."

"Anna?" I nodded. "There was something about her that didn't ring true, but even under hypnotism I couldn't get at anything other than a normal worried mother with a family that might be in danger."

"That's her story, but she doesn't have a family. She isn't telling the truth. The reason may not have anything to do with the problem, but she is in a convenient spot."

Mike frowned. "I can't help feeling too many people are involved to keep it a secret much longer. Can I contact you here and exchange information? You will keep Minlek updated on events?" He asked the United Nations Representatives.

"Normally, we would not cooperate with a private agency, but under the circumstances, you seem to know more than we do. We're willing to pool information if it in no way jeopardizes lives or interferes with our mission."

Mike smiled ironically. "OK, you've made your speech. None of us want our lives endangered. Let's keep it that way."

Minlek said hesitatingly, "I do not wish to insult your country, Mike, but you said the police in the United States were working with you. Won't they inform the military there? I feel that this piece of UN information should be withheld from them for the time being." Mike nodded in agreement.

"Also, the CIA man is waiting in the outer office. What can we do about him?"

"I suggest you tell him there have been some disturbances about the holograms. The Zinla Agency has promised to shut down the soundtracks which may have a subliminal message within them. That they were made without her knowledge and consent. They may prove to be harmless.

"By the way, did the models have the instrument they stole when you picked them up?"

"Yes, we have the police lab checking it now. John had tried to open it with little success. I've cautioned them to treat it like a bomb. There was a notice on the bottom saying that the instrument would explode if tampered with."

"We seem to be dealing with some very intelligent people. I'd take the message at face value, and any others that you may receive," Mike advised.

The office phone buzzed. "Mrs. Zinla is on the phone, Mike."

She sounded tired. "Everything's set here. Your plane to the coast of Italy is at 6 p.m. Anna will meet you at the airport. Your partner, Ted will be in this afternoon. They land in Rome within an hour of your flight. I booked all of you from Rome to Bari and a car to drive from Bari to Brindiski. The boat leaves at 4 p.m.

"Anna said she left a message for her sister to wait in Brindiski for her. Should I book all of you together on the boat?"

"Put Ted, Jean and the baby on the ship. Get Ted a separate cabin. I want them to be seen together as little as possible in

Brindiski. Anna can go with her sister. I'll have a separate cabin near Jean and the baby. You've done a fine job, Zin. Thanks." Mike felt it would be better at this point not to tell her about Anna's deception.

"Is it OK if I turn in after I've arranged the tickets for the boat, I'm exhausted.

"Sure." Mike was feeling weary himself and yawned in empathy.

"I'll have all the office calls switched through to my house. If anything important comes in, I'll try to get in touch with you.

"By the way, do you want to stay in Athens? That's where people usually go? I booked reservations for all of you for one night there. A bus takes all passengers from the boat to the city."

"That will do for the time being. Keep our schedule flexible. We may have to change our plans and move fast. Thanks Mrs. Zinla and goodnight."

"Just find my baby, Mike." He nodded sadly to a dead phone.

Looking out a one-way window into the reception area, Mike saw a tall slim man in a light nondescript jacket and glasses. The man from the CIA glanced up as though he knew he was being observed. Mike would know him if he ever saw him again. The others followed his gaze.

"At this point," Mike said, "I'd feel safer if my country was in the wings for a while longer. I'm sure you can handle him, Commissar. I appreciate your tact and cooperation."

Mike asked, puzzled, "I wonder why he couldn't wait until tomorrow? Try to stall him as long as possible. I'll go out with these gentlemen and we'll let him think we're all together." They walked to the door. "After you," Mike said.

The group left, chatting as though they were old friends. No one seemed to notice the CIA man as the group walked by. He looked intently at each of them and raised his hand as though in greeting. Mike wondered if he should smile for the camera that would be hidden in the sleeve.

Outside, he shook hands with the UN representatives. They agreed to contact him on the evening of August 10th to bring one another up to date. Zinla would have his Athens number.

What a relief to get to his hotel. "Call me at 4:30 a.m. he told the operator and fell onto the bed. The message indicator blinked.

Mike could hardly keep his eyes open as he returned the call to Troy.

"Hello darling. You called, "he said teasingly.

"Oh, Mike, I didn't expect to hear from you again tonight. You must be dead tired. I thought you should know. After talking to you, I remembered a dream one of my patients told me about. It stuck in my mind because another patient had a similar dream.

"Both dreamed of a lover who planted a seed in their wombs and told them they would not want to have sex with anyone until a year after their child was born. They believed they carried a fish in their wombs and were surprised when the child was born and was not a fish. Each of them came to me over a year ago, worried their babies would not be normal. Is it important or not?"

Mike yawned into the phone. "You bet it is, but I can't go into it now. I'm beat."

"I know you're tired, so I won't keep you. Have you had any new leads?"

He quickly updated her on the evening events, following their earlier conversation. "So you see, your call's very interesting. Can you get one or both women into the office and regress them to that night? Have them describe under hypnosis how they became pregnant."

"It is tomorrow here, love. I'll try, but one of them is going on a trip. Oh, my God. To Europe."

"Find out when and where if you can. If she insists on going, have Larry get her a tracking bracelet. Ted and Jean are already on their way and I leave in a few hours. Goodnight, Troy. I miss you."

"Good morning, Mike. I miss you too." She did not tell him she had just been elected president of the United States.

Mike felt as though he closed his eyes when it was time to leave for the airport. If he had not been in a rush, he would have tried to discover who was following him, but as it was, he barely made his plane.

As he walked down the aisle, he saw the CIA man. Had the Commissar de police told him he'd be on this plane? It was not likely. Was Zinla's phone bugged? She would know nothing of the UN operation until the day of the meeting.

I'd rather he followed me than the delegates, Mike thought. Normally, he would have confronted him. Mike was not ready to tell what he knew, so he continued on to his seat. Before the plane took off he fell asleep and did not wake until they touched down at the Rome airport.

On the next flight to the coast, Zinla had booked seats together. Ted and Mike ignored one another until the plane took off.

Mike boarded early with the children and Jean. She and the baby sat in the front seats. Mike inspected the baby and winked at her. The little girl, Shauna, talked well for such a young child. "Hello, Uncle Mike. We fly to big ocean. Go swim home. You swim too?"

"Will you show me where to go?"
"Shauna swim home."
"Where is home?"
"Home in water. You funny, Uncle Mike."
"Why am I funny?"

"Uncle Mike lost, Mommy. Can't swim home."
Out of the corner of his eye, Mike saw the other passengers loading. He wanted to be where he could inspect each one and not be caught being familiar with Jean at this point. Mike winked at Jean and headed for his seat.

The expense account didn't call for first class. He hated the crowded seats and lack of legroom. Either seats got smaller each year or he had gained weight since the last time he flew. Then again, the more people on each plane the less we pollute the environment, I suppose. The new wing and engine design saved a great deal of fuel, but with more people using planes each year, the environmental damage continued to get worse. An hours discomfort wouldn't hurt him. At least he had an aisle seat.

He dozed before the plane took off. Pushing back sleep, he made himself stay awake so he could talk with Ted once they were off the ground.

The CIA man was not in his section. "He may have known I spotted him and changed with someone else," Mike told Ted as they talked quietly, sitting with closed eyes. They speculated as to the possibilities and impossibilities. Could there be a race of fishlike people on earth? It seemed highly unlikely.

"Remember the press statement that we know more about the moon than we do our own oceans?"

Mike chuckled, "Troy always adds, 'Or then we know about ourselves."

Ted nodded. "Aliens might find the ocean a more hospitable climate than our polluted air. It's fun to speculate, but it's probably just another case of greed," Ted muttered gloomily. They sat in silence for awhile.

"Why do you suppose they chose Arles for the center of the operation? Or, are we just being thrown off the trail? Mike mused.

"Are you sure Zinla is not one of them?"

"Fairly certain, and I'm just about convinced her secretary is a great actress and one of 'them'."

Mike filled him in on the balance of the night after their phone conversation. "The UN investigation could not turn up a past on her farther back than three years. At first, I believed they operated from greed, too. And why not? Doesn't the world function by nearly everyone trying to sell everyone else something for more than it's worth? No one wants to plod along. Get rich quick and the devil take the hindmost, seems to be the motto of our age." Mike knew he was sounding bitter. In his job he often saw the worst side of people but, as Troy reminded him, there are still some people who would give you their last dollar."

"Where children are concerned, most people have a soft spot," Ted said.

Mike nodded. "Women can become fierce when their offspring are involved. They give up their young sons to war only because the sons choose to go. Most of them would call off a war rather than lose a member of their family. What would women give or make a world do, if the lives of their babies were at stake? It was an interesting thought. "If only we could hypnotize a couple of the women who have these babies."

"Well, Jean's aboard. There is time."

Ted sat beside me doodling. He thought with paper in hand and doodled words, diagrams and maps. Much like dream analysis. Mike glanced over and saw geometric symbols with lines drawn to meanings: Movement, water, flexibility, fish, alien, air, BABIES, OCEAN, MEDITERRANEAN, Atlantis, aquarium, Aquarius, aquanaut, aquatic, waddle, mystery, duck, deep, Quaternion, Quantra, Quinn, A. Aqua, Anna Quince, pithecanthropine, etc.

"What the hell is pithecanthropine?"

"Oh, an extinct race. Remember Atlantis?"

"Come on Ted. That's been overworked."

He laughed. Ted was big, slightly overweight, blond, and good-natured, except when he encountered evil. Where most of us used the word crime, he divided acts as grades of evil. An old word, but it put a finger on an act of violence more precisely.

"I'm just trying to stir up my imagination. For example, an advanced scientific civilization, Atlantis or an ancient city, foresaw a possible destruction of their world, went underseas instead of underground. Volcanoes, earthquakes, even meteorites may have destroyed advanced civilizations that we can't study because they're under the sea or have been covered over during the ice age." Mike yawned and listened.

"What if one of these groups survived? Atlantis was supposed to be off the coast near the entrance to the Mediterranean Sea. Someplace near Gibraltar or in the Atlantic.

"Remember? About ten years ago a whole group of divers and their highly advanced equipment, as well as the latest diving bell, disappeared in the Atlantic?" He added divers, advanced technology, atomic submarines, cultures . . . .

"Also, that atomic sub about two years ago near Fargo, Portugal. There's a large aquatic garden and an underwater city there. It was built by the famous Aquavits, Nemo Sono. He won a Nobel Prize or something. A lot of dollars. He also did something in genetics with fish. Didn't he have a baby who retained its gills and could either live in water or on land? A group of radicals protested and tried to get stringent laws set up against experimenting with genetics."

Mike sat us straighter. Bells were ringing in his head. "The child was said to have died. Because of the hue and cry from the religious fanatics, he promised no more experiments. Then there was the lab explosion and he died from injuries."

They sat quietly, thinking. Mike took Ted's pad and let the words float in his mind, hoping they'd form a subconscious pattern. "I wonder," Mike said. Ted looked at Mike and grinned. He had lit a fire as he intended. "You think we're going in the wrong direction, don't you?"

"Well, when I talked to you on the phone, I hadn't had time to think about some of these things. Jean and I were talking on the plane. We met skin diving off the cost of Florida. Her degree is in Aquaculture and Anthropology. She feels we spend too much time and money studying the earth's surface and not enough in the ocean and under the ice caps.

"Anyway, she has agreed to go to Fargo, Portugal, seek out Mrs. Sono and see what she can dig up. In college, she spent a month at a workshop there. Although she didn't meet Prof. Sono personally, she listened to some of his talks in the auditorium. She says he was a tall, slender, soft-spoken man who would not let himself be compromised, if he had a purpose. He was old then. His wife also taught, but she only saw her from a distance. We might just rent a little boat and go skin diving in case this cruise doesn't pan out. Want to come along?"

"You bet. It would seem that we have arrived. Better wear that nose filter. There's a lot of smog on the coast. Even with the European public transport system and all the propaganda to walk or ride a bike, it's as polluted as California. We're lucky we're special licensed and can rent a car."

"Since we're on the wrong track anyway, let's take a car together to Brindiski," Mike suggested. "I need to talk with Jean. May send you two off to lay the groundwork while I go to Athens with Anna, if I can track her down."

"You must let Jean have a day or two in Athens or she'll never forgive us. On such short notice, she had one hell of a time getting off at the Aquarium. Only the baby and Athens could have made her risk her job. She told them it was the baby's health. They don't want to lose Jean. Neither do I. She's one hell of a woman, as you know. Integrity is her middle name. That's why this baby thing didn't throw us for a loop like it did some of the other couples."

Mike patted his arm. "You're a lucky man, Ted.

"So are you," he countered. "I hope you don't fool around too long and lose Troy."

He looked surprised when Mike laughed and agreed with him.

"Have you seen today's headlines?"

"No. Should I?"

"Troy is now president of the United States."

"Oh, my God. What a selfish son-of-a . . . I never even asked her about the election—just filled up with my own concerns. She'll never forgive me for this."

"You do tend to have a one-track mind. That's why you're good at what you do."

"As soon as we land, I'm going to send her the biggest bunch of flowers . . . hell, I'll send a whole greenhouse."

"I think Troy of all people understands you, Mike. She . . . " Ted paused and let it go. Mike must find his own way.

Ted located the car and picked them up outside the baggage section of the terminal. He drove toward the coast. In the back seat of the car, Mike had a chance to study Shauna. She was certainly active and observant. The lips were very prominent. In a pout, but she smiled often and seemed extremely healthy and intelligent. "How old is she," he asked Jean.

"A year and five months. She's large, and advanced for her age. Very few babies say sentences at one year, but she did. However, she should be walking better. Let me show Uncle Mike your feet sweetheart."

Jean pulled off her socks. Between the toes were small webs. The fingers were the same.

The little girl said, "Swim, Swim, Mommy. Go home. Shauna go home." She seemed very excited and pointed toward the ocean. By this time they were driving down the coast, and until she pointed, Mike had not realized how close they were to the water.

Shauna tried to lean out the car windows. Jean rolled them up. "Later baby. We'll go swimming later on." Shauna shed crocodile tears. Jean laughed. "Do you think we could stop and let her go swimming sometime soon, Mike?"

Quickly the tears changed to smiles when Mike said. "OK. We'll have lunch by the ocean and all go for a swim. Might as well enjoy ourselves. There's plenty of time before the ship sails."

In the past the roads would have been crowded. Due to TV propaganda, the automobile was becoming socially unpopular, even in crowded Europe.

"I'll bet Jean is the one missing the water," Ted teased, giving her an affectionate glance over his shoulder. She laughed. "I hardly brought anything--three swimsuits. Working daily in an aquarium doesn't do much for the wardrobe."

"I like you best in the buff anyway, love."

Jean she tried to pat down Shauna's rough mane of hair. She had fluffed it out at the sides so that the heavy layer in the center top was not noticeable at first glance. Jean looked up and smiled at Mike, but the worried smile didn't touch her eyes. What a brave woman you are, Mike thought. Here she is, knowing her child may disappear, but willing to take the risk to save it and others.

Mike put his arm around her shoulders and gave them a sympathetic squeeze. For a moment she rested her head on his arm as though grateful for the comfort. Tears rolled silently down her cheeks and fell on the child's bare legs. Shauna continued to point toward the ocean and chatter. Ted's eyes met Mike's in the mirror. He nodded and continued to drive with a stubborn, determined look in his own eyes.

"Look at Shauna's necklace and bracelet," Ted said. Mike recognized her jewelry as two of their latest monitoring devices.

Jean held the arm and hand in the sunlight. Not only were the fingers slightly webbed, the silky smooth skin was made up of minute, iridescent scales.

"I had already written to Dr. Sono about this months ago." Jean said. "Mrs. Sono's answer came in the mail last week. She said she had heard of a few other cases and would like to see Shauna. I didn't show the letter to Ted because he was away. I applied for a month off after Troy's election. Shauna may need some extra help to learn to walk well."

What luck, Mike thought and continued to give her words close attention.

"Our older children, Melody, was an early walker and Jeff, a late one. I haven't been too worried about it until recently. It's the other things in addition. She's in the water more than she's out. I often take her to work so she can play with the turtles and dolphins. Sometimes I'm sure they communicate. She seems to be developing lines around the neck and ears, almost where gills would be. I showed her to Troy and she assured me she was alright."

Mike frowned and wondered why Troy hadn't mentioned it. He ran his fingers over the red lines. They seemed a bit hard compared to the baby skin, but otherwise they were okay.

"Has Troy known about Shauna since birth?"

"Oh, yes. When we visit her, she and Shauna often go swimming in her pool. They can both stay underwater an incredible length of time, but then Troy was practically raised in water."

"What do you mean?"

"Didn't she tell you? She was raised in Florida at an Aquamarine Boarding School, and then went to Sono's Portugal aqua garden and studied at the University near there. That's where I met her."

"She did mention something once or twice, but I guess I was too preoccupied. There was something about it in the news recently, but I was out of touch with the hologram virus."

Shauna began to fuss and Mike turned his attention to her. "Do you talk to the turtles, Shauna?" The little girl nodded and smiled but kept her nose pressed against the window on the ocean side.

Jean continued, "Ted suggested that we keep her out of the water for awhile, but if she's away from it, even a day, she seems to go into a slump. We took her on a ski trip last winter. She climbed right out of the car and slithered through the snow like a seal. We finally took her back home. A young lady who's training for the Olympics stays with us. She and Shauna spend most of their day swimming.

She's very strong and can take good care of them both." Jean gazed abstractly at Shauna, hugged her and brushed a tear from her cheek before continuing, "I showed her the articles about babies disappearing in water so we've been extra careful. We rebuilt the fence so it's now eight feet high. The gate and front door are locked at all times."

Mike had an uneasy feeling. They had taken such good care of Shauna; she had not escaped, so far. None of the children had been much over a year as far as he could tell. What happened to their appearance after a few more years, Mike wondered.

"Jean, Ted, are you sure you don't want to call this whole thing off?"

They looked at the child. Ted bit his lips and glanced at Jean in the mirror. Tears continued to roll silently down her cheeks. She wiped them away with the back of her hand and then reached into her purse for a tissue.

"You know it will happen one way or another, don't you?" Jean asked. "It's happened to most of the others already. Do they die, if they don't disappear?"

Mike shook his head, "I don't think so, but I can't be sure."

"We'd rather be there and know when it happens, hoping it might not be the end. Maybe there's something we can do. If we can put a stop to it for all parents, we must try," she said bravely.

Shauna turned, leaned over and licked the salty tears from Jean's cheeks. "Mommy cry. Shauna go swimming. Shauna be back Mommy. Don't cry. Shauna go, Shauna come back to Mommy and make Mommy happy. Laugh Mommy. Give Shauna a smile." She was such a jolly little girl. They couldn't help smiling as she tried to cheer her mother up.

"Where is Shauna going?" Mike asked.

"She always says that," Ted commented. Mike signaled him to be quiet.

"Shauna. Where are you going?"

She looked at Mike and then the ocean. "Shauna go swim in ocean. Help all Daddies like all Daddies. Shauna come home, Mommy."

"Are you going to an island or a boat?"

"Big island with big bubbles underwater. Mommy and Daddy come see Shauna. Uncle Mike come, too, Mommy?"

"Yes dear, Uncle Mike can come visit you under the water. She has a play cave under coral at the aquarium. I've timed her at three minutes, sitting there feeding fish and swimming in and out of the cave."

Ted said, "I have a feeling she doesn't mean that one. Just suppose that a genetic mutation or experiment was made and people could live underwater as easily as in the air. The first babies would need to be very intelligent and strong. There would have to be a program so it was 'instinctive.' A call to the water at a very early age. We have always supposed people would do the experimenting. And, we know Dr. Sono had. Did he really succeed or fail? Why did he drop out of the limelight? Is he really dead?"

"The more I think about it, Jean, the more I think you're right, we may be going in the wrong direction. We'll go to Athens and then head for Portugal. If we're nearer the source when Shauna goes, we'll be closer to getting her back. What do you two think?"

"Shauna hungry, Mommy."

They laughed. "I think both of you are right. Let's eat and talk about it."

They found a nice little seaside cafe in Ostuni. The outdoor deck was built over the sea. Seagulls circled leisurely above. A cool breeze kept the sun from feeling too warm. The wine and food were excellent. For awhile they drank, chatted and enjoyed the atmosphere. Shauna leaned against the glassed-in deck and stared longingly at the ocean. Finally, over coffee, they took up the problem again.

They would go to Brindiski and see if Anna and her sister showed up. Then, take a day in Athens, if Jean had her heart set on seeing it. By that time, they would know what the people from the United Nations had learned.

Mike glanced at his watch. "I think I'll check in with Zinla. That lady is a whiz. Maybe she can send Troy flowers and has talked to her. Take your time with coffee. Go ahead and have a little swim, if you want to risk it," Mike said over his shoulder.

He had just finished his calls and was returning to the table when he heard Ted shout. "Mike, call the coast guard and the police. It's Shauna. She's gone. "

Mike rushed to the edge of the deck as Ted dived into the water. Jean surfaced about a hundred feet out and dived again. Turning around, he saw the owner hang up the phone. "They will come, right away. A boat comes too, see?"

"Thanks," Mike shouted. He slipped off his shoes and slacks before diving into the water. All three adults were excellent swimmers. For exercise, Ted and Mike swam a couple of miles daily in the YMCA pool near the office. Sometimes they knocked off at late hours and went to Ted's huge backyard pool at night. Shauna had been in bed at those times.

Mike swam in the direction he had last seen Jean, but she no longer surfaced. Treading water for a minute, he looked out over the smooth calm sea. None of the three came up for air.

"Damn," he said and dived deeply again and again. One time, he thought he saw a large dark form in a distance, but the shadow moved away quickly.

When he surfaced again, a speed boat pulled up alongside. Hands pulled him out of the water. Other divers with fins and tanks dove into the water for a long time and found nothing.

Mike sat in a state of shock. To lose all three at once was too much. He tried to tell himself Mike and Jean were with the babies, but he knew of no other adults who had disappeared along with them. He went back to the sidewalk cafe on the boat. The police questioned the other guests and the owner. Mike gave them

Commissar de police Milek's number, and promised he'd find a hotel nearby and let them know where he was staying in case something came up.

They didn't want to release him.

A shadow fell across the table. He looked up to see the CIA man holding out a badge. The man spoke in fluent Italian to the police.

Finally, they nodded. He turned and said, "You're free to go with me."

Mike stumbled toward the car, he kept telling himself Mike and Jean weren't lost. They had expected to lose Shauna and find her again. "Her monitor," he said and ran to the car. They had left their jackets inside. Both Ted and he carried monitors. Looking up, he saw the man watching with interest as Mike noted the light on both monitors moving west, rapidly.

"Mr. Lambert, I'm Donovan with the CIA. Let's talk a bit. Perhaps we can help one another." He again extended his identification.

Mike nodded. "I'd like to thank you for talking them into letting me go, but you have no authority over me in this country. I really have nothing to say to you."

"Did you have anything to do with your friends drowning, Mr. Lambert?"

"Not a thing. How do you know my name?"

"Let's not play games. You and Ted are detectives, investigating the disappearance of babies and the holograms that have appeared all over the world. We thought they were two different cases until recently. I'm willing to share information, if you are."

Mike looked at him. He appeared to be intelligent and sincere. If he fed him a few things, maybe the exchange would be worth it. "OK, you tell me what you know first and I'll see if we're on the same case." They stood by Mike's car and Donovan talked.

"A couple of years ago a US atomic sub disappeared, and in the past year, both Russia and the United States have each lost another. We had given them up for lost units. Recently, one was detected in the Mediterranean Sea. We followed it to the Strait of Gibraltar where it disappeared. Just when we had given it up, another report came from the other side in the Pacific. It seems as though someone is playing tag with us. Now we see them, now we don't.

"We have also been detecting small, swift underwater craft recently with a different kind of power. Fusion is our guess. A plane dropped some depth charges. We got one. It was manned by an alien, a fishy-looking man. We are moving a fleet into the area. It's in the mid-Atlantic now."

"My God, you must stop it."

"Why must I stop it? Besides, it isn't in my hands, I'm afraid."

"I'm afraid, too, Mr. Donovan."

Mike felt a chill move along his spine. "During the last year hundreds of babies have disappeared. No bodies have been found. We believe there's a connection between the babies and the holograms and the babies are still alive. A group of war vessels might endanger their lives."

"Have you seen the holograms?"

Mike nodded and saw Donovan's face twist in an ugly expression before he pasted blandness over it again. "Then you know how they affect people. Haven't you been receiving reports on them?"

"We had anonymous phone calls about them and, at first, let the FBI handle it. They decoded the underlying messages in some and found out a few things, then called us in. The messages are programs which hypnotize people with sound into wanting to go on trips, which on the surface, seems all right." He looked vacantly into space, reminding Mike of Larry, shook himself and continued. "The tapes have specific suggestions regarding sexual activities, minority groups and going to the sea. Suddenly, this week, the tapes were switched to plain music. Someone knows we're listening." He paused thoughtfully.

Mike shrugged my shoulders. He was impatient and wanted to monitor Ted and Jean.

Donovan continued, "I went to Zinla's but the source of the supply had been stolen by a group of models. You were just leaving when I saw you at the station. I hope you got more out of the authorities at Arles than I did."

Mike said nothing. His gaze searched the sea. He hopefully told himself the flashing light on the monitor meant Ted, Jean and Shauna were together and safe for the time being. Glancing at it again his body trembled. The light had gone out. He tried to make himself listen to Donovan, then get away as quickly as possible. A police car was still at the restaurant and the boat still circling in the water. Divers appeared on deck. .

"The French have been difficult to deal with these past few years. Europeans seem to blame the United States for world pollution and the economic failure of their cooperative market."

Mike nodded. The police boat made several sweeps back and forth across the area where Jean, Ted and Shauna were last seen.

"Did you know that Zinla's grandmother was with the French Underground and her Father was a Nazi? However, her secretary is the most devious one of the two and we suspect has some connection with all this. She's disappeared."

"Anna?"

"She fooled you too?" He smiled for the first time. "I confronted Zinla with our information and she told me what you were up to. By the way, what were the men from the United Nations doing in the office? You may as well tell me where they're headed. They're being followed, not only by us, but someone else. They may be in danger."

"I don't know. Maybe the whole race is in danger." Mike began to use his words in a play back hoping to get Donovan at least partially under his control and dig deeper.

He decided to be frank and told him the story as he knew it, leaving nothing out except the UN message. The Spanish police kept looking in his direction. He needed Donovan's help to get swiftly to Fargo, Portugal. Perhaps he could enlist Mrs. Sono in his search.

"Dr. Sono may be the only person in the world who can solve the mystery in a hurry, in time to save Mike, Jean and the babies. We must do something before the fleet arrives in the Mediterranean. The babies, if they're alive, might be killed if US forces move in and attempt violence. It they have the atomic submarines, there might be an exchange of nuclear warheads." You could bet those atomic subs were armed.

Mike tried to put Donovan in a trance, but the man knew all his tricks and more he suspected.

"Never mind. May I call you Mike?" Mike shrugged and he continued, "I know what you're trying to do. It isn't necessary. I called a helicopter when there was trouble. It should be here soon. We'll head for Faro. Let's hope Dr. Sono is cooperative."

"He'll have to be, if he's alive. Apparently, his wife runs the show now. Their lives may be at stake, unless they can help us."

"I too lost a child," Donovan said. "Let's check the baby Shauna's monitor." He reached under the steering lever and pulled out a small listening device. He had heard every word Mike, Jean and Ted had spoken in the car. Mike gave himself a mental kick in the seat for not checking the rental.

Again Mike checked the one he held. Their signals was faint flicker now and then. Was Ted managing to get a signal out once in awhile? It went off again. They were definitely moving west at a fast pace. Too fast for a swimmer, and the line too straight for a fish.

Perhaps a nuclear sub? Were Ted and Jean with Shauna, he wondered?

Donovan talked on his two-way radio. Mike tried to hear the message he received, but it was coded.

"The helicopter will be here soon. What shall we do about your car? I can call and have mine picked up. Shall I have them pick up yours, too?"

Mike nodded. "Can I bring our luggage? I feel certain we'll find them with Shauna, near Portugal."

"Already there," Donovan reported. "We checked the radar directional for small underwater craft. One was reported following your car down the coast. They were sending out signals in the same code as the background of the holograms. It was calling for the little girl to swim to their boat. I think there's a good chance her parents are with her. Like the sub, the craft disappeared suddenly near Gibraltar. We're sending some divers into the area and a eulogist to do some soundings. Only a deep underground passage could cut off the radar and sounds so quickly."

"Unless their equipment is better than yours," Mike could not help saying.

"I wouldn't be surprised." He dug out a map. Mike studied him in the sunlight. This man was tough. About 5'9", sandy-haired, swift and sure in his movements. I'd rather not tangle with him, Mike decided.

"Oh, yes. Anna was followed to Madrid. We lost her there. The UN men went to Zinla's, then flew to Gibraltar, rented a small boat and disappeared.

"We've had Dr. Sono's aquarium under observation for years. Except for a couple of labs that are carefully locked, all is normal on the surface. If he lives he has not been seen. We aren't certain he's still alive. He would be over a hundred, according to his birth record in Spain. His wife and an assistant run the gardens since Anna Quince has been working at Zinla's."

Mike looked up in surprise and he grinned in amusement.

"Nearly all of his people were handpicked at an early age and trained at his aquarium. They seldom go to outside schools. In fact, his school was so good that over half the Oceanographers in the world were trained there at one time. Anna lived and trained there in underwater photography. She went to Zinla's as a partner to monitor the holograms after her brother set the snare." He grinned at Mike's surprised look. "We checked them out but nothing seemed out of order, except he disappeared. Now, so has Anna."

"That's where your lady friend, our new President, spent a great deal of her youth. But I guess you already know that."

Troy? Lived there? Then what Jean had said was true. He remembered vaguely hearing she and Jean talk about the Aqua gardens in Spain. "She did mention it," Mike muttered, not wanting to let Donovan know how little he actually knew of Troy's past life. He realized how selfish he had been in not taking more of an interest. Or, had she deliberately not told him? Before he could follow through on this idea, the CIA agent continued. Donovan seemed to need to talk. What was bothering him?

"That's where my wife and I encountered the holograms. She was a counter-agent during the 90s. We met in Spain and had been seeing one another off and on for years. She stayed home after we married. Both of us wanted children, but to our regret we had none. Then, a couple of years ago, she became pregnant. It was shortly after the first holograms appeared. Things didn't seem to work out as happily as we'd planned. The baby was strange. Didn't look like me and not much like Heather. We seemed to lose interest in one another. She said we needed time apart. I objected. She took the baby and disappeared. I traced them to a ship. Neither of them were on it when they arrived on the other shore."

Mike nodded in sympathy. "Maybe they never got on."

Donovan stared toward the sea, remembering. Finally, he shrugged and continued, "After decoding the messages, I began to think more objectively. Maybe, just maybe they were still alive and had been kidnapped. If . . . if anything happens to them, I'll wipe out the whole nest of vipers." His voice trembled, his face pale.

"Take it easy, Donovan. You're letting your emotions ruin your objectivity. Maybe you should let me handle this."

"No!" With a great deal of willpower, the agent took control of himself. In spite of his calm veneer, Mike felt as though a bomb ticked beside him. Would the CIA let a man like this handle a case? Or had they intentionally sent someone with violent intent? Donovan went on as though there had been an emotional explosion, "The part about the babies didn't seem to fit, until I remembered our own child's reaction to water. She would have slept in the bathtub had I allowed it." He paused. Mike wondered if he was going to cry.

Donovan straightened his shoulders and said in a determined voice, "I want them back, safe and sound . . . Just as much, or more, than you want Ted and Jean returned. I promise you one hundred percent cooperation, in spite of red tape, if you promise me the same. OK?" He extended his hand.

Mike studied him for a couple of seconds. He sounded authentic. But then that was his job. He wished Troy was along to check the man out. She had an instinct for smelling lies. If he went with Donovan, he could keep an eye on him and perhaps the agent would let him know what the CIA was up to. He could talk to the new President; perhaps she could slow the Agency down a bit.

They shook hands.

The helicopter landed in the parking lot but the pilot did not get out. They loaded their luggage and left the cars to be picked up. The pilot took off as soon as they sat in their seats.

Inside, Donovan opened his briefcase and unrolled maps. They were onion-skin. One could be overlaid upon the others. Small crafts had recently been sighted all over the Med and along the coast of Portugal and Spain. Many of the crafts were related to the school of Dr. Sono. These had an x beside them.

"Several years before he disappeared, Dr. Sono designed a small craft with a strange engine. We've never been able to get hold of a design. A network was set up to capture one, but they proved very elusive. It's as though they've been teasing us lately. As though someone wants us to know they can become invisible; if they wish and keep us guessing as to how powerful they really are. The Pentagon is uneasy." He pulled out a photograph.

"This is what the alien looked like," said Donovan as he laid a sheet of paper before Mike and a couple of photographs.

"She was slightly damaged on the lower part of her body."

Mike stared at the picture. Rather like a mermaid. Her hair grew thick on the top center and down the middle like a fin attached to her spine. It thinned out and then thickened the tail of a fish but there were feet and legs.

"The Assyrians had a fish god called Dagon. There is a palace relief of him at Nimrod. Do you suppose these people could be descendants of his?"

Donovan gave Mike an amused smile, but Mike saw his forehead wrinkle thoughtfully for a moment before he continued.

"She had skin like a rainbow trout. Soft to the touch and only by looking closely could we tell it was scales and not normal skin."

The face in the photograph was human, with large eyes, protruding mouth, extra high cheekbones and a rather elongated cranium. Mike wondered if the old tales of mermaids were ancestors of this creature. It was easier to think they'd come from space than believe Earth had been host to an unknown race.

Mike's mind whirled and darted between possibilities. Had they been in our ocean all along, or were they from a water planet in space as Donovan indicated the military thought? It was then that the secret knowledge nagging in the back of his mind hit him like a hammer. Troy! Troy had the same cast of features. Not as prominent but the look was there. Maybe she was a distant cousin or? No! She couldn't be one of them. She was too concerned about the babies. Now she was President. Jean and Madge would have known. Donovan was watching him closely, so he plastered a smile on his face and looked at the maps.

"One of Dr. Sono's 'so-called' students designed an air-sea craft. It flies so close above the water that it's nearly undetectable by air radar. Appears as a ship on navigational detectors. We believe he's cooperating with these beings. Perhaps he's in charge of the whole operation."

"You've been busy. How long have you been aware of these activities?"

"Just random spotting since before WWII. But they were discreet until last year. Our equipment has been getting more sophisticated. We think they're ready to come out of hiding. With the UN contact now, it seems even more likely."

The pilot turned around and said, "You've about to land at Dr. Sono's Aqua Gardens."

Both men gave startled exclamations.

"Do not reach for your guns. They will do no good. There is a protective screen between us."

Mike finally found his voice. "Mr. Quinn, I presume?"

"You presume correctly."

"What does this mean?" Donovan asked.

"It means that our Kingdom beneath the Sea is going to meet your Kingdom. It means that we both survive together, or we both go down together."

"Are Ted, Jean, and Shauna still alive?"

"And my wife and baby?" Donovan leaned forward eagerly. For a moment they were no longer detective and agent, only concerned, worried human beings.

"Yes. All of them are well. We are not murderers. I must communicate with Dr. Sono. Please remain in your seats and soon you will know all."

Mike felt the man beside him tense. He looked at Donovan trying to decide if they should act or remain passive. To meet the enemy face to face for the first time was both terrifying and a relief.

He wondered if this was A. Quinn himself, the romancer, seducer and father of hundreds of children.

"Let's wait and take a chance," he whispered. "Too many lives are at stake."

Donovan nodded and looked grim. Mike felt a tilt of the craft as it swooped low over the water toward an unusual city. Both men craned their necks for a better view. From the air, the whole city looked like an enormous pile of shells turned inside out. The free-formed roofs were tiled in iridescent blues, pinks, and lavender. Buildings seemed to float in ponds of water. The capitol of the undersea world, Mike thought. Hopefully, the secrets would be as lovely as the view.

Each building was a subtle shade of pastel. Bits of Formica sparkled in the sun. Pools were shaped like giant sea shells. Some contained colored water. Mike leaned forward and asked, "Mr. Quinn, you the father of all those babies?"

"You presume incorrectly," he said, but did not enlighten him further. He laughed at Mike's expression as they landed at the renowned Aquarium.

Mike thought of a fish when Quinn gave his toothy smile and removed the pilot's cap. He was rather handsome in a fishy sort of way and did waddle a bit as he stepped from the plane and waited for them. Bet this was Zinla's photographer and lover.

Mike wanted to see what was behind those dark glasses. He believed eyes tell a great deal about a soul, be it man, woman or beast. Quinn motioned them to follow him into a building.

The helicopter took off again. They must not want it found here, he thought. Or, could they make it disappear, too, if they wished?

"Could we be decoys?" he asked Donovan.

"By thunder, I hope not."

Mike drew a sharp breath as he caught a glimpse of the maniacal gleam in the agent's eyes before he turned away.

The Babies

Inside the room was a large, varied group of people. Many he recognized as heads of state.

A tall, handsome woman in a brief bathing suit and a light gauze wrap-around skirt caught up in a cluster of sea shells, greeted them. She had gray hair and very green eyes. How old was she, Mike wondered. There was something about her that reminded him of Troy. The rounded green eyes, he thought. Beside her was Anna, the pilot and the four gentlemen from the United Nations.

"I am Dr. Sono," she said extending her hand. "You know Anna, my daughter, Mr. Lambert, and you've met Alan Quinn Sono, my son?" Mike took her cool hand in his and found a strong grip.

"This is Mr. Donovan of the CIA."

"Mr. Donovan, this is a peaceful meeting. It is not about just one country, it is about a whole Earth. Our world." She gave him a penetrating look. "This is about two societies that must learn to live together."

Donovan hesitated for only a moment, and then nodded. "I'm for that, if it's possible."

"I must have the word of both of you that while you're here, you will remain neutral, act as human beings and not just a representative of a country, or a pseudo, patriotic James Bond?"

"I wasn't aware we had a choice," Donovan said.

"Not making a choice is a choice, Mr. Donovan."

Mike had a feeling she didn't like the agent and wondered why? Had the death of the alien been someone close to her?

"All right!" Donovan burst out. "I want my wife and child back. Also, my curiosity is killing me. Where and what is your society? If it isn't from space, it must be under the ocean. Am I right?"

"You may see for yourselves, if you slip off your clothing. If you're modest, leave on shorts. Most of the people you will be meeting are in their natural state. It is a custom with which we hope Landlings will soon become familiar and use."

Both she and Anna slipped out of their clothing. All that remained was a soft, gauzy entwining seaweed vine that covered the essentials. It also looked very charming. Mike was reminded of the fig leaf of Adam and Eve. Quinn wore the same. He quickly stripped to his briefs and the others in the room followed suit. It was simpler than a body search.

"For the time being, you will be blindfolded with dark goggles. For your own sake, remember, if you try to escape the oxygenated and depressurized rooms where we are going to hold our conference, you will be under such intense pressure your body will collapse.

"First, we'll take a short ride. There is a great deal for you to see and learn. I doubt that many of you have had much sleep so just relax, sit back and close your eyes. I will tell you about this undersea world, about its people and show parts of it to you; you will not know where it's located.

They were seated in the room in comfortable seats. Mike heard a hum but no motor sounds. A seat belt held him in the seat. In spite of himself, he felt very relaxed and felt that some form of hypnotic state had been induced. Or, perhaps it was a result of tension release.

He tried to be objective and estimate the time, speed and distance of the trip, then gave himself up to the adventure. He definitely needed to visit a restroom. Mike made his needs known by raising his hand. Anna gave a soft laugh, squeezed his arm as she guided him to a facility, removed his goggles and closed the door.

"Knock when you're finished," she said and stepped outside.

The bathroom was a round cubical, much like that of an airliner. However, the color was mother-of-pearl, the basin was a twisted shell, and the stool was made of a bone or shell composition. Everything was familiar, yet made of natural material as much as he could tell.

When he returned to his seat, Dr. Sono began.

"In the centuries before the last great Ice Age, there were several advanced societies scattered over the earth. Advanced, that is, in genetics, philosophy, arts, mechanics, engineering, and technology. These civilized cities were often constructed of stone to deflect the simple war weapons of primitives. Since our city was on a large island, and many of the occupants on the continents were primitive and warlike, our ancestors used the seas as gardens. Swimming was as natural as walking on the shore.

"Not all of evolution has taken place on land. Mermaids, mermen, amazons, sea horses as large as your land animals, sirens, and even dragons lived in the sea and still do. . Sea monsters as savage as land warriors wrecked a great deal of the first under-water city built, until someone discovered they were easily controlled with mind hype, a bit like your hypnosis. Then, the monsters were trained for deep sea work until underwater technology became more sophisticated.

"There were no rockets to the moon, but many experiments were made in underwater vessels and tanks as Aquaculture developed.

"They developed fission. Your technologists are still struggling with this." A murmur of awe arose from people Mike assumed were scientists and reporters in the audience around him. Donovan took a deep breath and expelled it.

Mike wondered what reporters would do with this talk. Before they were blindfolded, he hadn't had time to study the people and didn't know how many were with him on the craft. Or, for that matter, if they were even on one. There was very little sense of motion. Are they fooling us, he wondered?

"We designed crafts of specially developed materials. They can withstand great pressures," she continued. "Genetic experiments were not a new field even then. They discovered how to help a baby retain the gills it used in the womb, as well as how to use it's lungs after birth to retain oxygen. The body temperature, through mind control, can be regulated to match the surrounding environment, if needed. This eliminates the need for bulky clothing or air conditioning.

"I hope you will pardon me if I say we. These people are my people. My husband, Dr. Sono, was one of their descendants who married Landings to keep the relationship between land and sea people from being so different they could not understand one another." She paused for a moment. A touch of grief in her voice.

"Under the sea, there is no need for expensive highways or living quarters. What we build, we take from discarded shells, bones and nature. If combined in the correct way, natural, existing products can be used to build nearly anything. We use nature as a pattern whether it be for seacraft or air."

Mike raised my hand? "You do have aircraft?"

"Yes," she said and continued as though he had not interrupted her. He had the impression she would tell only what she wanted to at this point, so sat back and listened.

"One night, before the last ice age, the astronomer, Quinn, saw a great light in space. It could be seen with the naked eye, even in daylight. There had been an explosion in our solar system. Through their telescopes and by mathematical calculations, astronomers predicted a large amount of debris would be falling onto the earth.

"Once before a meteorite landed in the ocean causing huge tidal waves and great destruction to the cities along the coasts, according to legends and ancient records.

"This time, astronomers and meteorologists believed there would be several meteorites falling on many areas of the earth. They predicted earthquakes, possible volcanic eruptions and large cloud masses composed of soot and earth. There would probably be a long cold period. The safest place to live would be under the sea.

"To be on the safe side, they built two cities, one on each ocean floor. Above each was a lighthouse. In those days it was used as both an observatory and air shaft. Underneath each huge elevator was a pump system that kept the domes beneath the sea pressurized and oxygenated, so they did not collapse. The old cities are still there, but now we live in large crystal bubbles that can be moved about easily. We can also separate the oxygen from the water so we no longer need air funnels.

"We have strict birth control. Unlike Landlings, Sealings know how cruel Mother Nature can be when there is overpopulation. We have always produced quality people and not quantity. Each birth, each child is planned. Everyone awaits each birth with happiness and each of us is responsible, in part, for the education of the children. Incidentally, we call ourselves Sealings and land people Landlings.

"Also, we pick up victims from sinking vessels from time to time. These people become a part of our genetic pool so we retain many features of Landlings. You may remove your blindfolds."

Mike heard several people gasp at the beauty before them. Their view window was rounded and covered the whole side of the room.

"The cities are of spun gold and glass. They are decorated with fluorescence and mother-of-pearl, coral and anything our architects and artists decide is lovely.

"Actually, they are little more than breathing ponds within water ponds. Most of us still need a great deal of oxygen. The water in the bubble cities is saturated with extra oxygen. At the top of each is a pure air space, but even you will be able to take enough oxygen from the water to stay alive for several minutes in the way we will show you as we disembark. Please follow Anna and Quinn as you leave."

"Many of us, who are used to living on land, carry a small breathing device. Others have concealed gills. During the next twenty-four hours we, will be in council to speak with peace-loving environmentalists' representatives from as many countries as we could get together. The murder of one of our people by the CIA, a United States Spy Service, has speeded up the process. We hope to achieve a meeting of the minds with Landlings before any more lives are lost."

Donovan and Mike exchanged glances.

"Our society is much more advanced philosophically and technologically than any nation of Landlings. Our economy is stable; our needs few. There are no taxes or roads to maintain. The city domes are non-deteriorating. Each of us work a few hours each week to maintain our technology. Most of our people are inventive and creative. They work to expand the limits of present knowledge and simply because they enjoy being creative. No one receives wages, but each has the supplies which are needed to explore possibilities or just to be creative. We have achieved a balance with our environment. We offer to help Landlings to do the same.

"Who governs and solves problems?"

She smiled in amusement. "Often the government is the problem. In the Sealings world, all participate in governing, health, and education. Food is readily available. We have undersea gardens for beauty and pleasure as well as food. Only from so-called humans is there a threat to our peaceful environment.

"I have no doubt that Landlings are more aggressive as a result of greed and their harsh environment, especially the male. That is why we have chosen to work through the female. Extra strength in water is not often necessary. Her body is better adapted to aquatics.

"My family and I have been appointed by the Sealings to represent them and we come and go freely. Our family is the link between both cultures, Landlings and Sealings. Much of our knowledge about the ocean and genetics comes from Sealings. They have been caretakers of the ocean for thousands of years. They would not consider letting a child be born by chance in an unhealthy state or with no means of being cared for. They do not pollute the water, land or sky.

"Their mental powers are extraordinary. The most important qualities prized by these people are freedom to come and go, eat, drink clean water, think, live and to make and do lovely things."

"Why are they interfering now?" The President of the UN asked.

"They are interfering now because the world is grossly overpopulated, over-armed, ruled by the ignorant, selfish and power-hungry politicians. Most male Landlings are a greedy grasping lot. Much of their development has taken place since the last ice age. Their scientific advancements have been many in the past century, but their human relationships are as barren as bleached bones on a desert."

A real male basher, Mike thought, but had to acknowledge the truth of her statement. Wonder if she includes Troy in her political condemnation? Could the money for Troy's campaign have come from Sealings? Would that be considered a foreign power? He had a dozen questions for her when they met again. What had she seemed on the verge of telling him a couple of times? He remembered the pearl jewelry on her dressing table. Could they have been crafted here?

"As I said earlier, we at the Aquarium have agreed to be the go-betweens for Landlings and Sealings. We can be killed, but these people are far superior to any one of you. You who have been exposed to the babies have seen a bit of this. If you have any questions, raise your hand."

"Why girl babies?"

"We believe Mothers of Earth will not let their children be sacrificed. These children are the best of both races. They can tie Earth and Sea together. Women will be able to live safely in the sea and not have to live in poverty with their children or become slaves to men in order to survive and raise their young. Also, due to an extra layer of fat, women's bodies are better suited to water than that of men's. Female forms evolved in the water during a drought--long before the ice age and adapted later to land. Males are essentially land animals."

Beside him Mike heard Donovan snort. This man represented a powerful force and was not being swayed by Dr. Sono. Where is the fleet now, Mike wondered. Would he be betraying his country if he informed the Sealings? Surely they knew of it. He'd talk to Ted at the earliest moment. In the meantime, he didn't want to miss a word.

"In the future, with our help, men will not need to fight fiercely to survive or earn a living for their families. When quality people are produced, birth control established worldwide, with help from Sealings, the land can become a paradise just as the ocean. In fact, many land areas have been Gardens of Eden in the past, but natural catastrophe and wars have destroyed them. A great deal of knowledge has been lost each time.

"One of the problems we can help you solve is fresh water. Sealings can make large quantities of fresh water from salt water inexpensively.

"What about the balance of power, fighting and war?" Donovan asked. "It seems to me you aren't looking realistically at the world."

She gave him a knowing smile. Her discerning gaze met his. She understood his indoctrination. He was mouthing the thoughts of the greedy, power-crazed leaders of the world, not his own.

"War is passe. Sealings can put up a protective shield which will render an area invisible. From a distance, they can make your engines fail. Even now the American fleet in the Atlantic, the Russian ships in the Baltic, and Arab tankers have been brought to a standstill. All engines in areas that are fighting have halted. Instead of shooting down planes and missiles, the engines and firing mechanisms of guns and rockets will cease to operate."

Mike heard Donovan gasp in surprise. Was he a bastard or a good guy, Mike wondered again. He decided to keep an eye on him. Looking up he saw A. Quinn had also observed Donovan's reaction. Their glances locked and Donovan nodded grimly. Mrs. Sono was continuing. "Medicine is much more advanced here. Sealings look at their lives with enthusiasm and realism. They choose to live and they choose when to die. Each person is a gift to mankind, but his or her body belongs only to him or her.

A woman asked, "Will they share their food with the starving people in the world?"

"They will feed the poor, if they consent to be sterilized and re-educated."

"How can you re-educate India, for instance?"

"Sealings have access to all fresh water. A few drops in a city's water supply and people not only regain their health, they become sterile."

"Wow! Why haven't you helped us before?"

"We hoped you would help yourselves. But to answer you question about adults fit to be parents . . . "To be allowed to be a parent, a person must be in excellent health and willing to take courses in parenthood. This has been advocated by advanced thinkers in all countries. There is a balance between the capability of the environment and the population of any species which decides how many children each person can have. As you know, nature destroys through epidemics, wars and natural disasters. If the world needs more people, sterilization can be undone and a person may bear a child after taking classes and signing contracts with a partner and the community to care for it until it matures."

She sounds like Troy, Mike thought.

"When a child is born, all of society must be responsible for its education, health and welfare. When the world population levels off and can meet the needs of its people, without polluting the earth, a Mother may be allowed to have more than one child.

"Life and problems are very simple. It's the inability of the average person to comprise, due to fear of survival that calls for a third person to make a decision for them. This third party becomes a thing called law, government, and thus powerful politicians evolve. The average Landling is not qualified to be a leader. But, neither will he vote for anyone above average to be the head of government. Thus, the vote leads to impoverished thinking leaders, more fear and greed. An endless spiral downward has begun.

"Why have they waited until now to come out in the open if, as you claim, the Sealings are all powerful? Why not take us over and make us do what you wish us to do or destroy us?" a man asked.

"The late Dr. Sono, my husband, with whose work many of you are familiar, urged them to wait until there was no other way. He did not trust the Landlings governments to keep their word. The Sealings must be all-powerful and infiltrate groups that would eventually be strong enough to elect an intelligent government. They have been instrumental in introducing a little psychology into schools in upper levels, aiding in Planned Parenthood Clinics and Peace Marches, demonstrations against atomic plants, etc. But it is not enough. Time is running out.

"The ocean and ozone layer is being polluted faster than Sealings can clean it up. If there is an atomic war, it will render the surface and the air poisonous. This will end up in the ocean and Sealings will die as well. "

"Are you saying that we must cooperate or perish?" another asked.

"You have no choice. At the first sign of resistance, all electrical power will be stopped, the next step will be communication and the third, all major city water supplies will become unfit to drink or use.

"Tomorrow, all radio and TV stations on earth will be flooded with this tape and others. Each nation can decide for itself if it will be regressed to a primitive state or, become builders in conjunction with Sealings to make a better future. With the aid of Sealings and the cooperation of any nation, they/we can literally make the land into a paradise in a generation or two."

"What a liar," Donovan muttered.

Mike turned and looked at him. "Let her talk. Have you anything better to offer?"

"Traitor."

Mike shuttered. Would his country fight to the death? Must he choose sides?

"They will aid the Landlings in their dream of going to the stars. Since Landlings are more ambitious, this may be a way in which to use their fear-based aggression. It may be their destiny to inhabit the universe.

"Here on earth, the number one problems will be dealt with first: Birth control, genetic improvement for quality, healthy people, and the cleaning up of the environment. Sealings will aid all countries in the economic transition from war economies and poverty to creative, sharing human beings. The goal will be one Earth with cooperative units according to resources available, not countries, states, provinces, etc.

"Self-actualized people will be the next stage in evolution. Each person will learn to 'know himself' and begin to understand the difference between true needs vs. wants."

Mike was startled. These words were familiar. Troy had said them to him.

"This will be the most important aspect of education and the first step taken toward joining of the two societies. In other words, the Sealings are willing to help each person gain self-confidence, and self-control through self-awareness. Many of your people who belong to the new age society are already moving toward this goal. The sign of the hundredth monkey will be in the skies within the week."

"What is the hundredth monkey? How can a monkey help us?" A few people laughed.

"It is a symbolic figure of speech based on observation and experimenting by your Landling scientists. It means that when a certain number of a species begins to act in a new way, it suddenly becomes a property of the whole species, wherever they are.

Second: The environment will be cleaned up whether the Landlings want it or not.

Third: All people will be fed, provided they volunteer to be temporarily sterilized, and submit to some simple educational courses about themselves and how to enjoy the wonders of living.

Fourth: There will be health care for all. Any who are aged, ill, or wish to die, will be helped to do so in a loving atmosphere, provided they cannot be made whole again.

Fifth: All laws will become obsolete at the end of the year. New regulations will be temporary and set up where needed."

"How are you going to get some people to behave? What about the people in jail."

"Each person can decide his or her own fate. To cooperate is to survive, to rebel is to choose death or stillness. We can instantly freeze a body and store it until their circumstance can be cured or dealt with."

"How will that be any different from the present system?" A disgruntled voice asked.

"Without self-awareness, people do not really have a chance to become human or make choices. Each of you can develop this gift with the help of Sealings. Then the choice of many things, including life and death will become clear pathways from which to choose.

Sixth: We will be one people. All boundaries to countries will be opened and border lines canceled.

There were startled sounds and satirical chuckles.

"Seven: All policemen and women will remain on their jobs and will be given training and immobilizers. Anyone committing a crime will be stopped temporarily and stored in a canister until his or her case can be studied. If rehabilitation is impossible at this time, they will remain immobilized indefinitely. The same goes for all prisoners in institutions. However, we foresee very few problems once they understand the choices and possibilities."

There was a restless stirring in the group as she continued. Few believed the hardened criminal would be anything but detrimental to society.

"Eight: Religion and state must cooperate, although I dare say that once people have nothing to fear, they will not need these institutions. In Sealings world, the entire Universe is a church and it has its own laws. People need only be trained to govern themselves.

"A great fleet will appear in the skies. This fleet will land at water sources all over the world. They will contain the babies, medical labs, and food.

"Mothers, women and children will be welcome to meet the Sealing Ambassadors first. Anyone who wishes to live beneath the sea for their own protection during the time of crises is welcome. Housing is available, but a visit to a ship will cure most people. Anyone trying to impede people who wish to visit the ships, will be immobilized.

"Your radios and TV stations will keep you informed. Later, our new Ambassador will speak to you. She is well known to many." For a moment her eyes locked with Mike's as though he knew who she was talking about. His heart froze and his breathing became heavy. No. Not Madge or Troy. Who? He asked himself. Then she continued.

"Eden awaits Earth. I believe Landlings, with a little help from the Sealings are ready to make it so. But first, you must visit one of our colonies."

Bubble City

Lights came on. Before the group were huge bubble cathedrals, some filled with water, others must have contained air. Their room was inside one. All around the pressure of the ocean must exist. Mike tried to think of the water pressure as he would the air pressure on a plane at high altitude. His breathing was emotionally ragged as he gazed in awe at the beauty before him. Lights kept coming on farther and farther away. It was immense.

Thousands of swimming fish-people surrounded the ship from various levels and in adjacent bubbles, waving and smiling. Jean, Ted and Shauna swam nearby in the next ball. They waved and threw kisses. Ted's lips moved and in Mike's mind he heard, 'We'll talk after the show. Isn't this wonderful?' They waved again and swam toward a group of people.

On the other side of him Donovan choked back a sob and he yelled, "Pam, Kelly." He moved over to the side and touched the outside of the wall. He was nodding and laughing to a woman and baby. The woman did not seem terribly enthused to see him.

There were a variety of fish people, mermaids, Quinn's and Landlings joining the group. Dr. Sono has me thinking of myself as a Landling already. In a distance he saw a tall red-headed woman talking to Dr. Sono. She reminded him of Troy. I must really be in love, he thought. Images of Troy keep popping into is mind.

Someone called over the speaker and the lights switched to another part of the city.

It was a lovely scene. Instead of the golden sunny bubbles, turquoise and soft white light sparkled around and through the globes. He wished Troy could be here to share this moment. Also Larry with his camera. They seemed so far away. He felt as though he was in a twilight zone, a dream world.

The loudspeaker, yet inside his head said, "You're invited to attend a party. It will give you time to explore one of the cities of Sealings and to meet them. You will find that in spite of outside appearances, you have a great deal in common. You will be able to 'mind-speak,' with nearly everyone, so language will not be a barrier. Just visualize what you wish to know and they will understand. The gravity is light inside the domes and you will find movement easy both in water or air domes. Each of you will be given a tablet. Take it and you will have several hours of ability to absorb oxygen from the saturated domes. Do not attempt to go outside the overall bubble as the pressure is too great for you to survive."

How Troy, Madge and Larry would have enjoyed this, he thought again, and then smiled as a lovely mermaid swam up and waved just outside the chamber.

Mike could hardly wait to begin this new adventure. In spite of the little sleep he had been able to grab in the last few days, he felt relaxed and rested. It was mind hype suggestions. Turnabout is fair play he told himself.

"Soon we will return you to your own homes. After you go back to land, we wish you to be available to the media to answer questions. You will be given further instructions on how to contact us in case you need help.

"You who are here may be only a few hundred. You will become an assistant to the leaders of the new movement and shown how to train others to become citizens of one earth. It was a pleasure meeting you." Dr. Sono signed off.

"She's taking a lot for granted," Donovan said in a low grim voice. Is he up to something, Mike wondered and decided to keep an eye on him as much as possible. He knew too much about the ability of CIA agents to trust any of them completely. They had been stripped and probably scanned-searched, but . . .

"Please get in line."

Mike moved past Anna to receive the tablet. As he went by their eyes met. "I'm sorry I had to deceive you, Mike."

He nodded curtly. "You could have told me."

"We needed time to check your environmental and emotional background. You've come a long way in the past couple of years."

"Thanks," he said dryly and wondered how she could know anything about his past. He decided it was a figure of speech and hurried on to catch up with the rest of the group. He felt her eyes following him and glanced back to see Anna, Quinn and Dr. Sono talking together and looking in his direction.

The water felt refreshingly and soft. Sparkling bubbles formed around him with each movement. For a time he treaded water and looked about him again, enjoying the breathtaking beauty.

Then, he heard the music. It was the siren song of the tapes, but more intense and lovely. Mike felt it move softly like waves over the surface of his body, then, it was inside pounding in his bloodstream. He wanted to sing and dance. His body floated on it, in it. He moved with the music, freed of heavy gravity as currents moved him along. He swam in quiet pools, through waterfalls and streams, refreshing his body in gymnastic exercise. Finally, he rolled over on his back to rest and enjoy the surroundings.

A figure at his side said in his mind, "May I join? If you wish, I will be your guide for awhile." A Dolph-man extended a flipper-like hand. Mike shook the projection realizing it worked much like fingers which spread into appendages, webbed between them. Apparently, fingers were more beneficial even under the sea. The man had the slick sheen of a dolphin, the physical characteristics of a male with finned arms which folded against his side when not being used. The genital area bulged under a flap of flesh. Altogether, he was a handsome looking fellow with heavy hair braided down his spine and interwoven with seaweed decorated rope. The large protruding lips were upturned and pleasant.

"How can you understand me without my saying a word?"

"We have intensified a mind-matching magnetic field within the globes. You might be interested to know we have mind tapes which anyone can absorb to gain knowledge in a few hours."

"You mean I can learn anything in a day?"

"You can understand a new language within a day but the tongue and facial muscles must develop in order to speak it fluently. As in art for example, the mind, hand and eyes must develop coordination. Music, calculus, sculpture, mechanics, math, government, psychology, medicine, biology, genetics, ancient languages, and more, are available in our library globe."

He motioned for Mike to follow him. They swam from one ball to another where people of all sizes and shapes lay quietly in the water listening to learning tapes. Others were working with strange tools and something that he suspected was computer related. Screens were non-existent but above them danced fascinating designs and holographic images. Dolph-man pointed at capsules with labels of the different subjects. There were many sub-headings under each like Psychology, man, woman, animals, fish, Sealings, Landlings, etc.

Mike pointed at Woman and said, "I like to learn about those." Dolph laughed.

"So be it. After the show, come back here and we'll see if you can learn anything you don't already know."

"What do you mean?"

"Probably you already know what you need to about women; you just do not have the self-knowledge to use it wisely." Mike frowned, trying to understand.

"Learning's must be taken step-by-step, like crawling or swimming before walking." He nodded, beginning to get a glimmer of what Dolph was trying to tell him.

He looked at his new friend. Now he knew what lay behind Quinn's dark glasses. The eyes were large and glowed with warmth and kindness only a child can direct at a loved one.

These people were vulnerable in their caring about people and the environment, but this might also be their strength. Love is a special feeling for only a few people in Landling society. It quite often traps innocent people. Or, do we trap ourselves because of an unwillingness to explore all of its possibilities, Mike asked himself.

Turning to his companion he said, "I've felt the euphoria of love from the moment I encountered Dr. Sono's presence. Do you always live in this rose-colored world?"

There was a touch on his arm and he felt himself being hugged from two sides. Ted and Jean had joined them. "Let us answer that."

He hugged them back and all three laughed with joy at being together again.

"We three have always had an especially warm feeling for one another. But, each held back. With social rules, 'three's a crowd,' or, you may take him or her from me, so each would feel threatened, if we let our feelings show," Ted said.

"In this world the threats are gone. Love is caring and caring is sharing. When a woman has a child, all take responsibility for its health, education and welfare. It takes a bit of understanding at first, but we're beginning to get there. I won't lose you to her or vice versa. Go ahead and hug her."

Mike hugged them both again in sheer joy. "Where is Shauna?"

They turned and pointed. Like schools of fish, several balls contained babies playing with turtles, dolphins, seashores, mermaids, and various fishes. Anyone could see they were having a great time and quite safe.

Mike felt healed and warm inside, rather like the feeling he got in Troy's kitchen.

"I only wish Larry and Troy could be here to share this with us. If I heard Dr. Sono correctly, we'll be home tomorrow and I can be with her."

Ted and Jean looked at Mike as though about to tell him something. He caught words that sounded like, "She is." Then the thought was cut off.

My companion waved to them. "Let me show him around and you can talk later. He needs time to digest what he's seen and heard so far."

Mike nodded and lay back in the water. Jean and Ted relaxed nearby.

For the first time, he let his feelings of need for Troy wash over him. There would be no more holding back, he promised himself. He had been his own stumbling block. Turning to Dolph-man he said, "Perhaps I need a tape on loving."

"It is a wise being who requests such help. I expected it to be different with you, although that is the first tape Landlings usually need. Very few humans weave their lives with love. Life is very cruel to Landlings," he said sympathetically.

"Each of you has learned to fight for what you need instead of sharing. Take a look at our world first. Then go to the library lab and absorb as many tapes as you wish. However, we don't recommend over three a day. A great deal of learning must be combined with experiencing and contemplating the new knowledge."

Dolph gave a large, toothy grin, "Learning easily is like turning a kid loose in an ice cream shop."

Mike chuckled and looked around. They were slowly gliding toward a large central ball. Where was Donovan? Hopefully with his family.

"You know, I've heard more good sense here today than I have in a normal lifetime of growing up."

"You've left your mind open today. Partly because of the possible loss of your dear friends and the world as you know it. Emotional wounds are often a pathway to new learning and healing."

"Now, I think you're getting in over my head. However, the next time I'll bring a Psychiatrist, Helene Troy with me. She will be in seventh heaven talking with you."

He nodded. "We know of her. She has been useful and a great help to our cause. We're looking forward to having her join us in our work here. Our Phylogenetic Department fed her tapes as a child. Her mother visited the sea gardens at Faro as a young woman, and remained. I hope you can accept this Mr. Lambert."

"What do you mean?"

"The real Helen of Troy lineage is still in existence. We have cells from many great minds from the past of which you have never heard, but you will in the future."

Ted and Jean had followed behind them. All three looked at him in astonishment. Jean recovered first. "You mean you can revive those people?"

"No. We do not wish to duplicate anyone. Our people and the people we feed into your civilization are not just from two parents. Genetically, their ancestors could be a bit of Odysseus, Jesus, Einstein, Dagon, or Juno. It depends on the characteristics we hope will compound into a strong central leader."

"You're saying Troy is a combination of more than two parents."

"Yes. She will become a strong figure soon. You must all three assist her in any way. Also, your sister, Madge, will be asked to come forth out of hiding."

"My God. My sister? You've monkeyed around with her genes?"

"No. Don't look so worried. Our representatives have met her at environmental rallies and she has been a great help to the president. She joined us two years ago of her own free will."

Mike was silent. His feeling of euphoria had become a knot in his gut. Dolph-man saw his distress and continued.

"We have made a couple of mistakes in the past, but have rectified them as our understanding of Landlings developed."

"What mistakes?" Ted asked.

"We gave the persuasive personality of Mark Anthony to Hitler."

"Lord. You were behind him?"

"We must take part of the blame. We were looking for a strong figure to father an environmental revolution which we could see would be needed in the future. His mother's character had a serious flaw and he was taken away from the influence of his teachers at a vulnerable age. His genetic engineering boomeranged and we hesitated to try again with a strong leader."

"Our best counter offensive against him were scientists like Dyson, Einstein, Eiseley, writers like Huxley and many science writers. If we had come from the sea, your people were not psychologically ready for us. We worked through Landlings and let them handle the secret of atomic energy in their own way. However, they missed the path to fission and clean power. We will guide them more closely in the future."

"Where can solving so many problems begin?" Mike asked.

"Again, with people. The world has a large quantity of people who are stifling the influence of quality people who could lead the cleanup of Earth if there was time, but time is running out for the polluted world."

Mike listened, puzzled. "And the babies?"

"With the babies, we have brazenly mingled our people with yours. With the love of mothers for their children, strong people like you, Troy, your sister and many other peaceful, environmental lovers, we hope to try another tack. A large group of people instead of one strong leader."

"You're aiming for a balance of power based on what?" Mike asked. "How can you hope to convince the people of the world to accept the tearing down of boundaries, government, fences, religions, social customs, in other words, the very foundations on which their lives rest, without a fight?"

In a distance he saw Donovan holding a heated argument with A. Quinn and Anna. How much had they told him, Mike wondered, as he waited for Dolph-man to answer?

"We do have a plan. You will see shortly. Now, they are waiting for us to join the program which is a special performance for Landlings. It is a combination of your music, dance and art forms with ours. A Transition Performance, it has been named."

Mike didn't want to be entertained. He needed to think. Looking around, he saw Ted and Jean flowing through an opening into a great cathedral.

Dolph waited politely for Mike to enter ahead of him. Outside the stadium were balls of many colors filled with people of all sizes and shapes. Many great whales waited along with porpoises, dolphins, sea horses and colorful fishes, mermaids, men and women.

All was silent as lights dimmed to a deep black. Slowly they came back on. One strange creature was spotlighted, then another. Mike felt a catch in his throat at the sight of the grace and beauty surrounding him. Each actor and actress added a voice, heard distinctly for a moment and then blended with the chorus.

Actors began to tumble among bubbles in time to the music. Huge bubble sculptures formed, then exploded in a profusion of color. They reached from the bottom to the top of the dome. Then holograms of the earth down through the centuries tumbled in the air. The earth from space a thousand years ago, a hundred years and now. The blue had been replaced by an ugly brown.

No one could keep his mind on problems with such a setting. Gradually, the low moan of whales became louder as they joined the siren singers. At times dancers and riders would come to a complete stop in the water. It was like looking at a great impressionistic painting. Then they would do synchronized aerobics to the strange, bizarre, yet magnificent music.

The air on Mike's side of the glass was heavy and damp but the temperature was comfortable. Finally, the show ended in a burst of dozens of sparkling, colored fountains of water, much like our Fourth of July.

Toward the end of the show the audience side filled up with water, opened up to the show and the audience became one with the performers. The oxygenated tablets they had been given allowed them to absorb oxygen. Mike could see air bubbles form around the sides and at the bottom.

The actors and actresses, mermaids, mermen, fishes and whales swam among the audience, inviting people on a guided tour into the lives and homes of Sealings.

A mermaid took Mike's hand. He became a part of a rhythmic dance as they moved through the water. It was another world and he felt a part of it. The worry in his mind ceased to exist. He wanted only to enjoy and be with the surroundings.

Several mermaids circled him. They were lovely creatures. One took his hand. They swam among florescent coral reefs, great whales, flowering seaweed and gardens. Mike couldn't spot the openings as they moved from one dome to another. They explored giant seashells, coral reefs, sculptured cities and forms made from seashells. Abalone colors glowed and shifted color with their positions and moving lights.

He wondered if they were outside the domes and somehow protected, and was informed that there were bubbles within bubbles, within bubbles. The area covered must be immense, he thought.

In a lovely cave they settled under filtered sunlight which must have been near the surface. It reminded him of skin diving in coral reefs. The couches and beds were of large mussels shells filled with seaweed.

Mike was fed grape-like pods which tasted like cinnamon and nuts, a sweetly-spiced fungus cake, prickly shrimp, phyllopod and seaweed salad, melon-like fruit and a salty apple, or so it tasted.

He was surprised when the mermaid tails were laid aside like a diving suit. The lovely legs of women had been tucked inside for more efficient swimming.

One goblet fruit was filled with liquor. It had a strange effect upon him as he sipped it through a seaweed straw. He felt a strong sexual desire to mate with these creatures. The water was scented lightly. They caressed and sang to him. His seduction was easy.

He felt both excited and contented as well as an acute awareness of the uniqueness of these creatures as they rested on the bed of seaweed. The taste of her mouth as she held a bit of food between her teeth was delicious. A third mermaid joined them. He was amazed that each had a different taste, smell and song. Vaguely he wondered if he was the father of a new breed and what was happening to Ted, Jean and Donovan.

Later, he learned from the tapes that sexual experiences were more exciting and fulfilling because the memories of an act shared with caring people were without guilt.

Return to Land

Once more they gathered in the room which had originally transported them to the Sealing city. Ted and Jean came in and sat on either side of Mike as if to offer reassurance.

"We're going to stay on for a few days, Mike. Both of us need a rest before taking up our new duties," Ted said.

Mike looked at him and asked, "What do you mean?"

"Dr. Sono will tell you. The main thing we must do now is keep an eye on Donovan. He's a devious character."

"But what could he possibly do down here? Would he try anything which would endanger his family? "

"No. I hope not."

They sat on seats behind and to the left of the CIA agent. Jean took Mike's hand and squeezed it in sympathy as the light lowered.

Dr. Sono, Anna, A. Quince and . . . . and Helene Troy appeared before them.

Mike's heart skipped a beat in joy and then seemed to freeze as the implication of her presence began to dawn on him. He must have jerked or made a noise. Ted's arm went around him. "It's all right," Ted said softly.

"My God!" He heard himself say. Several people turned and looked at him. He felt betrayed as he thought of all the things she had not trusted him to know. How could she? He wanted to get up and run. Never see a woman again. Once again love had betrayed him.

Troy's eyes met his from across the room.

In his head he heard. "I'm sorry you have to hear it this way, Mike. Please bear with me. I'll meet you at my place when this is over and we'll work it out. I love you."

This failed to soothe Mike. He wanted to jump up and shout, "Traitor. You used me. Don't listen to her."

Ted's arm felt like an iron bar as it restrained him. "Don't be pigheaded, Mike. You can take this."

"Don't lose all you've gained by being macho," Jean hissed.

He collapsed against the seat as the light fell upon another figure. His sister, Madge, stepped up to Dr. Sono and said something. Then she left the low platform and came to Mike. She took his hand, pulled him to his feet and embraced him. "It's alright, Mike. You weren't ready. Be patient and you'll understand."

They sat down together. In all his years of detective work there had been many surprises and shocks, but none as great as seeing the two people he loved in the enemy camp.

"We are not the enemy," Madge said distinctly into his mind. He turned to her.

"You're doing it, too."

"Yes and so are you." Her eyes twinkled in the way he knew so well.

"As they say in the comics, trust me for just a little while, Mike. And trust Troy, too. You won't regret it. Please . . . "

Mike made an attempt to smile as he looked into her grave little face. Madge had always been there for him. He had never known her to be stupid or dishonest. Unless someone had misled her . . . Under her pleading gaze, he relaxed, reached out and patted her hand. After all, the danger was not down here. It would be on the surface when Earth was conquered by the Sea. In spite of her words, jealousy and mistrust filled his stomach with bile.

Dr. Sono began to speak. "Welcome back. I hope you enjoyed the show and your tour." At first there was scattered applause, then it grew louder and louder. The United Nations delegates stood up and were soon joined by the rest of the audience.

Mike glanced around. Donovan remained seated. Just behind and to his right stood Ted. He nodded to Mike and in the direction of Donovan. Mike wasn't certain what he meant, but it was Ted's look of warning. They were still in their shorts. There was no place to conceal weapons. Each had been machine checked when they came onto the craft. He's being overly suspicious, Mike thought.

"Look who's talking," Madge mind spoke into mine. Mike smiled and stood up beside keeping an eye on Donovan.

What the hell, Mike thought, and joined the applause. They seem to be trying to make a better world. The least he could do was hear them out.

Again his eyes made contact with Troy's. She gave him her Mona Lisa smile and nodded slightly. He returned the nod. Their minds connected for a moment in a flash of white flame. He had a glimpse of what their togetherness could be now that he understood. Understood . . . he understood, but not the way she . . .

"It will be done," rang in his mind. Mike touched his ear. Was this mind act really happening?

Dr. Sono raised her hand. She gave a brilliant smile and pointed upward. Above them the population of Bubble city gathered.

As one they sang, "Hallelujah!"

The lights dimmed again and she continued to speak.

"We are happy you enjoyed your tour. Each of you is invited to spend a week here before going topside. Any of you may refuse. If you choose to take on the strenuous task we are going to request of you, it will be our pleasure to train you. "You may think you are not up to the immensity of our request, but you will have plenty of help. Mainly, we ask you to act as ambassadors of goodwill between our two worlds.

"As you know, yesterday was election day in the United States. My sister, Helene Troy, has been elected President." She raised her hand. "Please do not applaud."

"In a short time, there will be no countries. Landlings will be guided by the United Nations under the advisement of a temporary Sealing and Landling appointed cabinet. Some of you here today will be asked to work on that project.

"On the platform with us is my daughter, Anna and my son, Quinn. Anna has been in charge of the hologram communications which drew all of you here in various ways. Quinn is the head of the genetics department. We three, along with many Sealings/Landlings who remain anonymous at this time, have taken over the goals of my beloved husband and the Sealing Kingdom.

Troy will introduce a few of your chosen people and give you a short briefing on what you can expect to happen during the next few weeks. You will be given memory tapes about various departments so each of you will be able to coordinate your work with the others. Nearly all of you chose to study three subjects of your choice today. We were pleased with this. Now, let me introduce Helene Troy."

Mike led the standing ovation this time. There was a definite sensation of being kissed when her eyes locked with his. She had won the election. The least he could do was give a belated applause. Finally, she raised her hand and the group sat down. Mike leaned forward in trepidation and anticipation.

"Thank you. I will be brief. Yes. I do carry the genes of the ancient Helene of Troy. You will learn about this from the genetic tapes.

"Many of the problems such as drugs, crime, dishonesty, greed for power, lack of purpose, hopelessness, poor health, the homeless and last but not least the pollution of the earth, have solutions. The tapes as well as many of my past speeches will offer not only solutions but the way in which we intend to carry them out.

"Ted Wentz and his agency will be directors of the training programs for the police department worldwide. As each of you know here, mind talk is possible. You will be able to use this in your contacts with one another because of the electrical-magnetic boost your brains were given when blindfolded.

"Soon the skies will be filled with our fleet. They will be setting down in water areas all over the world. As the women and children, then men come through the ships, they will have much the same reception as you have received in the undersea review, and a mind taping, not brainwashing, as well. When they return home, they too will be ready to aid in the project for a clean, peaceful earth. All babies who disappeared have Sealing/Landling DNA. They will be returned to their parents and grow up to be future leaders trained to weave goodwill between our peoples.

"Dr. Sono has briefed you on the television and radio programs during the next week. All war-related motors and factories have been shut down as of today. Police weapons will be replaced with freezer lazars within the week. They are not effective against our people.

"Madge Lambert Burton is in charge of Environmental Coordination, Jean Wentz, Water Adaptation, and the gentlemen from the United Nations coordinators of One Earth Leadership ... ."

"Mike. Quick." Ted spoke in my mind. Ted turned to see him striding toward the restroom sign. "Donovan is gone."

Mike rose quickly. Troy paused for a moment and continued, but he got a brief message ... "Help is on the way."

In the tiled hallway Ted was trying to force the bathroom door. Fortunately, it was of fragile shell construction. Donovan was inside pulling a jelly-like capsule out of his ear.

He saw them in the mirror, turned and said, "Stay back. This can blow us all to kingdom come."

"What's the problem Donovan? I thought you were happy to see Pam. If you hurt the city you will destroy your wife and your child."

"It's not mine. She's not mine. She won't come home with me. They brainwashed her just as they have you." For a minute Mike thought he was going to cry, then his eyes glazed over again and he looked angrily at Mike and Ted.

"Who's this?"

"My partner, Ted Wentz."

Ted reached out to shake hands and he jumped back. "Don't touch me or try to pull any tricks. I know all of them and more, too."

"I'm sure you do," Ted said in his quiet mild way. "But that capsule is a new one on me. What is it?"

For a moment Donovan looked puzzled at the capsule in his hand. It was then Mike realized he was reacting to a post-hypnotic suggestion. Probably one given him back in training school. It wouldn't have mattered what happened here. He would try to destroy anything different whether it was bad or good.

"Together." Mike heard Ted mind speak. They had done the trick a dozen times and it usually worked. Mike grabbed his heart and began to gag. He sagged toward Donovan, then to the side as he moved back a step, Donovan's attention centered on Mike. Ted pounced. There was a flash of light. Mike passed out.

When he came to, Mike was on a small watercraft headed into the San Diego harbor. A sailor stood at the wheel.

"What happened? Did Donovan blow up the city?"

"No, Sir. Just as Mr. Wentz dived toward the CIA man, a Sealing used a freeze stick on him. Both of you caught a bit of it and passed out. You'll be fine now. Mr. Wentz is staying down under a few days."

Mike nodded and worked his fingers and arm. They still felt slightly numb. His ears rang, but otherwise, he felt fine physically. Had it all been a dream, he wondered?

"Where would you like to be let off, Sir?" The seaman asked.

Mike looked at him closely. "You're one of us. A Landling," he said in surprise.

The man laughed. "There are lots of us. Nearly always when a ship sinks, Sealings save the people. We have our choice to stay with them or drown. After a week with them, who would want to live on land again? Wars, bad government, work, work, work and the dirty air. Ten minutes top side makes me feel like a filthy pig. No thanks."

Mike nodded in understanding. "I'm Mike Lambert. Do you know where Helene Troy lives on Coronado Island?"

"Sure. She hoped that's where you'd want to go. Helene says to tell you she'll be along soon. Wait for her."

Mike was surprised when the boat dived under the water and let him out inside her boat house. The sailor saluted and handed Mike's clothing over the side.

"See you when the air is clean," he waved and left without a sound or even a splash in the water.

Surprises

The sub/boat delivered Mike to San Diego and Troy's yard in Coronado bay. It was probably better she was not home yet. He needed time to think and her backyard was a good place for it. Besides, he felt a strong desire to sleep. Mike looked at Troy's house with new eyes. How could he call himself a detective and not have been more observant? He yawned.

How long had it been since he had a good nap? This was no time to sleep. He drug himself up to her bedroom. I'll just lie down and relax. The educational tapes of the Sealings recommended for relaxation came into his mind. He breathed deeply and tried to get a handle on the swirling phantasmagoria in his mind.

When Mike woke the dull morning smog/sun shown in the window. He felt rested and energetic. As he stood in her shower, everything came back to him. Once again he felt betrayed by Troy, Madge and even Ted knew. They hadn't trusted him. Why?

Did they know him so little? Perhaps he hadn't trusted them, came a thought. How long since he had really let anyone other than Madge, into his heart?

And then there was his country? Could he have kept still when Troy was running for President when he knew she represented an alien race? Or was he the alien? They had been here before the ice age . . .

Mike went downstairs and put on a pot of coffee and toast. While his breakfast cooked, rain fell outside the window. Good. The air would be breathable for awhile. He went into Troy's office and found a notebook and pen. Carrying breakfast and a large apple out onto the porch, he looked up. A rainbow glowed against blue sky. The horizon was still brown over the ocean, but . . . hope. He had lost the hope in his heart, he'd thought, yet suddenly it was there. But had anything really changed? Forgetting his breakfast, he began to write a poem about rainbows and the hope and the inspiration they'd given him over the years. He remembered a rainbow he had seen on a snow-covered land, one in France with Crystal and here on this very porch with Troy . . . Troy. Would he once again be left without love close to his heart? The tape had said, now . . . . Live now . . . he looked again at the rainbow and smiled:

> Coat I don to greet cold natures morn.
> I step outside, and mixed up weather
> Pierces me with shafts of sunbeams
> Through blue-sky clouded mists.
> Nature smiles—I feel so light.
>
> A sailor's dawn—colorful sight,
> Flickering on dewy lawn from spotty clouds.
> Wind sweeps over Black-green water
> To flat prairie lands.
> Natures beams—a bird in flight.
>
> Cautiously, I slide,
> Along a black and curvy road, dreading ice.
> When overhead, streaking lights,
> Merge into
> Rainbow colors—pastel, then bright,
> Painting themselves across orange clouds, blue sky.
> Nature sings—what a sight!

After the rains her fish pond was covered by blooming water lilies. Pink and yellow buds laced the emerald green pads with color.

Baby frogs croaked and leapt into the murky depths. Everything was alive and singing with the joy of life. Even the still water moved with fish; tiny whirlpools formed here and there. A straw or spider which got too near was pulled into it's grasping mouth.

Water, he wrote. He who rules fresh water, rules the world. Such a simple, natural thing.

Water, the juice of life, nourished our conception and birth. It protects while exuding the clarity and luster of a gem. Our sack-filled bodies drink, seep, ooze, drip and sweat, Water.

Water speaks in the heartbeat, the gargle of creeks, the creaking of shrinking blue ice, the rat-a-tat-tat of raindrops on tin roofs, and the soft sigh of a snowflake finding rest. Water dresses in Sequined Snowflakes, insisting that no two be alike. At 32 degrees she may salt soil with sleet. Her skirts are often waterfalls, her face a placid pool.

Sometimes she hides in shadowed caverns from the brightness of Sun who sucks her upward into a frosty sky. When sun and water forces wrestle, throwing bolts of lightening and roars of thunder across Sky, creatures of Earth stand at attention, ready to run for cover.

Sun is both an enemy and friend. They play games, but deep down, Water knows Sun can be a dreaded enemy, so she attempts to keep on the cool side of her.

Once when she tried to run away, Sun reminded her, "There are whole planets barren because they angered me."

Waterspouts, quicksand seas, hurricanes, monsoons and lionized waves, hiss and roar with her power. She likes to play hide and seek with weathermen.

But, Water is as gracious as she is fickle and devious. She enjoys supporting red blood cells, cleansing bodies and bathing Earth's hot sweating brow. She kisses roses, ferns and leaves with dewdrops and says of herself, "I may look like a brook and roar like a lion in a storm, but I'm really as sweet as a spring lamb . . . "

On a granite coast, anchored in rock...a
Glacier shaped destiny, all laced with bays
And coves...washed...by fogs & mists,
Stinging ice, winter's glare...the many faces of Water!

Mike thought about the average person going about the common business of daily life while politicians and the greedy salesman tried to sell them on an illusive world where things are more important than people and nature. Selling the idea that other countries are reaching out to take over theirs, take their things.

The unthinking are swirled away and sucked down into a world of evil and hatred. Yet all over Earth, the average person is much like me, he thought. Often, if I pay too much attention to the TV praying mantis, warmongers, and super advertisements, I lose my way until I come back to nature.

How can people who never leave the city streets keep a handle on reality? The whirlpool spins people round and round. Many are killed off in political wars; others believe the ravings that say mankind is not OK and commit suicide. Many inundate themselves with things, business and busyness. Often we could regain our equilibrium by simply taking a walk in the woods, a smile and touch of love, some exercise, releasing competitiveness, or by taking time to watch the butterflies dance, but we've destroyed most of our natural heritage.

Mike agreed with Sealings. Life is simple but in our anxiety and fear, we lose our way. How can we avoid it, I wonder. Will the hyper-suggestions from the tapes really be enough?

They suggest that failing to reach out to our friends and neighbors in caring and sharing, makes them more inclined to withdraw and hide like bugs under the lily pod, seeing only the shadows cast below. That we can change our lives.

The tapes said it was simple: Today give everyone a smile, tomorrow a touch, the day after a hug, an invitation for coffee, a bit of time to listen, or sing a song together. It's the bits and pieces put together that relieve us of fear and gives us strength to pull back from the whirlpools.

He thought of the essay he'd written on civilization. How did it go? Mike went in the house and got a dictionary.

If his future depended on living a civilized life, he should at least know the definition. Would it be different from the Sealings? How much had they infiltrated the educational system in the past? Not enough. Apparently, the power unleashed by Hitler, scared them and slowed them down. Could the world forgive them for that?

The dictionary blandly defined Civilization as an advanced stage of development in the arts, sciences and complex social, political and cultural structures. Pretty cool and abstract. Needing to see it more clearly he did his old word trick—let the word speak for itself.

Civilization says, "I am the safe future for which all men search, yet out of fear and ignorance, they destroy that which they blindly pursue."

Civilization agrees that this may be the goal, "But individual men and women are the foundation on which I stand. These people live in the winding streets and twilight cities of everyday life. They work, plow, plan, dream and play. They dress me with clean streets, are courteous and thoughtful to one another and are honest in their dealings."

Civilization continues thoughtfully, "The breath of a civilized man or woman smells of cosmic dust. She may be bare of foot, but knows herself to be the mother of mankind. Loving is her greatest attribute. He has compassion, raises violets and bridges, and has fetish oddities, boundless dreams and a smile as sweet as maple syrup for his family and friends.

Civilization is elastic and demanding. She believes criminals are a wart on her blushing face. A sign that those teaching virtues, the wonders and joy of life, have failed. Like a blade of grass pushing through a cement highway, crime is an erosion of the evolution of the human soul, a destroyer of civilization. It can be as small as littering, rudeness and vandalism, or as large as taking another's life.

"These diverse genes of wild forbears must not be allowed to reproduce," the Sealing warns, smiling sadly across chill vapors of time and space.

Evening shadows creep across autumn's party splendor as her mystical face becomes one with purple shadows in a forest green garden.

Civilization says, "You will know me when I come. My middle name is Peace."

Was the choice really as simple as one between peace and a painful death to life on this planet? Mike thought he understood human nature. How could Sealings hope to change a whole world for the better? For better or worse . . .

Troy. I was going to ask you to marry me. I felt so close to you. Now we're worlds apart.

He sat back and looked at the long shadows falling across the garden. Where was she? Turning around he watched the ocean waves pounding on the beach. So familiar but now so strange. A whole world he never suspected was out there, someplace. He remembered the freshness of the water, the songs and music and felt a great longing.

What had Dr. Sono said about women being from the sea? Yet, we're sons of those very women.

He remembered reading with amusement from Desmans Morris. Who said, "A woman's body is a sexual flag for men."

Musing he began to write:

When Eden's God in Africa
Gave drought to fertile soil,
Driving early man to other lands,
And woman, afraid for child in arms,
Looked for a home to rest.
There was no place to on land to hide or food to eat.
They were prey for man and beast,
Until . . .
Until she took up refuge on a friendly water shore.
A place to rest sometimes by wading out,
Out beyond the reach of snarling,
Hungry animals and shaggy demanding man.
The fish, snails, sweet coconuts,
Were crushed by rocks and feet.

She rolled them to her babies,
Threw them to defeat, and rushing into water,
Found protection and a friend.
Her children swam with dolphins, manatees played around.
They mated and their children had on hair upon their bodies,
Some had mermaid tails or naked feet.

With all the swimming, body spines began to flex,
Giving birth in friendly waters, larger heads and brains,
But a landing birth gave pain and misery.
Her body changed again as layers of fat gave buoyancy.
Breasts so full of Mothers milk, became rounded,
Longer yet as children clung and suckled.
She sat upon the rocks and sand,
It clutched a lock of hair. Her bottom rounded out.
Sexual organs slanted forward, like the fishes of the ocean,
Sex changed gear, moved forward not reverse.
The nostril of her nose grew out and down,

Becoming covering flap. Lips that nursed for several years,
Were soft, muscled, round and full.

The eyes removed all excess salt, through crocodile tears.
To bring her back to land again, the ape-man-child
Began to swim, bring her gifts, play love games,
Protect both woman and child.
Thus, FAMILY LIFE BEGAN.

Desmans Morris, Great Father, Macho Man, John Wayne's—
eat your heart out.

Mike yawned, stretched, and realized in spite of all the
emotional upheavals he'd been through he was having a great time.
He felt he had time to write from his soul. If the fish took over the
world, would he be free to write as much as he wished? Could good
and evil really be gotten rid of so easily? Was he supposed to help Ted
train policemen all over the world? An impossible task. He sighed
and decided to take a swim.

Pulling off his clothing, Mike dived into Troy's fish pond-pool.
This time when he swam among the fish, he wanted to reach out and
touch them. All creatures are kindred spirits, he realized. Always
before it had been someone else pushing the thought onto him and
he'd pulled away. Now, today, he really felt it. So Ted had volunteered
their firm to train policemen without consulting him—quite an
undertaking. Would he be expected to help? Would he? If he and
Troy didn't make it . . . Mike felt the old emptiness tugging at his
heart. "Now, now," he said aloud, trying to get back to the contented
feeling he'd had when writing.
Mike pulled himself up and climbed back onto the porch. He
dried and went inside the kitchen to fix a sandwich. All he wanted to
do was write.

It felt as though years of pent-up feeling-thoughts gushed out and needed to be considered. Taking a sweater, he returned to the porch.

Tomorrow? What would that bring? He tried to imagine the changes needed. Or was it as simple as Dr. Sono said? "The change only need come from within each person."

Tomorrow sits on Yesterday's memories. Memories of giants, dinosaurs, reptiles, and redwood forests. Memories of a time when no flowers glowed jewel-like above graceful stems; the earth was warm, animals slow-moving. Tomorrow was bored. Her middle name was Yesterday. She dreamed of another time, a time of beauty and romance, so changed her name to Today.

Today gave a party. With upheavals, and shifting climate she decorated Earth with creeping grasses, extinguished giants--mindless, instinctive creatures who would trample and eat her new-born flower decorations--except for a small knobby creature, a ne'er-do-well, a social outcast with a gleam in his eye. When he shambled out on the grassy rug and held a flower to the sun, her laughter tinkled across the earth as she welcomed her guest . . .

She called it Human, nourishing it like a baby with seeds of flowers and fleshy fruit. The weakling became more alert, but it's body was weak. There were no hooves on his feet, his teeth were not the tearing sabers of great cats, nor could he run gracefully like the gazelle or use the bulk of the bison. But Today enjoyed his curiosity and began to educate him in the ways of seeing, hearing, smelling. "The weight of a petaled flower changed the face of Yesterday to Today, and you were born, my child."

They shared the wine of fruits and the seed of flowers. Extolling their exotic beauty, she planted inside a desire for something beyond his reach.

One night he saw the stars, up there, waiting. He became impatient because he could not grasp them. Like an angry child, he trampled Today's gifts of grasses, jeweled flowers. In his grasping, flexing fingers he picked up a rock and flung it into beyond.

Today's child had given birth to Tomorrow.

Today watched in sorry as her child destroyed great herds of Earth animals. He reproduced without thought. His offspring gobbled up the wheat, fruits and even jeweled flowers were trampled under feet.

Today's party wreaths were soiled and her green Earth became desert. In desperation she watched the thrown stone fall back to a changed environment. A place where once again reptiles, rats and instinct ruled.

In desperation, Today changed her name again and retreated to yesterday, hoping a muse could show her offspring a wisdom-rock he could ride to the stars.

Today is gray-haired, weak. Aged memories bring both tears and smiles.

Tomorrow rests in the hands of this knobby party-child. Sometimes the thoughtless, ruthless twinkle in his eyes, lights up with wisdom. He looks at stars for guidance and tramples more lightly on his heritage.

Sometimes, sometimes he reflects on a flower and holds it to the sun. Sometimes he tries to plant a garden and protect it from the herd of thoughtlessness.

In this Sometimes, Yesterday hopes she can find her youth once again and her Human-child will become a man of wisdom. She dreams of giving another party, of clean air, blue skies, pure water and a flower covered Earth.

Mike contemplated what he had written and some of the things he'd heard on the learning tape on love. It hadn't emphasized the word love as much as other words such as, "In a civilized world, self-reliance could dispel fear and make independent beings."

He thought about it and wrote again until shadows of darkness fell across his pages. With reluctance he realized the day was over and his body felt stiff. Quickly he scanned the pages and began to edit. The word self-reliance kept nagging then wrote:

Self Reliance woke from the realm of dreams to the pounding hoofs of reality. The unearned luxuries of his past were gone.

The world, a series of surprises, unpredictable, unreliable, stood in his path, dressed in an army of shapes and events.

Old men in suspenders chewed the tobacco of gossip and malice. Friends, with greed in their eyes, took advantage of his kindness.

Unseen forces in the form of government claimed much and gave back pittance.

"Unfair," he accused. At their laughter, he slunk away as though he were guilty.

Wandering in brooding silence into the green forests of remembrance, Self Reliance sulked. His strange, gray iceberg brain listened to the night cries of faceless creatures. Cowering in the chill vapors of regret and remembrance of ashen splendor, his body trembled under an icy moon.

In nagging shadows of genetic memories stood his ancestors, with only a club standing before the wolf of hunger, cold icy winds, the sharing of food and body warmth. With this instinctive knowledge came the dawn of self-realization.

Sunlight sparkled cleanly on bubbling water, dewdrops rode rainbows, his clumsy hands tenderly stroked the lilies of the field, a kitten rubbed his leg, and a rib-thin dog snarled, barked, sniffed his hand and waited to be patted.

From the tree on which he leaned, an apple fell. Along the vine-covered path of life he wandered. A limping horse followed him with hanging head, as though he, too, were condemned. Self Reliance now had a family to feed.

At first he saw only the seeds of a thistle to harvest. His eyes begin to pierce the shadows, the green, his nostrils the odors blown on a vagrant wind. Ears heard nature's music of whispering winds, babbling brooks, and animal walks. With pride and the fruits of the earth, he was able to survive. A discarded mansion became home. The horse provided transportation, the dog and cat brought food treasures. A lonely widow hired him.

Arms which had known silk shirts and soft woolens now wore sunlit tan; muscles bulged from labor which left him exhausted but with a sense of accomplishment . . . Entertainment which had been sought in theaters and museums was all around in the beauty of nature, the frolic and courtships of animals and birds.

Self Reliance had known many women but never love. In the arms of a simple widow, the purr of a stray cat, the greeting of a rib-thin dog, a limping horse and the pride in his own accomplishments, he found himself.

Emotions within Mike which mixed and churned in the morning gradually vanished with his writing. Perhaps Troy, Madge and even Ted and Jean had deceived him, or it was his own lack of ego-maturity which held him away from them?

True, he wouldn't have been ready to accept who or what she was; but now, would she give him another chance? Would she even have time for him now?

And Ted? He seemed ready to go along with the plans of the Sealing. Apparently, he had known about them since Troy spent the night at their house three years ago. His wife, Jean, had been one of them for years and kept it a secret. Mike went inside and paced recklessly. He'd stay here tonight and in the morning go back to his apartment. What would tomorrow bring? He hadn't even turned on the TV. The phone had rung behind him, but he had wanted to write without interruption. Just one day before life came rushing back, he wanted silence and limbo.

He fixed supper and again took up the pen. When he thought of Troy his mind rejected, his body desired.

"Come, back, Troy. If you can hear my thoughts or feel my feelings, come back. Help me understand . . ." She had won the election for president and might not have much time for him. Hadn't her mind assured him she would meet him here?

God! Round and round went his mind . . . .

A tape labeled, Swirling Phantasmagoria, kept pace with his mind. He fumbled in his jacket for his little poetry book . . . He felt lost and lonely. Where was Troy?

Phantasmagoria
Spinning, throbbing, where am I,
Among throw away art, one shot sitcoms,
Polaroid snapshots, Xerox copies,
Beliefs challenged undefined threats?
Celebrities pirouette moral slogans,
Political contradictions assail me,
Accelerated information,
Jetting by like rockets,
Bursting loudly on the 4th of July.
Ideologies crack about me
Swiftly fade away!
Driving here and flying there,
Live my life just anyway, who cares?

Well, I do and so do you!
I care so much I dare not think,
And then I must. Where do I start?

I QUESTION,
Why must leaders of a country,
Twist and warp our sense of view?
Take our kindness, give back hatred,
With fear and power they turn our screw.
Revengeful politicians, soul-less beings,
Selling might is right, hate and greed.
Out to take our money and simple way of life,
By keeping all on edge of starving fright
Using the implements we give them.
Never, never enough, as they claim their dues.

Look outside my smoggy window . . .
See Black Visions . . . Birds without a place to light,
Bushes, trees, no blooming anywhere.
A green-blue planet, paradise lost . . .
Before my eyes it burns to black!

Sighing, tearful, I turn and close my eyes.
Thoughts of death no longer frighten,
Thoughts of death do now invite,
As I sit here silently!

Suddenly,
A bird sings, orange blossoms fill the air,
A New Vision comes to me ... Saying, "Take things one by one.
What really is . . .?
What just seems to be?
What do I want my life to be like?
What part of law, religion, customs,
Meaning of words, should I adopt, hang onto?
What really counts? "

I see you and me, people all around the earth,
Working, playing, giving birth.
Fearing me as I fear them.
Knowing that their fear is useless,
If that's so, then mine is too.

So, I sit here silently,
Vowing that my place I'll keep,
Clear my vision as it clouds up,
Making space with others like me
Keeping Earth all blue and green!

As usual, writing a poem had a tranquil affect on Mike. He felt at peace with himself, the future and life. It was like floating bits of words on the whirlpools of his mind . . . like watching a spider free itself. He walked out onto the porch and looked at the lit pool. A dragonfly rested for a moment on a water lily. A gentle wind blew against his cheek.

Troy Returns

Mike heard a movement. Troy rose from the pool all dripping wet and stood before him. He felt as though he have never really seen her before. She was wearing the bit of wispy gauze of the Sealings. Light sparkled on glistening droplets of water clinging to her body. Pale freckles stood out against white skin. Red hair glowed damply orange, a familiar sea-perfume emanated from her body.

For a long time, they simply looked at one another. Slowly, she raised her arms and reached out to him. There was no question of his turning away. Within him the siren music called. He knew this was the love he had waited and longed for all his life, but had been too fearful of being hurt to accept.

He walked toward her, their arms entwined. Silently they slipped into the pool and made love.

Mike felt their minds as well as bodies mingle. Her experience of the Sealings and Landlings was his, just as his knowledge became hers.

Eventually, they entered the basement through the strange door he had failed to investigate before he met her. Mike shuddered, thinking of what might have happened if he had.

Troy paused, looked at him and smiled. Hand in hand they went up to her bedroom and out onto the balcony.

The mist over the ocean had cleared. They watched as a great mirage slowly formed above the horizon. One of the ships from the Sealings fleet had arrived. They would soon be in the air above cities all over Earth. The surface of the ship, even in the moonlight, twinkled like a million, multi-colored stars.

Troy and Mike sat on the balcony and talked watching the luminous ship above San Diego and the night. "It will be a new and better world," she assured him.

For the first time in years, Mike felt hope for the future.

For a week the Sealings delivered messages of peace and good will via radio and television. Instead of sitcoms and soaps--plays, music and songs, art, sculpture and news of the Sealings way of life were broadcast.

Helene Troy, the President of the United States, declared peace instead of war. She clearly stated the intentions of the Sealings and the ways in which each individual could clean up his own space, contribute to solutions of pollution problems. An invitation was extended to each individual to visit a sea spacers.

"We of the United States will work with the United Nations to become one world, at peace with one another at long last. It will happen. There is no choice. All engines for peaceful use will be allowed to run until our new fusion engines can be adapted. Your fast moving world will seem to slow down, but you will not be bored. With the mind tapes, you will be as intelligent as you wish to be. You will have time to become creative, not destructive. When we, you and I, have let Earth regain it's natural state, Sealings promise to help mankind venture into space.

"To become Star men and Star women will take a great deal of training and knowledge, but since it has been one of Landlings few idealistic goals, Sealings feel it must be important and they are ready to help us succeed. Young people can begin their studies and training within the month. With the mind-training tapes and work, any person can achieve his or her goal . . ."

"People of the land will have a week in which to meditate and consider their new lives. Those who try to attack Sealing ships and people will cease to exist. All war machines have, from this moment on, ceased to function. Guns may be delivered to the nearest police station to be recycled. Anyone needing help may also seek refuge by calling this number. PEACE.

"Sealings welcome you to their world. The future begins N O W! During this week, we ask food merchants to continue to operate stores and their providers to deliver products. Honesty, caring and sharing and creative work will be your future way of life. With the help of the Sealing, this will not be too difficult. This message is being repeated in every language all over Earth." Troy raised an open hand to the smog-filled sky and smiled, "May your future hold abundant clean air and water."

After a week, the tails of the ships began to separate and land in waterways and on land all over the world. Women and children were invited to come first, visit the new world under the sea and partake of its knowledge. After they returned, the men were invited. When all had been on this journey, there were large-scale adjustments in transportation, communication and the United Nations governing body.

Mike woke up before Troy and went to the balcony. It had not been a dream. The ships of hope for Planet Earth were still there. The morning sun was not as blurred with brown, smelly air. A salt breeze caressed his cheek.

In Mike's mind he pictured people's reactions to what was taking place with the new hope of youth for the future. He wrote a summarizing poem, which became a legend among the Star men and Star women from the Earth . . .

EDEN REVISITED

"What is that," asked the child,
As he watched through the eye of the Statue of Liberty.
The phones kept on ringing, countries called back and forth.
"Should we shoot off our warheads?
Where shall we aim?
Why doesn't the radar, give us a signal?"

"It's a hologram, a trick, an illusion or star."
"It's the Russians," said some," Or the Yanks, Arabs, or Jews."
Each hoping the other would give them some clue.

For over a week, we'd been getting a message.
"The thing in the sky just keeps growing bigger.
Now, it's hanging, over New York. There's one in the Baltic,
one near Bombay, another in
Australia," they say.

The ships were all frothy, like miles of
spun foam. Translucent the wingspread,
Opaque in the center.
The tail about five miles long.
Net covered body with crystal spun coral,
It glittered and sparkled, both day and night,
with millions of rainbows, all covered with dew drops.
"A giant of the sea, a blue-green crystal sting ray,"
said an artist today.
"It's not of the church, so it must be the devil.
We'll sing and say prayers,
DESTROY," said the clergy.

"WAIT," said the scientists,
"Their mission seems peaceful.
Let's send invitations, invite them to lunch."

Armies turned rockets, this way and that.
They raised and lowered their sights.
Afraid of the MESSAGE now covering the earth.

A swat team stood by on a submarine deck.
A madman drew a pistol and shot at the net.
The bullet came back, blew up the revolver.
Each time an explosion, came close to a ship,
it returned to the sender in violent reprisal.

"SEND US YOUR LEADERS," we'll talk said the Landlings.
The message came back loud and clear.

WE'VE SENT YOU OUR LEADERS, OVER THE YEARS.
YOU'VE FALSIFIED WORDS, KILLED MANY, AND
IGNORED OTHERS.
WE'VE TRIED GLACIERS, DROUTH, FLOODS,
LET YOU START OVER.
NOW IT WOULD SEEM, YOU'D DESTROY OUR
EARTH.
THE HOME THAT WE SEEDED, LEFT YOU TO TEND.
WE EXPANDED YOUR BRAINS TO HELP SOLVE
YOUR
PROBLEMS, BUT WE LEFT YOU A FLAW,
AND HAVE COME TO CORRECT IT.

A SICKNESS CALLED FEAR,
TURNS TO POWER AND THEN GREED,
WHEN YOUR INSTINCTS, MIND, AND BODIES

ARE NOT IN SYNC.

BRING US YOUR PEOPLE,
LET THEM WALK THROUGH OUR SHIPS,
WE'LL HEAL ALL THEIR BODIES,
GIVE BACK PEACE OF MIND.
YOU WON'T NEED TO KILL, HANG ON TO, GET
MORE,
TO EASE THE ACHING OF FEAR!
BECOME ONE WITH THE UNIVERSE,
BRING PEACE AND BLUE SKIES BACK TO EARTH!

The greedy and powerful laughed with each other.
Defense departments
conferred with their warriors.
But . . .
The tail of the spacers, began
breaking up, landing pieces all over the earth.
Out came the sick, the wives and the mothers.
Bringing their children, then husbands and lovers.
They walked into rainbows of crystal spun coral.

When they walked out, came back to the land,
All were healthy and happy, with a spring in their step,
a twinkle in eyes.

Now the ships that had come,
to visit from space, were really from down
under in the Pacific Trench.
No one knew, but the fishes themselves,
and the mermaid-merman crew, that the ship
was built, by the minds of peace, by the
ones who lived in the sea.

Through hypnosis,
they took away fear, re-balanced our hormones,
re-trained egos, took away cultural warp.
Cut mankind loose, to look to the moment and future at last.

Ignoring the commanders, soldiers dismounted the rockets,
threw guns in a pot, melting them down, reshaping for tools.
Cleaned up their homes, streets and towns,
Traded pots for computers, lent someone a hand.
Life became simple so little was needed.

Knew the difference between needing and wanting.
There was always a boat when wishing
to sail or yarn for some weaving, and neat little homes for all.
Scientists designed, what comforts were needed,
divided the labor, divided it's fruits.

Mankind became seekers, life was an adventure,
new discovers exciting.
People lived longer, a thousand years or more.
Just like Columbus, they built large space ships, mined the
moon with some robots, went farther out . . . explored our galaxy,
went looking for more.

Now that we've, stopped fighting our brothers,
taking care of the place where we are,
we enjoy our living, sharing with others,
There's more than enough for us all.

EARTH IS AGAIN EDEN,
THE UNIVERSE IS OUR PLAYGROUND,
AND THE MIND MAKES IT FUN FOR US ALL!

Avonelle Kelsey